RYDER

RYDER

AN AYESHA RYDER NOVEL

Nick Pengelley

HarperCollinsPublishersLtd

HarperCollins Publishers Ltd
2 Bloor Street East, 20th Floor
Toronto, Ontario, Canada
M4W 1A8

www.harpercollins.ca

Library and Archives Canada Cataloguing in Publication
information is available upon request

ISBN 978-1-44343-897-1

Printed and bound in Canada
WEB 9 8 7 6 5 4 3 2 1

For Pamela, always

CHAPTER 1

The phone buzzed. Ayesha Ryder ignored it, as she had on the three previous occasions. She flicked her long black hair away from her face and resumed typing on her laptop, her back propped against her living room sofa. At the end of a paragraph, she picked up her drink and drained the glass. As she put it down her glance fell on the glossy brochure that lay on the carpet beside her.

PEACE IN THE MIDDLE EAST, CAN IT REALLY WORK?
Keynote Speaker: Ayesha Ryder Ph.D., Director of Research Walsingham Institute for Oriental Studies
PALESTINE, A NATIONAL IDEA

The words were splayed across one of those so familiar photographs of Jerusalem's Temple Mount, the golden Dome of the Rock rising above the limestone walls of the old city. The title of the talk was not her idea; she'd been overruled by the conference planning committee. Too dry, they called her suggestion for a title.

It needs to be sexier, they said. Attention-grabbing. She snorted at the memory. The conference, timed to coincide with the summit meeting between the Israeli and Palestinian leaders—to be held at the Tower of London for security reasons—was already fully booked. The attention of the whole world would be on the summit, and on everything to do with the talks in which so much hope was invested. It would not have mattered what they called her paper.

She frowned at the screen. Words usually came easily to her. Quickly, too. Tonight she was struggling. Procrastinating. She kept swapping to her browser, surfing the Web for the latest news on the summit. Checking the weather—all anyone could talk about was whether they'd have a white Christmas. Her bank account. Browsing the latest book reviews. Anything but what she had to focus on. *Dammit*, she scolded herself. *Concentrate*. The paper had to be finished by morning.

She stretched her arms high. She repeated the exercise with each of her long pale legs, wiggling her toes into the plush pile of the Aubusson carpet. Slowly, over the course of a year, she had adjusted to the idea that these things—the apartment itself, the carpet, and much more besides, like the fur coats she would probably never wear—were hers. The wealth, the sheer luxury of owning her own apartment near London's Vauxhall Park—something she could never hope to do, even on her very decent pay—was so far removed from the surroundings she grew up in as to be laughable. She had a sudden flash of herself as a child, leaving the rough cement-block structure in Gaza City she and her parents called home, walking the mile to the nearest well and spending the day in line to fill two iron buckets with water.

She pushed away the memory. With a fluid movement, she rose to her feet and raised her arms high. On tiptoe she just brushed the bottom of the chandelier with her fingertips. She dropped back, padded across the carpet to the bathroom, relieved herself, washed her hands in the basin, and splashed water on her face. She blotted it dry with a face towel, raised her head, and looked at herself in the mirrored cabinet. She stared into the green eyes of her reflection, then grasped the bottom of her ribbed cotton tank top. It and panties were all she had on—the building's furnace provided more than adequate heating, even in the depths of an English winter. She lifted the top back over her head and looked down.

The scars were old. She was thirty-four; the wounds were inflicted when she was sixteen. Few people had ever seen them. Only two of them were men: the man who had tortured her, and one other. With her left hand she probed the scars, feeling their rough texture against the soft skin of her fingertips. As she did this, her eyes rose to the mirror once more. Memories swarmed. She pushed them back and pulled her tank top back down over her head, took a deep breath, and closed her eyes. Centered herself. When she opened them again she avoided the mirror and opened the cabinet door. She took down her toothbrush, making a mental note to clear the cabinet of Harriet's drugs.

The apartment was still full of her aunt's things—clothes and knickknacks. She had to clear them out. Give the clothes to a charity. Somehow she'd never gotten around to it. The presence of Harriet's things meant she was still there. Sort of. Her father's sister had been everything to her—mother, sister, friend. Harriet had rescued Ayesha from the asylum in Gaza, adopted her, provided her with an education—and seen that she got the years of mental therapy she needed. More than anything, though, Harriet's love helped her . . . not heal, but survive.

She was still staring at her toothbrush when the doorbell rang.

She threw a bathrobe on. "Yes?" She spoke through the crack in the door. "Who is it?"

"Detective Sergeant Kaleb Bryan," a deep male voice replied. A photo ID appeared in the crack. "Metropolitan Police."

She slipped the chain and opened the door wider. A powerfully built black man loomed in the hallway, six foot one or two, with buzz-cut hair and wearing a tailored suit.

"Sorry to disturb you so late," he said. "I did try calling."

"What can I do for you?" She glanced at her watch. It was just after nine o'clock. She made no move to invite the detective in. Whatever he wanted, she wasn't interested; her lecture was in two days and she was nothing like ready. She *had* to get back to her computer.

"I work for Detective Inspector Holden," Bryan said. "There's been a murder. The boss wants you to have a look at some documents."

Ayesha grimaced at the mention of Holden. Three years before, the inspector had consulted her on a case involving antiquities stolen from Iraqi museums. Discovering she was a mine of information on the Middle East—its peoples, cultures, languages, and politics—Holden had developed the habit of calling upon her whenever he thought her expertise might save him some time. Sometimes she found the work interesting. Not tonight, though. Whatever it was would have to wait until she'd finished her paper. She shook her head, started to close the door. "Please tell Detective Inspector Holden I will be at his disposal tomorrow. I can't possibly come at the moment."

DS Bryan grunted. His eyes flicked downward.

She followed his glance. Her robe had fallen open. She pulled it tight. When she looked up again, Bryan held her gaze.

"The boss said you wouldn't want to come," he said. "He thought you might know the vic, though."

She waited, impatient to close the door.

"He was a professor, lived over in St. John's Wood. Expert in your field."

"Who?" she blurted, her computer, her paper, forgotten.

"Sir Evelyn Montagu."

She forgot to breathe. She stared at the detective, willing him not to be there, willing this not to be true. Finally she spoke. "How?"

Bryan didn't answer. She saw it in his eyes, though. Whatever it was, it was very bad.

CHAPTER 2

Judah Ben David's right hand ached from the pressure applied to it by so many well-wishers. Everyone who had attended the dinner in his honor at Israel's London embassy wanted to meet the new prime minister. There was only one person Ben David wanted to meet: his old friend Sir Evelyn Montagu.

As his hand was grasped yet again by a man who seemed to want to squeeze the life out of it, he felt a touch on his arm. He turned his head and looked into the hazel eyes of the person he most wanted to avoid: Diana Longshore, the American secretary of state. He freed his hand, trying not to wince as the blood surged back into it, and managed an affable nod.

"Mr. Prime Minister." The American leaned in toward him, the better to be heard over the hubbub in the embassy's majestic reception hall. Her soft Virginia accent did little to disguise the steel that lay beneath. "Judah. When are you going to tell me what you're up to?"

"I truly am sorry, Madam Secretary. Diana." He forced a smile, grateful the American's presence was deterring the approach of other guests. "I'm afraid you'll have to wait till Wednesday like everyone else."

The secretary's eyes blazed, just for a second, but enough for Ben David to know she was furious. Diana Longshore was a very attractive woman who could be good company. Right now, however, she wanted answers—answers he was not prepared to give. He placed an arm around her slender waist. She stiffened at his touch, then relaxed and allowed him to guide her across the noisy room. "I want to show you something," he said, determined to make nice—too much depended on the Americans.

Near the door that was Ben David's objective he spoke to a waiter carrying a tray laden with drinks. "Bring me a bottle of Krcmly, would you please? Make sure it's chilled." He glanced at his companion. She nodded, with the hint of a smile. "And two glasses."

He took a last look around for Evelyn. Not seeing him, he opened the door and ushered the secretary into a library, intimately appointed. Bookcases lined the walls. A Louis Quinze writing desk covered in papers sat in front of French windows. A guard was stationed outside, his chiseled form silhouetted against the glass. Ben David shut the door and the noise of the reception dropped from a roar to a low hum.

"This is what I wanted to show you." He gestured toward an antique map. Nearly five feet tall by four feet wide, framed in dark wood, it rested on the floor, propped against a bookcase to the right of the door.

The secretary stepped forward to look at the map, which showed the eastern Mediterranean littoral. A knock at the door was followed by the entry of the waiter. He carried a bottle and two shot glasses on a silver tray.

"On the desk, please," the Israeli said. "We'll help ourselves."

"It's quite wonderful," the secretary said, still studying the map. "Seventeenth century?"

"Late sixteenth. Petrus Plancius." He lifted the bottle of vodka and poured measures into each glass, handed one to the secretary, and raised his own. "*L'chaim.*"

"To life," Diana Longshore replied, and knocked back her drink. She gestured to the map. "It was Palestine back then."

"Yes, Palestine." He refilled her glass. "The Holy Land. No Israel. No occupied territories. No division of the land many Jews regard as ours by right from God."

"That's been the problem since the beginning. The trouble is the other people who live there. We want to know what you plan to do about them." She tossed back her vodka. "We don't really care how you go about it."

Powerful men and women had quailed beneath Longshore's gaze, but he didn't blink. *So now I know,* he thought. He and Sayyed Khalidi had been right not to take the Americans into their confidence. "It's time to end the bloodshed," he told her. "We've had more than half a century of that."

"I know—"

A knock on the door cut the secretary off midsentence. Israel's ambassador entered. "Excuse me, Mr. Prime Minister. Madam Secretary, the American ambassador is looking for you."

Alone in the room, Ben David pondered his latest acquisition. He could never resist old maps, had fantasized about crewing on an old-time sailing ship, setting out on a voyage to who knew where. The map in front of him showed a place plenty had set sail for, only to die there. The Crusaders. Knights and peasants of Europe, their blood and bones had fertilized the soil of his land.

RYDER

Some of his blood, too. And that of those he had killed in war. He sighed, put down his glass, and left the library.

Back in the reception room, his gaze swept over the crowd, his height giving him advantage. His gaze locked with that of a sultry-looking blonde with come-hither lips on the far side of the room. He smiled and took a step toward her, then, feeling a hand touch his shoulder, he turned and found himself looking into the smiling face of his closest friend. That hadn't always been the case—for most of their lives they'd been mortal enemies. Two years ago they'd met at the scene of a gas explosion that left dozens of civilians dead and injured—Israeli Jews and Arabs. To the surprise of both men, they'd found they had much in common. They also liked each other.

"No sign of your friend?" Sayyed Khalidi asked him.

"No. I hope it means he's on the trail of something."

"Less than forty-eight hours." Khalidi spoke close to Ben David's ear. Not that they were at much risk of being overheard. The reception was formally over but few people showed signs of leaving and the noise level had not abated. "What do you think the reaction will be?"

"We need to be prepared for anything."

"You've told your people?"

"The day before I left for London. I've sworn them to secrecy."

"You trust them?"

"I have to. Nothing's got out—yet, anyway." Ben David grinned. "Have you spoken with the secretary?"

"Oh yes. Diana is one unhappy lady." Khalidi laughed. "What are the chances your friend, Sir Evelyn, is really on to something?"

"After all this time? Do you believe in miracles?"

"Indeed I do. Tell me, Judah, how many times did your Shin Bet try to kill me?"

"More than I know. Thank God we failed."

"And you—that day on the Golan in '73. You've told me often that you should have died from your wound."

"It was a miracle I didn't."

"Well then, we have two miracles. Why not a third?"

"True. But I'm counting on Evelyn to give us an edge." Ben David peered toward the other side of the room. "So where the hell is he?"

CHAPTER 3

Ayesha stopped outside the door of Evelyn's apartment to pull off the black boots she'd hurriedly put on, along with black skinny jeans, T-shirt, and black leather bomber jacket, before leaving her apartment with DS Bryan. She put on a pair of disposable blue plastic booties and stepped through the open doorway, her heart torn at the sight of the Christmas wreath on the door. No Christian, Evelyn had nevertheless loved the traditions that went with an English Yuletide.

Inside the apartment she made her way along the hallway, squeezing past the investigators, members of Death's bureaucracy, who moved briskly in and out of what had been a home and was now a sepulchre. Everything seemed just as she'd last seen it. Except for the plastic sheeting covering the hall carpet runner. The same pictures crowded the walls—framed paintings and photographs of Evelyn's distinguished ancestors and relatives.

One of the photographs had been knocked askew. It showed Evelyn and Ayesha together at a formal dinner. He was elegant in a dinner suit, she in the formal gown he'd bought her for the occasion. She swung away from the photograph and saw Bryan watching her. The black man was waiting beside a doorway farther along the hall. He jerked his head toward the doorway, then watched her approach.

She thrust her hands deep into the pockets of her jacket, braced herself, then stepped across the threshold into the study. The room where Evelyn spent most of his time, writing, surrounded by his books and mementos of his travels. The room, whenever she had been in it, was immaculate. The books arranged just so. Papers on the desk piled and squared away. Framed documents and maps hung on the walls with military precision. Evelyn required everything around him to be in order before he could think. Clutter and mess were anathema to him. He would hate what had happened to his holy of holies.

Most of the books had been pulled from the shelves and lay scattered on the floor. Many of them were rare and valuable and she grimaced to see the damage done to centuries-old bindings. Papers were strewn everywhere and the contents of the desk drawers had been emptied on the carpet. Fingerprint powder spattered the great mahogany desk, once the property of the Duke of Wellington, part of the spoils captured after his defeat of the French at Vitoria. Three white-garbed Scenes of Crime Officers photographed and measured.

She was aware of the shrouded shape in the corner, but could not bring herself to look at it. Easier to examine the mundane, catalogue the devastation wrought upon property. Until she could put it off no longer.

A sheet covered Evelyn's body and the antique wood and leather swivel chair in which he sat. One leg of the chair was visible. And one of Evelyn's feet. Naked and smeared with blood. The sheet, too, was spattered with blood. More blood stained the carpet around the chair. Ayesha took a step forward. A man stepped in front of her, blocking her view of the shrouded corpse.

"Thanks for coming. I'd like you to take a look at a few things here. Did you know the vic? He was pretty well-known in your field."

DI Holden was casually dressed—in blue jeans, white cotton T-shirt, and black leather jacket. His fair hair, which always needed a comb, flopped forward across his forehead. He looked at her with engaging blue eyes and smiled the boyish smile that, so rumor had it, had won him a succession of female conquests.

"What sort of things?" She ignored the other part of Holden's question.

"Some of these are in English." The DI gestured to the papers scattered on the floor. "Some are in what I think is Arabic. Others I can't identify." He turned and pointed to the wall behind the shrouded form in the chair. "And there's that. Can you tell me what it says?"

She lifted her eyes to the wall. Spray paint? *No.*

"It's blood." Holden nodded at the sheet-covered form. "His."

"It's Arabic." She forced herself to focus on the words. Written in Evelyn's blood above his corpse. "'Death to the Zionists. Freedom for Palestine.'"

"Palestinians." Holden nodded. "Terrorists."

She opened her mouth, but she didn't want to argue. Not yet. "I want to see," she said.

"Why? How well did you know him? It's bad," he warned.

"I have to."

Holden studied her, his eyes narrowed. "All right, if you insist."

He gestured to a metal wastepaper bin. "If you have to barf, use that." In two strides he crossed to the chair and lifted the sheet.

She couldn't breathe. Her eyes saw what was in front of her, but her brain refused to let her comprehend. Instead she absorbed it as a series of snapshots. Lips, stretched in a rictus of agony. Blink. Nose, smashed and ruined. Blink. Eyes, massively bruised, swollen shut. Blink. Splintered bone and cartilage. The left knee? Blink. A signet ring, the gold shining through blood and gore. It rested on something blue and twisted. A finger. Other shapes, grotesquely bent.

Evelyn's body was naked. He had been tied to the chair with phone and computer cables that had cut deep into his flesh. These injuries were minor in comparison to what else had been done to him. She saw it all, understood everything in its full horror. Until this moment, she had feared how she would react to the sight of his body. Whether the reality of seeing Evelyn dead, and what had been done to him, would cause her to crack.

She looked again at the corpse in the chair. The *corpse*—not Evelyn. He—the essential he—had gone. What was left was something for the pathologist to examine and report on. He, or she, would have to start by washing away the blood. So much blood. It had matted in the chest hair and dried in rivulets down the torso. She smelled it. Tasted the sharp iron tang in the back of her throat. She swallowed and turned away. Then she swung back, her nose wrinkling, took a step forward, and bent closer, searching. Her eyes widened. Images from the past rose up, and this time she could not push them away.

"Anything to tell me yet?" The voice. Smooth, calm, oh so rational, it belied the ferocity of the treatment its owner relished meting out. Ayesha bore witness to that. Every part of her body throbbed from the punches he had expertly applied. Each time she breathed, pain stabbed at her chest. Her ribs were cracked or broken. She had to breathe through her mouth—one of the first punches had broken her nose. She'd lost teeth, and her jaw was a mass of hurt. The least of her injuries was a wound made with a knife that had sliced through the skin of her neck from below her ear to her collarbone. The Voice had stretched her nerves exquisitely, almost to the breaking point, running the blade over her skin, stopping, then coming back and touching her in a new place—her face, breasts, stomach, between her legs. Not being able to see, not knowing where the blade would prick next. It was the worst form of torture. *My parents will never know what happened to me.* That thought haunted her more than the knowledge of her own impending death.

The Voice told her he intended to slice off her ears, slit her nose, blind her. He had not done those things—yet, but she was at his mercy. The Voice could do anything he wanted. He whispered in her ear other things he would do. In graphic detail he described how he would defile her before he killed her and had her body burned in a pit.

The Voice was not the first to inflict violence on her. She'd been beaten by her captors. Kicked, punched, dragged by the hair, her body groped, spat at, abused. All that before they hog-tied her with rope and threw her into the back of a truck. On top of the dead bodies of the other members of her team. She was the only one to be taken alive after the attack on the colony. An accident of fate she bitterly regretted.

The journey in the truck took an interminable time, part of which she spent unconscious. For the rest, unable to move, even to feel her limbs, she was forced to breathe in the fetid stench that the bodies of the *Fedayeen*—her friends—were already giving off in the heat of the day.

When the truck finally stopped, she'd been hauled out and dropped to the ground inside the gates of a place she recognized: an old stone fort, dating from Ottoman times. It was outside Beersheba, deserted since the British used it in the days of the Palestine Mandate. Before she had time to wonder why the Israelis were using it, she was picked up by two soldiers and half carried, half dragged to a room beneath the old barracks building.

The soldiers dropped her onto a wooden table, untied her, then used the same ropes to lash her limbs to its legs. Laughing and making lewd comments in Hebrew, they ripped and tore every shred of clothing from her body. Expecting to be raped, she tried to shut her mind to the horror to come, but the soldiers left, slamming the door behind them.

She thought she was alone. She strained at the ropes and tried to force some feeling back into her arms and legs. Cursed herself for being taken alive. Heavy, booted footsteps rang on the stone floor, coming toward her. They stopped. A fist smashed into her jaw.

All the time he beat and tortured her, the Voice asked questions. "What is your name?" "Who is your commander?" "Where does your group hide their weapons?"

She stayed silent, determined to give no information. No matter what. A thought occurred: if she angered the Voice he might finish the job quickly. From somewhere in her throat she summoned up an ounce of phlegm and spat in his face. He chuckled. Lit a cigarette. Its pungent odor filled the room. He leaned over her. She flinched from the heat of the cigarette on her cheek. Then a searing pain pierced her breast and she passed out.

Ayesha turned to Holden, her head pounding, the palms of her hands slick with sweat. The old memories had surfaced suddenly, taking her unawares. "Cigarette burns," she said.

"Yes, several by the looks of it. Bastards." The DI studied her face. "You didn't answer my question. How well did you know him?"

"Well. I knew him well." She turned back to the corpse and counted the roundish red lesions. One at the base of the throat. One at the top of each side of the chest. A matching pair at the hips, and one at the top of the groin. "Look," she said, pointing.

Holden stepped forward and followed her finger as she showed him the location of each burn. "You're right. I missed that. Whoever did it liked symmetry. I'll run it through HOLMES and see if we get a match."

The Home Office Large Major Enquiry System, known by the backronym HOLMES, was a giant database for the management of major incidents like murders. One of its aspects was the matching of features from other investigations. If there had been other cases involving torture with cigarette burns, especially where the burns were made in a pattern, Holden would soon know about it. A voice inside her head said there would be no match. The same voice said she knew who was responsible for Evelyn's torture and death. She stared at the cigarette burns on her lover's chest. How could she prove it?

CHAPTER 4

Moses Litmann, Israel's foreign minister, stared at the doorway on the other side of the embassy's reception chamber through which his prime minister had just vanished, smiling, with the Palestinian leader. *Let them enjoy their moment,* Litmann thought. Just a matter of hours now, then everything he wanted would be his. He felt a surge of exhilaration, then his eyes flicked back to the woman in front of him. He needed to get away. Make his phone call. Find out how his plans were progressing, although at this point he expected only good news.

"You know what they're up to," Diana Longshore said.

"I'm sorry." He forced a smile. "I really can't talk about it."

Before the American could reply, the two diplomats were joined by a large man in a tight-fitting suit. His florid face was shiny from too much drink and he was holding a plate of canapés. "Diana," he said, then dabbed at his lips with a napkin. He nodded to Litmann, wiped one huge paw on a trouser leg, and extended it in his direction. "John S. Danforth," he said. "The Third. Good to meet you."

The third what? Litmann wondered as his hand was squeezed in an iron grip. He started to introduce himself but the big man cut him off.

"I know who you are, Mr. Litmann." Danforth swallowed a smoked oyster. "Seeing as I have both foreign secretaries together, ours and that of our best buddy, Israel, maybe you two can enlighten me on something."

"John is an old friend of the president's." Diana Longshore looked at Litmann. Her smile contained a hint of pleading.

"Of course, Mr. Danforth." He got the message. *Please be nice to this man.* He summoned up one of his best smiles. "What is it you want to know?"

"Call me John," the Texan insisted. "And I'm going to call you Moses. Unless you prefer Mo?"

Litmann suppressed a wince. "Moses is fine."

Danforth lifted a glass of champagne from a passing waitress with the practiced ease of a rancher lassoing a steer. He drained most of its contents in one swallow, then asked, "This group, calls itself *Shamir*. What's it all about? Did I pronounce it right, Moses?"

"Yes, John. The name comes from Jewish mythology. Supposedly the *Shamir* was the hardest substance ever known. It could split open stones just by touching them; its mere presence would break iron. The group is outlawed; we're doing everything we can to hunt them down. Other than that, I'm not sure what I can tell you that you haven't already read in the newspapers or online yourself."

"I don't have a lot of time for reading." This was said with an aw-shucks kind of grin. "Didn't they put out some sort of manifesto a while back, after killing a bunch of people? They're a what? Sort of a Jewish Al Qaeda?" Danforth pronounced it *Al Kay-ee-dah,* dragging out the syllables.

Litmann bit back a groan. Americans. How did they make so much money and yet remain ignorant of what happened outside their own country?

"That's right, John," Diana Longshore interjected. "*Shamir* massacred the inhabitants of a Palestinian village. They killed men, women, even children. Some of them were burned alive in their houses. They tortured many of them, too, in very horrible ways. Then they flooded the Net with a video showing what they'd done."

"Now just why would they do that?" Danforth directed his question to Litmann. His grin had disappeared.

"*Shamir,*" he answered, putting up a hand to hide the tic beneath his left eye, "claims all of the biblical land of Israel for the Jews. They believe it is ours—theirs—by right from God." He grimaced. "Unfortunately they have a great deal of support. For their aims, not their methods."

"The Bible lands—that'd include the occupied territories then?" Danforth asked. "Palestine?"

"Yes. They want all of it."

"So I guess with these atrocities they aim to take up where you guys left off in '48?"

"What do you mean by that?" Litmann had no idea where this was going, but he was desperate to end the conversation.

"Deir Yassin. You know—the massacres committed by the Jews against Arab villages to scare others into running away."

"That was not official policy," Litmann replied, managing to keep his voice calm. Most people, even many Jewish Israelis, didn't know about the slaughter of more than two hundred men, women, and children in the Arab village of Deir Yassin by Jewish paramilitary forces outside Jerusalem in 1948. "Certain . . . fanatics got out of hand."

"Ri-ight," Danforth drawled. "Fanatics." The Texan chose another canapé from his plate. When he swallowed it he looked at Litmann again. "So who's the leader of this *new* bunch of fanatics? Their—what do you say—Eminence grease?"

"That's *grise*, John," the secretary corrected. "Nobody knows who is behind *Shamir*. CIA is working with Shin Bet—Israel's internal security agency—to try to find out, and to destroy them before they can do more harm to the peace process."

"I see." Danforth nodded. "So there's no chance these guys are ever going to get into power?"

"Of course not!" Litmann was shocked by the question. Did Danforth know something? "They're *terrorists*."

"Terrorists." All trace of drunkenness had vanished from the Texan's expression. "You mean like your Irgun and Stern Gang? Back in the forties when you boys were trying to get the British out of Palestine. They killed a whole lot of Arabs, as well as Brits. You say they were fanatics who got out of hand. But wasn't Irgun led by Menachem Begin? He became your prime minister." Danforth jabbed a finger at the Israeli. "Those people were once considered terrorists, Mr. Litmann. You tell me, what's different about *Shamir*?"

He opened his mouth to respond, but Danforth threw his head back and let out a huge roar of laughter that caused heads to swing in their direction. The Israeli flushed.

Danforth clapped him on the arm, then wiped his eyes with the back of his hand. "Oh boy," he said, "you should have seen your face."

"I'm sorry," Diana Longshore told Litmann. "I should have warned you about John's sense of humor."

"That's quite all right, John." He painted a smile on his face. "You touched a sensitive nerve, I'm afraid."

Danforth beamed. "I do have a knack for doing that."

The Texan lurched off in search of more canapés and the secretary apologized again.

"No need," Litmann told her, calming. After all, what did it matter? Danforth was gone; now he could slip away and make his phone call. "Really. He's quite a character."

"He is. And a huge financial contributor to the president. So thank you for being nice to him." The secretary glanced at the room into which Judah Ben David and Sayyed Khalidi had gone. "What do you think of the prospects for a permanent peace agreement? Is there any hope?"

"Let's just say I'm not overly optimistic."

The secretary grimaced. "I should have known. I've been around this block too many times to believe that anything would come of it. I'm going to be long dead before it's resolved." She hesitated, glanced behind her, then leaned close. "I know I shouldn't say it, but what John said, his comparison of *Shamir* with the Irgun and the rest. Do you ever think about it?"

Litmann recoiled as if she had slapped him. First Danforth, now her. He stared at the secretary, his eyes wide with shock.

"I'm sorry." The secretary, evidently mistaking his emotion for outrage, placed a hand on his arm. "Please forget what I said."

When the American moved away, he hurried from the reception hall and stepped into the embassy foyer. It was deserted except for two uniformed security personnel at the front doors. He walked away from them, toward the doors to the enclosed garden at the far end, withdrew a cellphone from his coat pocket, and entered a number. He stepped through the door into the garden, relishing the feel of the cold December air on his face after the heated air inside. He spoke quietly, then listened, a frown creasing his forehead. "Ayesha Ryder," he said, repeating the name he had just heard. "Who the hell is Ayesha Ryder?"

CHAPTER 5

Holden picked up the sheet and draped it back over Sir Evelyn's body. Ayesha watched, scarcely breathing, but with her emotions under control. She'd seen Evelyn's corpse. Accepted the reality of his death. She had an idea who might be behind it. Now she had to prove it. And do something about it.

"Now, perhaps you'd have a gander at these papers?" Holden waved a hand to encompass the study. "Get them into some sort of order, could you? Give me the gist?" The DI held her gaze until she nodded, then he turned to DS Bryan, who stood waiting for orders.

"'Death to the Zionists.'" Holden pointed to the blood-streaked wall. "'Freedom for Palestine.'" He read the words aloud with a satisfied air, as if he'd translated them himself. "Terrorists, Sergeant."

Bryan opened his mouth to reply, but Holden kept talking. "Palestinian terrorists. Some of these Hamas or Hezbollah people, trying to screw with the big meeting this week between the two leaders. I'll have to bring in Special Branch." The DI referred to the unit now known as SO15, or the Counter Terrorism Command.

But Special Branch had been around, like Scotland Yard, for more than a hundred years and, thanks to countless books and movies, was now firmly fixed in the popular imagination.

Ayesha, kneeling on the carpet by a slew of papers, frowned at Holden's ignorance—Hezbollah was Lebanese, not Palestinian—as well as his assumption that Palestinians were behind Evelyn's murder. She stared at the papers in front of her, not seeing them, forcing herself to think past the fact of Evelyn's murder and the presence, just feet away, of his mutilated body. Impossible not to look once more at the silent, shrouded form, one blood-streaked foot protruding from beneath the sheet. Tears pricked at her eyes. Evelyn's life and work . . .

She rose to her feet. How to articulate what she was thinking? How to persuade Holden? It was him or Special Branch. At least he knew her. She looked at the two detectives. Holden had opened his cellphone and Bryan was turning away. The tall DS stopped and faced her. She recognized something in his face. Just for a moment, then it was gone. Doubt? He must have a deal of it, she thought, if he has to take orders from Holden all the time. "I disagree," she said.

Holden lowered his phone, one eyebrow raised. *Probably thinks it makes him look sophisticated*, she thought. Some women would find it so. It was wasted on her. "You disagree with what exactly?" the DI asked.

"With the idea that Palestinians did . . . this." She nodded at Evelyn's corpse. Almost, she lost the will to continue, to battle with Holden. She took a deep breath and started again. "I can't think of any logical reason for a Palestinian group to have come after Evelyn, let alone torture him."

"He was Jewish, wasn't he?" Holden was amused. "And

there's that." He jerked his head at the writing on the wall. "Their signature. In his blood. It's not the IRA or the friggin' Scottish nationalists."

A snort of laughter from one of the SOCOs greeted this remark.

She scowled and glanced at Bryan. The DS's face showed no expression, but she saw a glitter in his eye. "Most Palestinians don't have any problem with Jews." She forced herself to speak slowly, confidently, using language Holden would understand. "It's the policies of Israel's government they take issue with." She gestured at the words written in Evelyn's blood. "It's wrong."

"What do you mean *wrong*? Wrong how?"

"Palestine is spelled *Palestina*. No Arab would write it like that—it's the way someone would write it in Hebrew. An Arab would write it as *Falastin*. And anyway," she continued before Holden could dismiss her linguistic argument, "Evelyn was a life-long supporter of Arab causes, especially that of the Palestinians."

"How so?"

"Read some of his work, you'll see what I mean. He's on record that Palestinians were robbed of their land—views he repeated whenever he got the chance." Her thoughts flashed to the *Mavi Marmara*. Sprawled on her back on the upper deck of the unarmed ship that had tried to break Israel's blockade of Gaza, blinded by the powerful searchlights beamed from the Israeli helicopters. Deafened by the noise. Her arm hurt like hell. It was broken—by an Israeli rifle butt aimed at Evelyn's head. Ayesha had gotten in the way at the last second.

"What has any of that got to do with his murder?" Holden stepped aside as two men entered the study carrying a body bag and stretcher.

She and Bryan moved back to give the men room while they

went about the grisly task of moving Sir Evelyn's corpse. Everyone, the SOCOs included, watched them for a few moments, then Holden turned back to her. He opened his mouth to say something. Stopped. "You okay? You look white."

The men had removed the sheet and sliced through the cables that held Evelyn's body in the chair, whereupon it sagged forward. The sudden lifelike movement nearly caused her to cry out. She dragged her eyes away. She turned her back so she wouldn't have to watch, but she couldn't close her ears to the grunts and low-voiced conversation that went on between the men. "That's right, Izzy, you take his feet. Nice and easy like. Just slide 'em into the bag."

She managed a nod.

The DI narrowed his eyes, glanced once more at the activity around Sir Evelyn's body. "Montagu was a prominent Jewish intellectual, member of an old Jewish family."

She forced herself to concentrate on Holden's words. Shut out the sounds behind her.

"He was wealthy," Holden continued, "or he wouldn't have lived here, in St. John's Wood. Couldn't he just have been a target of opportunity for some Palestinian group who maybe didn't know his sympathies?"

She stared at the DI. "He was interrogated, Holden. Tortured. It must have taken a long time. Whoever did this was looking for something. Something they wanted badly enough to do that." She glanced behind her to where the ambulance men were zipping up the body bag.

"What, then?" Holden was losing patience. "You're the Middle East expert. You tell me. I've got a dead Jewish academic, a Knight of the Realm to boot, with evidence—superficial evidence anyway—that makes it look as if he was killed by Palestinian terrorists. And"—he glanced at his watch—"in less than forty-eight hours, as I'm sure you know, this city is playing host to a conference between the heads of the Israeli and Palestinian governments. I should be calling in Special Branch right now."

She did not answer. She, Holden, Bryan, and the SOCOs moved aside as the stretcher was maneuvered toward the door. After it had gone, on the start of its journey to the morgue, she felt as if a weight had been lifted. It was less difficult to breathe, and to think. She scanned the room—easier now that it did not hold Evelyn's body. She visualized it before it was ransacked. The books. Evelyn's framed degrees. Maps. Pictures. They had all been stripped from the walls. Mementos of his travels, mainly in the Middle East. She'd loved lingering over them. Before. She spotted what remained of his collection of terra-cotta figurines from Hellenic Egypt. Most were smashed beyond repair. A bronze Tibetan Buddha seated upon the Lotus was undamaged, though. As was, remarkably, a Greek amphora Evelyn was particularly proud of. A pair of Moorish pistols, inlaid with turquoise and gold, had spilled from their wooden case. Pieces of a gold Turkish coffee service lay scattered next to a Rodney decanter that once belonged to Nelson.

Any of these objects would fetch a lot of money at auction. Robbery was not the motive. She thought she could account for everything in the room. But it had been two years since she last saw it. Who knew what Evelyn had acquired in that time?

She knelt down and reached out to the papers that lay nearest to her on the floor.

Holden stopped her. "Here." He handed her a pair of disposable gloves. "Use these."

She slipped on the gloves and picked up a sheet of paper. The writing was Arabic. She scanned it. Picked up another. This one was in French. The next in Hebrew. She looked up at Holden. "What was he working on?"

"You tell me."

She lowered her head and read silently. When she looked at Holden again, he was watching her from his perch on the corner of Evelyn's desk. Bryan was no longer in the room. "Lawrence," she said. "He was working on Lawrence. A new biography perhaps. He often talked about it."

"Lawrence who?"

"Him." She gestured to a bronze bust that lay on its side on the carpet in front of the desk. It was a copy of the famous sculpture by Eric Kennington. The original was in St. Paul's Cathedral. "T. E. Lawrence. Lawrence of Arabia. Evelyn had a lifelong fascination with him."

"I see," Holden said. "I saw the movie when I was a kid," he added.

She rose, stooped, picked up the bust of Lawrence, and replaced it on the desk. She made a small adjustment to its position, then she glanced down at the blotter—not something you saw much anymore, but Evelyn had used a fountain pen. He preferred records to CDs, would only read "real" newspapers, never their online progeny, and preferred trains and ships to airplanes. The one exception to his preference for the old over the new was the computer. Even Evelyn had to admit that writing was easier on a computer than a typewriter.

She looked at the doodles that covered the blotter, feeling herself close to tears, pushing them back, nearly losing it again when her gaze was caught by a small sketch. Evelyn had drawn himself as a Lawrence-like figure, robed and sitting astride something vaguely camel-shaped. She froze, her attention riveted by a single word below the sketch. It was scrawled in capitals and enclosed in a box. *VINCEY.*

"What is it?" Holden asked.

Her pulse had quickened at the sight of the word scrawled on the blotter in Evelyn's distinctive hand. *Vincey.* She'd reacted, and Holden had seen it. The DI was watching her keenly now. "That," she said, tapping the word.

"*Vincey?* It was probably the last thing he wrote."

"How do you know?"

"It's smudged. And there are fresh drops of ink around it. We found his fountain pen. The cartridge was leaking, and Montagu's fingers were stained with ink."

Her brain raced. The last thing he wrote, she thought. A message. It had to be. For her.

"Tell me, Dr. Ryder." Holden studied her with narrowed eyes. "What do you know? What does *Vincey* mean to you?"

She did not reply. Instead she knelt by the nearest pile of books and started sorting through them while Holden looked on with an annoyed expression. Many of the books she picked up were familiar—from her own studies, research, and work. How many discussions she'd had in this room with Evelyn, late into the night, sometimes through the night! They had agreed on some topics, fought and argued over others, to the accompaniment of old brandy and, usually, one of Evelyn's favorite operettas playing on the expensive sound system that fed to speakers throughout the apartment. Music was one of the few things that reached past the dark places inside her.

She picked up a copy of T. E. Lawrence's great work, his auto-biographical *Seven Pillars of Wisdom*. She opened the cover, reading once more the inscription on the flyleaf, from the author to Winston Churchill. This was one of Evelyn's most treasured possessions. Other works by and about Lawrence lay nearby. Collections of letters. *The Mint*, the book about his time in the Royal Air Force, after the war. Books about the Middle East. She had many of them herself, although, unlike Evelyn's first editions with rare bindings, hers were mostly much later reprints and paperbacks. Finally, she found the book she was looking for. Evelyn's small collection of fiction, readily identifiable by some of the lurid covers, had landed together. Beneath a copy of Dashiell Hammett's *The Maltese Falcon* she spotted the dark blue cover, stamped in gold, of the book she knew so well.

She carried the book to the desk and laid it on the surface. Despite its rough treatment, the book did not seem any the worse for wear. Luckily. It was a first edition, signed by the author to Rudyard Kipling, and worth many thousands of pounds.

Holden stood beside her. He glanced down at the book—Sir Henry Rider Haggard's classic novel *She*. "Okay," he said. "I read it when I was a kid. So what?"

She hesitated. "You know what *She*'s name was? The name of the character in the story, I mean. *She* was just a name used by the tribes that worshipped her—*She who must be obeyed*."

"No idea."

"Ayesha." DS Bryan spoke. He'd returned to the room unnoticed by her.

Holden's face was a question mark.

"Ayesha was the real name of the character referred to as *She*," Bryan explained to his boss.

"Your name." The DI's jaw dropped a fraction. "That's a hell of a coincidence. What's it got to do with *Vincey*?"

"In the book, Leo Vincey was Ayesha's lover," Bryan said.

Holden glared at Bryan, then he swung to face her. "You." His face whitened, then it reddened. "You're his lover?" A glance at the now-empty, bloodstained chair. "Montagu's?"

"I was. For three years." Calmly. "It ended two years ago."

"Bitch!" Holden spat the word.

She didn't flinch. She held her head up high and looked at Holden steadily, which seemed to inflame him more. She'd seen him angry before, but not like this. He kicked the desk, raved about stupid women who kept things back and contaminated crime scenes. The paperwork he'd have to fill out. The explanations he'd have to give to his superiors. She said nothing, waiting until he'd vented his spleen. At one point her eye caught Bryan's. She saw a flicker of something in the man's expression, instantly concealed. The SOCOs proceeded about their work, seemingly indifferent to the explosions emanating from the infuriated man in charge.

Holden stilled finally. His jaw tightened so much she thought she heard his teeth grind together. "Detective Sergeant," he said. "You can take Dr. Ryder home. She will be taking no further part in this investigation."

CHAPTER 6

Who is Ayesha Ryder? The man known as Nazir was puzzled. He opened a fresh pack of cigarettes. Gauloises. He extracted one from the pack, lit it with his lighter, and sucked smoke into his lungs. He exhaled and leaned forward over the laptop computer on the table in front of him. He reread the email. Then he opened the photographs that had come with it. He scrutinized them one by one, taking his time—methodical, as he was in all things. Ayesha Ryder. Senior researcher at the Walsingham Institute for Oriental Studies. She was extremely beautiful, like a fashion model. He could acknowledge the fact objectively, although he experienced no feelings of lust.

Was this woman any more than she appeared? Was she a threat to his plans, and those of his employer? On the surface, no. She was simply the consultant Scotland Yard called upon in any case with Middle Eastern aspects.

Ryder's career was well documented: stellar Ph.D. at Oxford. Internationally renowned author and speaker. Palestinian rights activist. Apparently Palestinian by birth, although Ryder was no

Palestinian name. Where had she come from? Nazir couldn't find any trace of her before Oxford. That worried him.

He closed the email window on his computer, stubbed his cigarette out in a take-out coffee cup, rose from the battered arm-chair—like the rest of the furniture in the Whitechapel safe house, it was a hurried purchase from a thrift shop—and walked through to the kitchen. He leaned against the doorjamb and watched the two men wearing rubber gloves who worked at a Formica-topped table, much chipped and stained, and liberally decorated with cigarette burns.

The smell of stale chips was strong in the confined space—the newspaper-wrapped remains of a large order from the local fish-and-chip shop were heaped in the kitchen sink, next to a pile of Styrofoam coffee cups and crushed Pepsi cans. The hum of nighttime traffic on Tower Bridge could be heard over the muted sounds of the BBC news from a radio on the countertop.

An array of materials was spread on the table in front of the two men. Bits of metal pipe, electronics, wiring, tools, and a block of some yellow substance. Trinitrotoluene. More commonly known as TNT. Put together in the right way—which could be discovered by any child with a computer and access to the Internet—these components would make a bomb. Exploded in a confined space, the results would be devastating.

A fly settled on his sleeve. Nazir stared at it for a moment, then, with a lightning-fast move, he caught it. He held it in his fist and felt its feeble flickering against his skin. He opened his hand slightly, caught the insect by the wings, then crushed it between his fingers until it burst with an almost audible pop. He flicked the mangled remains to the floor and wiped his hand on the door-jamb. "How long?" he asked.

RYDER

Both men stopped what they were doing and looked at their chief. He could see the fear in their eyes, was used to it. Nazir knew that people who met him for the first time found it difficult to believe a man with his reputation could look so harmless—like an accountant or insurance adjuster. It was an image he cultivated; his stocky build, chubby features, the round, cheap-looking spectacles through which he blinked owlishly. His generally benign demeanor had led many an opponent to underestimate him, forgetting physical appearance is often no indicator of the man beneath. Heinrich Himmler, after all, looked like a schoolteacher.

His men had worked with him for a long time and knew his appearance for the mask it was. He'd given these two a graphic example, just a few weeks back. They'd been present when he questioned a suspected informer. The man was stripped naked and tied to stakes in the ground, then his body was smeared with honey. This was in the desert, in an area with large ant nests. Nazir had read about this ancient form of torture and had been intrigued. The man, a former commando, pissed himself and talked before the first ant even reached him. But Nazir wanted to observe what happened when the ants swarmed over him. What would happen to his body. How long it would take him to die.

It took a long time. All the while the man writhed and jerked, screaming until his heart failed. When it was over they left the body there. What the ants didn't finish, other desert scavengers soon would.

"An hour." One of the men at the table, a bullet-headed ex-paratrooper, replied to his question. "It'd be much faster if we used our own stuff," he added, after a hesitation.

Nazir did not reply. He stared at the man for so long the ex-paratrooper started to tremble and a bead of sweat ran down his broad face. Nazir waited a moment longer, then glanced at his watch. "You have thirty minutes," he said. "Make sure it's ready." Turning on his heel, he walked back into the living room, sat down, reopened his laptop, and contemplated the biography of Ayesha Ryder—all of it that was known. Something, possibly much, was missing.

CHAPTER 7

The duty officer suppressed a yawn. He took a sip of tea, grimaced at the lukewarm temperature, then turned back to reading the file on Sir Evelyn Montagu. His assignment was to determine whether Montagu's death held any significance for national security, particularly in light of the imminent Tower of London peace conference.

The duty officer was a slim, fit-looking man in his late thirties—a receding hairline made him look older. The windowless, high-tech room in which he sat took up much of the space on the second floor of Thames House, the headquarters of MI5, a few hundred yards south of the Houses of Parliament. With the heightened alert for the conference between the Israeli and Palestinian leaders, he was not the only one on the floor. Three other desks were also staffed, and the director-general was in, too—although that was by no means uncommon, even if there was no alert.

Sir Evelyn Montagu had led a busy life. His file was an extensive one with linkages to many other files. The duty officer's eyebrows arched, although with no hope of meeting his hairline;

Montagu once worked for MI6, the British foreign intelligence service, as a consultant. He had played a leading role in persuading the Shah to leave Iran in 1979. He read on, intrigued.

At the end of the nineties Montagu became involved with members of several Palestinian organizations. His dealings with Arafat led the Israelis to declare him persona non grata, and this in turn caused him to be blacklisted for further work with the British government. During the Second Intifada in the early 2000s, he was vocal in his criticism of Israel's treatment of the Palestinians. This criticism grew during the 2006 Israel-Hezbollah war; then, at the end of 2008, when Israel invaded the Gaza Strip and killed more than 1,400 Palestinians, many of them women and children, he'd taken a very visible role as leader of a group of British academics protesting Israel's actions.

Montagu's activism culminated in his presence on board the *Mavi Marmara* during the spectacularly failed attempt to break the Gaza blockade in 2010. His subsequent imprisonment by Israel caused a major diplomatic furor. The queen issued a statement saying how personally distressed she was at the treatment of an old and dear friend. The duty officer muttered a fervent prayer on behalf of his organization that they would not need to get involved. People this well connected invariably caused all sorts of problems. Even after death.

He read on, pausing now and then to make notes. Montagu had known many people regarded as problematic. Not just Arafat— everyone had known *him*. Muslim clerics on hot lists kept by every intelligence organization in the West. Hezbollah leaders. Hamas militants. *But he was Jewish.* Longtime friend of Israel's new prime minister, Judah Ben David. The officer remembered something. His fingers danced across the keyboard, making connections. Montagu was on the guest list for tonight's reception at the Israeli embassy.

He made more notes, until his interest was distracted by some of Montagu's writings. The Israelis wouldn't like this stuff, he knew. So how did the Ben David friendship figure? He clicked on another link, to a file on a former lover of Sir Evelyn's. He reached for his tea, put it down untasted.

Ayesha Ryder, he read, *researcher at the Walsingham Institute for Oriental Studies. Palestinian. Former member of the* Fedayeen. *Terrorist.* He picked up his pen and scribbled furiously. He had the answer to his question. Montagu's death was now a matter of national security.

On the far side of the windowless room, a woman in her late thirties sat at another desk where a row of Christmas cards bespoke a degree of popularity—or at least a desire to be thought popular. The woman was attractive, with blond hair cut in a pageboy bob that had gone out of fashion years before. She did not care—like most things, her hairstyle would come back into fashion. Right now she was not thinking about her hair, but what the balding man—the duty officer—was finding so interesting. She glanced around the room. Her other colleagues were occupied. She tapped a series of keys on her computer and opened up a program. It had been installed by an expert, a master who assured her it would never be detected, and that, if it was, it would disappear if anyone tried to access it in anything but the right way.

When the program opened, she entered a series of numbers. Another screen appeared. It was full of text. A file. The same file being read by the duty officer.

CHAPTER 8

"Holden! No!" Ayesha couldn't let him send her away. She *had* to stay. Stay and find out what had happened to Evelyn. Who tortured him. Who murdered him. "I can help," she said, almost pleading. "*Vincey*. It's a clue. Evelyn left it. For me."

Holden grimaced. She knew he'd been shaken by her revelation she was Evelyn's lover. Shaken and angry. Angry with her for not telling him about her relationship with Evelyn right away. Angry with himself for not knowing. His immediate reaction had been to order her out of the study, out of the apartment, and get Bryan to drive her home. But now he hesitated.

She stared into his face, willing him to let her stay. She could guess his thoughts. If *Vincey* was a clue to Montagu's murder, Holden could not afford to ignore it. She had worked with him on four separate occasions now. She knew he respected her ability. It was why he kept using her. That, and because he was very attracted to her. He'd made no secret of that. After her part in the Iraqi antiquities investigation came to an end, he'd asked her to dinner. She refused. Holden had seemed surprised, as if "no" was not a word he'd ever heard from a woman. He hadn't taken the rejection lightly and she doubted he'd give up. It wasn't in his nature.

The DI returned her stare. "How can you . . ." The question died on his lips. He tried again. "If your relationship ended two years ago, why would he have left a clue for *you*?"

A wave of relief swept over her. She fought not to let it show. "Evelyn knew you called me in on cases with Middle Eastern elements." She drew breath and slowed down. "He would have thought it likely—if you got the case—you'd call me in on this one, too. So he left that." She looked down at the blotter. When she raised her eyes Holden was staring at the chair that had held Evelyn's body. Again she guessed his thoughts. What was it about Evelyn that she'd gone to bed with *him*? What kind of man was he?

Holden faced her. "So you think he left something inside his copy of *She*?"

"It seems like the obvious place to start." She opened the book and turned the pages. The inscription on the flyleaf to Kipling was ancient. There was nothing else. Nothing written, nothing inserted between the pages.

"That's that, then," Holden said, when she came to the last page.

"No! There has to be something. Evelyn wrote that word with a purpose. I was meant to see it and guess its meaning."

"I'm open to suggestions." Again, Holden glanced at his watch.

She looked around the study, thinking back to her time with Evelyn. Rider Haggard's *She* was something of a joke between them. Evelyn often compared the single-minded determination of the fictional character to her own. She glanced at Bryan. He inclined his head. She saw respect in his eyes, and something else—understanding? "I want to see the other rooms," she told Holden.

The DI blew out his cheeks, hesitated, then shrugged.

The master bedroom was next to the study. She looked at the neatly made-up bed, the tallboy with Evelyn's silver-backed brushes arranged on top. The top two drawers had been hers. A framed painting, an original watercolor by Winston Churchill, lay on the floor. The door of the small wall safe it normally concealed hung open, a wad of cash visible within. Evelyn's passport. Under torture, he must have given them the combination.

Holden cleared his throat. "We don't know what, if anything, was taken. Did he have anything else particularly valuable?"

"His books, paintings, the sort of things you've seen." She brushed past the DI and left the bedroom, Bryan sidestepping out of her way. The dining room seemed untouched. The dark surfaces of the mahogany table shone with the fresh polish applied by Evelyn's housekeeper. Decanters and bottles gleamed on the sideboard. The chairs were neatly arranged. The paintings on the walls, an eclectic mix of old and modern masters and complete nonentities, were undisturbed. The sitting room was the same. Recent editions of magazines and newspapers were piled on a coffee table. A book lay next to them, its pages marked with sticky notes.

"*Palestine Redux*," Holden said, picking up the book and reading the title, "by Ayesha Ryder." He turned the book over and studied the author photograph on the back.

Evelyn had practically had to tie her down to get that photograph taken. Abruptly she turned on her heel and left the room. Her lip was quivering and she did not want the detectives to see.

She inspected the bathroom and the guest room. Then she

came to the kitchen and saw it. On the wall next to the fridge. The gift she had given Evelyn on his birthday, the second year they were together. She remembered the day she'd found it. She'd been killing time, browsing in a little shop—the Witch Ball—in Cecil Court, off Leicester Square. She'd flipped through a rack of unframed prints and posters and found the perfect present. An original poster, so the shop owner said. Evelyn had loved it.

She glanced around the kitchen, saw the teapot and the cup and saucer next to it on the sink, then she looked back at the poster. Ursula Andress, a statuesque blond movie star, best known for *that* scene in *Dr. No*, was engulfed in red flame. *SHE who must be obeyed! SHE who must be loved! SHE who must be possessed!*

How often Evelyn had teased her with those words. Now, while the Scotland Yard men watched, she lifted the framed movie poster off its hook and turned it over. Holden sucked in his breath. Stuck to the back of the poster was a folded square of paper.

In Evelyn's study, she tried to restrain her impatience while a SOCO, summoned to the kitchen by Holden, took his time returning with the folded paper from the back of the poster. She had started to remove it but Holden stopped her, insisting proper procedure be followed. Bryan stayed in the kitchen to supervise.

She stared at the empty chair, stained with Evelyn's blood. Sometime in the next few hours an autopsy would be performed. The cause of death officially established. Evelyn's already mutilated body would be further violated, cut open, his organs removed. A formal identification would take place. Holden had not asked her to do it. She glanced at him. He was speaking on his cellphone again, not looking her way. Who would do it? Evelyn had no close relatives. One of his cousins perhaps. *The funeral.* She'd go. Of course she'd go. Did Evelyn want to be buried or cremated? What was the Jewish tradition? Not that he was in the least bit religious. He never observed the Sabbath, or any of the high holidays. Like her, he did not believe in God, anyone's god. He had no time for it all.

With Evelyn religion was an exercise in logic. He could not believe in anything without proof, let alone the thousand and one rules of Judaism with their intrusions into daily life. What you could eat and not eat. What food you could not wash in the same sink. She shared his outlook, but for her it was more. No God would permit what passed for life in the Gaza Strip. No God would permit what had happened to her. Or what happened to her parents. Or, if He did exist, then He was not a God she wanted anything to do with.

The SOCOs finished their work and packed up their equipment. They said good night to Holden, still talking on his cell, and nodded to her as they left the room. What would happen to Evelyn's apartment? All his things. His books and mementos. Would his cousins sell them all off? Perhaps they'd let her buy some of his books. Who would move in, once everything had been cleaned and sterilized? Someone who'd never heard of Evelyn Montagu. Would his ghost haunt them? She shivered, not from cold, and pulled her arms tight about her chest. She might not believe in God, but she'd always had a vivid imagination. As a child she had loved ghost stories. She did not want to think of Evelyn as some lost revenant. Surely, if there was an afterlife, he'd gone somewhere . . . better.

Bryan came through the doorway. She pulled herself out of her reverie and focused on the clear plastic evidence bag he held out to Holden. The DI ended his conversation, put away his cell, took the bag, and laid it down flat on the desktop, next to the blotter.

RYDER

The cheap writing paper was yellow with age, and there were dark creases where it had been folded. It was dated, in the top left hand corner—13.V.1935. There was no superscription. Just the text of the letter, inscribed in copperplate script that flowed across the paper. The ink was faded, but it was still easy to make out the words:

Dear Winston,

The treaty is signed. Tell R.M. HMG's copy is in safe custody, proverbially speaking. 9.1, 26, 327, 15. In passing, 25:10.

T.E.S.

A treaty; the government's copy in safe custody. She wanted to take the letter away and study it until she had probed all of its secrets.

"Well?" Holden asked her. "What does it mean? *Winston*." A trace of excitement crept into his voice. "A letter to Churchill?"

"Probably. T. E. Lawrence wrote this. They were old friends."

"Lawrence?" Holden was puzzled. "The initials are T.E.S. How do you get Lawrence from that?"

"After the war—World War One—Lawrence of Arabia was a hero to millions. He was incredibly famous. Hounded by the press. Think of today's top movie stars, or Princess Diana and the paparazzi. Lawrence was that big. He couldn't stand the publicity, so he joined the RAF as a common aircraftsman under the name John Hume Ross. When that identity was discovered by the press he took another name—Shaw—which he kept until his death after a motorcycle accident in 1935. He was T. E. Shaw. *T.E.S.* Also," she added, "I'm familiar with his handwriting."

"Okay. Fine. So what does this letter mean? What's this treaty he's talking about? And what do these numbers mean?"

"I don't have the first idea. But Evelyn thought the letter important enough to hide it for me to find, and"—she glanced down at the blotter—"for leaving a clue to be the last thing he did. My guess is this is what whoever tortured him was after."

"So Montagu was working on something to do with Lawrence of Arabia. That's ancient history. Who would care about that now? Enough to torture him?"

"Lawrence supported the Arab cause." She formulated her thoughts as she spoke. Working it out in her mind. "He was their advocate at the Paris Peace Conference in 1919. His proposals were ignored, but it doesn't mean people have forgotten them."

She bent, picked up a small globe of the world that lay on the carpet. Evelyn had haggled for it in a tiny shop in the Grand Bazaar during a trip to Istanbul. He'd been absurdly pleased with his bargaining skills. She forced back the memory, spun the globe, then stopped it and tapped with her finger on the eastern end of the Mediterranean. "What has been the most contentious part of the world for the past few decades?" she asked. "The Middle East. It's all about land and resources, and where the borders are drawn. What if Evelyn discovered something that shed new light on an old problem? And what if somebody else found out?" She put the globe down on the desk. "Somebody who thought whatever he found might hurt their particular cause?"

"Enlighten me," Holden said sarcastically.

She glanced at Bryan. He leaned against an empty bookcase, his face impassive. She focused on the bust of Lawrence. How to explain the life and thought of such a complex man? "You said you've seen *Lawrence of Arabia*? The movie."

"Years ago," Holden said.

"You know then that the Arabs helped the British fight the Turks—the Ottoman Empire—in the First World War?" The DI nodded.

"They didn't do that just for the hell of it. The British promised the Arabs their independence; in an Arab nation that would have encompassed the present-day Saudi peninsula, Iraq, Jordan, Syria. And Palestine. A Palestine that included all of what is now Israel."

"Oh."

"'Oh' is right. Do you think the Arabs would have risen up against the Turks if they thought the British would go back on their word, and instead promise a homeland to the Jews in Palestine? A place, incidentally, with an Arab population of well over half a million at the time, and only a few thousand Jews?"

"I see." Holden shook his head. "No, actually, I don't. Spell it out for me."

"There would have been no Israel if Lawrence'd had his way. Palestine would have been part of an *Arab* nation. A treaty worked on by Lawrence and important enough for him to have concealed by a code could be of huge importance to the Palestinians. And the Israelis." Holden looked skeptical. "I know it looks like Palestinians killed Evelyn, Holden, but it doesn't add up. I've told you about the writing." She gestured at the words daubed in Evelyn's blood on the wall behind the now-empty chair. "No Palestinian, no Arab, would write 'Palestine' that way."

"Even if you're right, it's hardly conclusive."

She bit her lip. She'd wanted to keep this to herself until she had some proof. She looked at Bryan; couldn't read him. "Do you have a pen and paper?" she asked. Taking the notebook and pen he produced from his jacket pocket, she sketched the rough outline of a human body, then drew a series of small black circles on the torso. "This is the pattern of the burn marks we saw on Evelyn's body. One at the base of the throat, one below each shoulder, a matching pair at the hips, and one at the top of the groin."

The DI nodded.

She connected the dots.

Bryan grunted when he saw what she had drawn.

"A pentagram?" Holden looked bewildered. "Satanism?"

"It's the Star of David." *Idiot.*

"If you're right," Holden made a face, "then the shit will really hit the fan. I'm not convinced, though. Why wouldn't a Palestinian do the same thing, as a gesture of contempt? Anyway, you said a Palestinian could be just as interested in whatever this code means." He tapped the letter in its plastic bag, then, reaching into his jacket pocket, he pulled out his phone and flicked it open. "It's time I brought in Special Branch."

She looked at the Lawrence letter, memorizing it, then back at Holden, who was punching a number into his phone. "Do what you have to do," she said. "I'm out of here."

"What are you going to do?" Holden looked at her with suspicion. "Do you have some idea what that letter means?"

She thought furiously. If she did crack the code, she'd need help. Holden had access. What was more to the point, he knew her. Which could not be said of anyone at Special Branch. No one there would trust her after they'd looked at her file. "I told you I don't," she replied. "But I'm going to have a shot at working it out. Who should I talk to in Special Branch if I manage to crack Lawrence's code?"

"Hold up." Holden closed his phone. "If you think there's a chance you can do this, then I can wait a couple of hours before calling them in. But that's all you're getting."

"All right. We have a library at the Walsingham Institute. You can come with me if you like."

She breathed a sigh of relief. She had a reprieve. Now she had to make every moment of it count.

CHAPTER 9

"What have you got?" Moses Litmann demanded as he thrust through the door into the brightly lit room two levels below the basement of Israel's London embassy. Mossad's domain. He'd hurried down as soon as he could decently escape from the reception, urgent to find out more about Ayesha Ryder, the woman he'd first learned about during his phone call in the embassy garden. That call had worried him. A second one a few minutes ago had put the fear of God into him.

Moshe Weinberg, the Mossad station head, was a career intelligence operative in his mid-fifties. He was nearly bald, with a fringe of graying hair, sagging jowls, and a lugubrious expression that gave him a strong resemblance to a bulldog. "Minister," he said, rising from a chair in front of a computer workstation, "you wanted to see what we have on a woman named Ryder?"

"Yes."

"I've pulled her file. You can read it here." Weinberg gestured to the chair he had vacated. "Coffee?"

"Cream and sugar."

When Weinberg placed an embassy mug beside him a few moments later, the foreign minister was bent forward, peering at the screen. It displayed a series of photographs of Ayesha Ryder. One was identified as sourced from the website of the Walsingham Institute, where she worked as a senior researcher. Another was a jacket photograph from her book, *Palestine Redux*.

"What's this?" He tapped the third. The photograph showed a very different-looking Ryder. Her hair was snarled. Her face was streaked with blood. She was cradling her left arm and appeared to be in pain.

"That was taken on board the *Mavi Marmara*. After our people stormed it."

"She's one of *them*?" Litmann's voice was full of loathing. The so-called peace activists who repeatedly tried to break Israel's blockade of the Gaza Strip were a major irritant. He wanted to tighten the blockade, extend the offshore no-go zone, and shoot the *mamzers* on sight—damn the consequences. He'd run into opposition from the prime minister. Judah Ben David was doing his best to push through a proposal to drop the blockade entirely and, to his chagrin, he had to appear to support him.

"Hmm." Weinberg leaned forward, moved the mouse, and clicked on a link. Another screen of photographs appeared. "These were taken during her interrogation."

Litmann studied the new photographs. Ryder had been cleaned up and now wore a fresh sling on her arm. Her face was devoid of expression. "Did she say anything?"

"Nothing. Like most of them she refused to give even her name or nationality."

"Arab-loving scum."

Weinberg moved the mouse again. "These were taken twenty years ago."

Litmann looked at the images of a young woman, barely more than a girl. She had light olive skin, high cheekbones, a long nose, a full-lipped mouth, and a firm, pointed chin. Her dark hair was shaved close to her scalp and one eye was swollen shut. "I don't understand." He turned to Weinberg, baffled. "This is Ryder?"

"Yes. She would have been sixteen at the time. They were taken after she was captured by the IDF."

"Captured?"

"Yes." Weinberg brought up another screen. Text this time. "While attempting to attack one of our settlements in the Gaza Strip. She was *Fedayeen*."

"A terrorist!" It took Litmann two attempts to get the words out. "Ryder's a terrorist?"

"*Was* a terrorist. Twenty years ago. You didn't know?"

Ryder a terrorist. What could that mean? Ignoring Weinberg's question, he swung back to the screen and read the report of Ryder's capture and interrogation, forcing himself to slow down to comprehend the words. The file had initially been marked *Unnamed Female Fedayeen*, with the date and place of capture, then the transcript of her interrogation. He jumped to the last screen to see who conducted it, then jumped back to the beginning of the report. He read quickly, absorbing the details of the IDF ambush and the death of all of the *Fedayeen* but Ryder. Her transportation to the fort outside Beersheba. The interrogator had put numerous questions to her. She refused to answer any of them.

He clicked on the next document. It was a report by the fort's commander, a Captain Aarens. In dry terms Aarens described how the interrogating officer had been found on the floor, unconscious and bleeding heavily from his groin. A broken bottle lay nearby. Next to the man's penis. The prisoner had used it to castrate him. Before she escaped. How was never established. She was not recaptured. Much later, through an informant, they found out her name—it was not Ryder then.

"We let her go," Litmann muttered. "After the Gaza flotilla business. Why?"

"It was only then that we made the connection and identified Ryder. Fingerprints. The decision to let her go was political." Weinberg shrugged. "Whatever she did in the past, she's now a British citizen. Highly respected, with an international reputation. At the time she was Montagu's girlfriend. You remember the furor over him. That must have played a part in the decision."

Litmann stared at the Mossad station head with unseeing eyes. Then he turned back to the photographs of Ayesha Ryder. What in hell's name did it mean? Montagu's girlfriend was a Palestinian terrorist. Did Sayyed Khalidi know something? If the Palestinian leader did, so would his friend Judah Ben David. A cold sweat broke out on Litmann's forehead. Was he walking into a trap?

CHAPTER 10

Tears pricked at Ayesha's eyelids. She forced them back. She would find who murdered Evelyn, she reminded herself. And they would pay. Assuming she could crack Lawrence's code and work out what his killers were after. She was confident in her ability, but she needed the resources of the library at the Walsingham Institute. She glanced up, caught Bryan's eyes in the rearview mirror. She looked away, out the window. "Next turn," she said.

The car slowed, Bryan uncertain.

"Round the corner," she directed. "Past the church." As they went by the darkened building she noticed Bryan peering at the stone gateway with its three grinning skulls, starkly silhouetted in the light of a streetlamp. "St. Olave's," she said. "It's one of the oldest churches in London—built around 1450, but rebuilt after being bombed in the war."

"It survived the Great Fire?" Holden asked.

"Yes. As did the Walsingham Institute. The flames came close, but the wind changed direction at the last minute. Samuel Pepys is buried in the church. His wife, too."

"Oh?" This from Bryan. "I've read his *Diaries*."

Holden snorted, but her respect for the DS rose another notch. "Then you'd be interested to know that those gardens"—she gestured to the left—"are where the Navy Office used to be. Where Pepys lived and worked."

Bryan stared through the window, almost as if he expected to see a bewigged figure hurrying along the street. "Awesome," he whispered, as they left the car.

Ayesha led the two detectives toward the wrought-iron fence that fronted the stone and half-timbered pile, once the home of Sir Francis Walsingham, principal secretary to Queen Elizabeth I, but more remembered as perhaps history's most coldly efficient spymaster. None of the three noticed an unmarked van turn into Seething Lane behind them, its lights doused. It parked in a pool of darkness beside the garden where Pepys's Naval Office once stood, opposite the grinning skulls of St. Olave's.

She used her keys to let them in through the front door of the great Elizabethan house that now housed the Walsingham Institute. Once inside she tapped a code on the wall-mounted security panel. The alarm system deactivated, she led Holden and Bryan through the ancient building, seasonally decorated with tinsel and a fake tree, and across an enclosed courtyard. In clipped tones, as they walked, she flung back over her shoulder various bits of information. There had been, she told them, many structural changes and additions over the centuries, including the construction of a new wing in the 1860s behind the main house. That was where the library was housed. In recent years the original building had been renovated to bring it back as close as was practical to something Sir Francis Walsingham would have felt at home in.

Many of the furnishings were original to the house. Some

items had been stored for decades and only recently brought out and restored. The simple but elegant Elizabethan furniture, much of it made of solid English oak, gleamed in the concealed lighting—not as romantic as the original candlelight, but much safer.

In the library, she sat down at the nearest large table, one of several arranged about the main reading room, the walls of which were lined with bookcases, packed so densely with books there did not seem an inch to spare. Dark wood, polished to a high sheen, with massive turned legs and green leather tops, the tables were designed expressly for the library. So were most of the other furnishings—except of course for the black, flat-screen computers.

"Tea?" Holden queried.

"There's a kitchen." She pointed to a door on the far side of the reading room, in the shadow cast by the overhang of the mezzanine floor above. "Help yourself."

Holden turned to Bryan, who stood with his head back, admiring the library ceiling high overhead. One of London's hidden gems, it had been painted by Frederick Leighton, the Victorian fresco painter, in the artist's distinctive vivid and sensuous style. It depicted a bustling scene in the Roman Forum. "Sergeant," the DI said.

"Hmm?" Bryan dragged his gaze from the ceiling. "Oh, right. Tea. Dr. Ryder?"

"No thanks."

She saw Holden's gaze linger on the portrait above the great fireplace. The man it depicted wore dark Elizabethan garb, his neck buried in the standard white ruff. He had a long, mournful face, with a full mustache and a trim beard. The institute's benefactor and namesake. Not for the first time she felt that Walsingham's dark eyes stared right at her.

"Lot of books," Holden remarked.

"You've got the letter?" she asked. She had memorized the text but wanted to see it again anyway.

Holden produced the clear plastic evidence bag from a brown leather satchel. "How do you even start trying to crack a code that's over three-quarters of a century old?"

She had been puzzling over the same question since they left St. John's Wood. She was already going over in her mind what she knew about Lawrence. Born, she thought, 1888. He was forty-six when he died. In 1935. She checked the letter. It was dated May 13, 1935. "When exactly did he die?"

"What's that?" Holden asked, looking up as Bryan put a tray with tea things on the table.

She brought up the Wikipedia entry for T. E. Lawrence. Hardly authoritative, but it contained a wealth of information and could presumably be relied on for basic dates. She clicked on the link to Death and read the information aloud. "'At the age of 46, two months after leaving the service, Lawrence was fatally injured in an accident on his motorcycle in Dorset, close to his cottage, Clouds Hill, near Wareham. He died six days later, on the nineteenth of May, 1935.'"

"May thirteenth!" Bryan exclaimed. Holden looked blank.

"Six days before May nineteenth is May thirteenth," she said. "Lawrence had his accident the same day he wrote this letter."

"Shit!" Holden exclaimed. "So Lawrence wrote this, then got killed." He rubbed his chin. "From the fact that he used code he must have had an inkling something might happen. You said his death was an accident. Any doubt about that?"

"In fact, yes. Quite a lot." Her mind buzzed with speculation as she typed *T. E. Lawrence death conspiracy theories* in the browser search engine. There were pages of entries. She clicked on one of the first and brought up an article from *The Independent*. It was dated a few years previously and concerned an exhibition on Lawrence's life at the Imperial War Museum.

She scrolled through the entry, stopped: "'One witness, giving evidence at the inquest, stated that he had seen a black car travelling in the opposite direction to Lawrence moments before the crash, though its driver, if the car ever existed, never came forward.'"

"A black car," Holden repeated. "Very sinister. But who'd want to kill Lawrence?"

"There were rumors he was a spy," she said. "Most speculation centers on the Germans. Or British Nazi sympathizers."

Holden snorted. "Why on earth would the Germans want to kill Lawrence of Arabia?"

"Remember the times," she said. "Nineteen thirty-five. Hitler is in power. Germany is rearming. Appeasement is the name of the game in Britain. Except for one politician."

"Churchill," Bryan supplied.

"Yes." She looked up at the DS. "And this letter is addressed to Winston."

"Fine," Holden said, impatient. "But I still don't get why the Germans would want to kill Lawrence."

"Remember what I said about him? That he was a hero to millions?"

Holden nodded.

"It might be hard to understand now, but Lawrence had an attraction that was almost Arthurian. Some people even thought he hadn't really died, but, like Arthur, gone to a sort of Avalon from which he would return to save an imperiled Britain. If Lawrence had come out publicly against appeasement, he might very well have rallied the nation into intervening against Hitler. We know, now, that if Britain and France had stood up to him in the mid-thirties he wouldn't have had a chance. No one knew that better at the time than Hitler."

Holden poured himself a cup of tea, adding milk from a carton. "That makes a kind of sense. I guess. But what relevance could it have now? A treaty connected to the Nazis? Old news. Who'd care now?"

"You're right." She slumped back in her chair. "It doesn't make any sense."

"What about the rest of the letter?" Bryan asked. "The second line — 'Tell R.M.' Who could that be?"

She went back to the Wikipedia entry on Lawrence. "No R.M." she reported. "But it has to be someone known to both Churchill and Lawrence. Someone important, presumably. What else was happening in 1935?" Not waiting for an answer she typed more words into the search engine.

"'World history 1935,'" Holden read, looking over her shoulder at the list of events displayed on the screen. "'Night of the Long Knives, King of Yugoslavia assassinated, Dollfuss assassinated.' Who was Dollfuss?"

"The Austrian chancellor," Bryan said.

"Austrian?" Holden cocked an eyebrow at his sergeant. "The Nazis?"

Bryan nodded.

"Hmm." Holden looked back at the screen. "'Stalin Begins Purges,' 'Mao Sets off on Long March,' 'Howard Hughes Slashes Speed Record.' Any of this dotting any *i*'s?" he asked Ayesha.

"No. But you can see how much Nazi-related news there

is. Look." She tapped the screen. "'Germany Rejects Versailles Treaty.' 'Saar Becomes Part of Germany.' This is the time when Hitler was really on the rise."

"Anything that looks like R.M.?" Holden wanted to know.

She typed a new search query: *UK 1935.*

"Holy crap!" Holden exclaimed. Bryan was silent, but she felt his hand grip the back of her chair.

"Prime Minister Ramsay MacDonald," Holden said, reading from the screen. "*R.M.*"

"Yes." Excitement boiled within her. She jabbed a finger at the screen. "Until June seventh. Ramsay MacDonald was prime minister until June seventh. Then Stanley Baldwin took over."

"So?" Holden, elated at their discovery, did not understand the significance of her observation.

Bryan did. "June seventh," he said. "That's less than a month after Lawrence was killed."

"Okay," Holden said, "so what does that tell us? What's the connection?"

She bit her lip. Holden was right. What was the connection? There had to be one. She was sure of it. But how to find it?

CHAPTER 11

M oses Litmann left the Mossad facility and entered the elevator, his mind racing. He needed to know what kind of threat the Ryder woman posed to his plans. What did she know? Who had she told?

How had Ryder got involved? he wondered as the elevator doors slid closed. On the surface it was obvious. Was it any more than that? He'd read her dossier. Her professional and academic record spoke for itself. The fact Holden was the officer in charge of the case . . . used Ryder on other investigations. It would have been strange if he'd not called her in. That she should have such a highly personal connection with Montagu, though. Nobody could have anticipated that. Now this new development. Not only was she a Palestinian, she was a terrorist. Former terrorist, as Weinberg put it. The distinction meant nothing to Israel's foreign minister.

Back in his room he went straight to the whiskey decanter and poured himself a large measure, draining it in a single gulp. He poured another, brooding over the report of Ryder's interrogation twenty years before. Or rather the nonreport. It must have been completed after her interrogator recovered. Not that he ever really recovered. Litmann's imagination conjured up the scene. What she had done to the man. He took another gulp of whiskey. That it should be the same woman now. All these years later. He shuddered.

He crossed to the writing table, put down his glass, and picked up a file that lay there. It was an old file, and starting to come apart. He leafed through the handwritten pages, browned from the years since Chaim Weizmann, Israel's first president, had penned them.

He had been stunned when he first read the dossier. He'd had to find out more, couldn't rest until he knew the truth and found any proof that still existed. His search led to the death of Sir Evelyn Montagu. And dead-ended there. Now Ayesha Ryder had discovered something. A coded letter from T. E. Lawrence—Lawrence of Arabia. *The treaty has been signed. Tell R.M.* Some would say it wouldn't matter if it all came out now. Too much time had passed. He knew better.

With the exception of the file containing Weizmann's own notes, everything had been erased from history. Weizmann's people in Britain had gone to extraordinary lengths to make sure of that. T. E. Lawrence was dead. Lawrence's sponsor, Prime Minister Ramsay MacDonald, resigned from office claiming ill health—thanks to Weizmann's notes he knew the real story. Nigel Clarke-Kerr, deputy chief of the League of Nations and almost the only other person in on the secret, died when the plane taking him back to Geneva crashed into the North Sea. That left only Churchill. He was out of office, though, in his "wilderness years," with little power to influence anything.

Litmann picked up the file once more and turned to the last page. The paper was different from the other pages. It looked like it had been torn from a notebook. A sketch took up most of the space on the page. Of a boxlike object on top of which sat two figures, rough approximations of angels. Anyone familiar with popular books and movies of the last half century knew instantly what it was. Although theories abounded as to its whereabouts, and many had searched for it, it had been lost for centuries. Two words were written beside the sketch, in Weizmann's crabbed hand: *Lawrence knows!*

T. E. Lawrence was long dead. Montagu had discovered something—what? But now he was dead, too. As with the other business, Litmann thought he was the only one who had an inkling that the Ark of the Covenant might still exist. Now he couldn't be sure. Did Ayesha Ryder know something, too?

CHAPTER 12

Where do I go from here?

Ayesha was frustrated. The knowledge that R.M. was Prime Minister Ramsay MacDonald, and that he had resigned from office less than a month after Lawrence's death, had seemed a vitally important clue. But so far it had led nowhere.

She stared up at the portrait of Francis Walsingham. *Spymaster, I could use your help now.* Why had MacDonald retired from politics so soon after Lawrence's death, or murder? She had looked at a plethora of websites pertaining to MacDonald and his premiership, trying to find links to Lawrence. They were there. Mentions in his memoirs. References in speeches by MacDonald recorded in Hansard—the verbatim transcript of Parliament's debates. Nothing that seemed to bear any significance, though. No mention of any treaty. It was like looking for the proverbial needle.

Proverbially speaking.

Impulsively, she opened up another website devoted to proverbs and their meanings. There were dozens, hundreds of them. In each one she looked for *treaty*, and carried out random searches for the numbers in Lawrence's letter. There were no proverbs that had anything to do with treaties.

The treaty.

She splashed water on her face. Patted it dry with paper towels.

Proverbially speaking.

She was glad of the quiet in the small washroom. Away from Holden and Bryan. Not that they had been distracting her. Not really. Just, it was good to be alone. *Evelyn.* He would have broken Lawrence's code by now. She pictured him sitting at the kitchen table, doing *The Times* crossword with his morning coffee. He never failed to complete it in less than ten minutes. Tears pricked at her eyes. Then she gasped. Evelyn and crossword clues. What if there was another clue? Could there have been something else on his blotter?

She pushed through the door back into the library reading room, her mouth already open and forming the request to Holden. To return to Evelyn's apartment. Bryan got in first.

"Dr. Ryder," he called, "what about the Book of Proverbs? From the Bible. Could that be anything?"

She stopped in her tracks, stared at the DS for an instant, then raced across the reading room, swiftly typing *Proverbs 9.1* into the search engine. A choice of Bibles confronted her. She chose the King James as being the version T. E. Lawrence would most likely have used. She read out the words: "'Wisdom hath builded her house, she hath hewn out her seven pillars.'" *Yes!* She clenched her fist and thumped the tabletop. "That's it!"

"So?" Holden grinned. "What does it mean?"

"*Seven Pillars of Wisdom,*" Bryan said, joining them.

"Yes, Sergeant, that's what it says." Holden's tone was heavy with sarcasm.

Ayesha, who was looking directly at Bryan, saw his eyes darken. "That's what it *means*," she said.

Holden looked blank.

"*Seven Pillars of Wisdom* is Lawrence's best-known book. His autobiographical account of the Arab Revolt. A huge bestseller in its day and an acknowledged literary masterpiece."

"Great." Holden shrugged. "We've got a letter from Lawrence to Churchill—maybe—in which he says a treaty has been signed and Ramsay MacDonald, the prime minister, should be told. Then a reference to his own book?" He reached across the table and picked up the letter in its plastic evidence bag. "How do these numbers relate to the book, then?"

"Page numbers?" Bryan guessed.

Ayesha strode across the room and stopped in front of a bookcase near the fireplace. She ran a hand along one shelf and drew out a volume, sumptuously bound in dark blue with raised bands on the spine and lavishly decorated in gold.

"Sergeant," she called, "give me the first number, would you?"

"Twenty-six."

She turned the thick, creamy pages until she got to page 26. It was the introduction to the first section of the book. *Some Englishmen*, she read to herself, *of whom Kitchener was chief, believed that a rebellion of Arabs against Turks would enable England, while fighting Germany, simultaneously to defeat her ally Turkey.* She scanned the next two paragraphs, all there was on the page.

"Well?" Holden asked impatiently.

"See for yourself." She held out the book to him. "It's just a brief explanation for how the Arab Revolt came about. If it's a clue, I don't have any idea what it means."

RYDER

Proverbs 9.1 led us to Seven Pillars. Her brain worked furiously on the puzzle. *So, logically, there must be something about the book. Or more likely in the book. Otherwise there'd be no point.* Think. *If 26 is not a page number, what is it? Chapter? Illustration? Map?* She pulled another copy of *Seven Pillars* from the shelf. Different binding. Different edition. She opened the contents pages. Skimmed back and forth. There was nothing that made sense. *Dammit. What did Lawrence mean?*

She returned the volume and contemplated the shelf from which she had taken it. It held several copies of *Seven Pillars* as well as Lawrence's other book, *The Mint*, written about his time in the RAF. There were also collections of letters by Lawrence, and others written to him. Her hand moved along the spines of the books, stopped at another edition of *Seven Pillars*. This one was plainer, in an off-white binding. It was the original 1922 edition, which had been issued in a very limited run. Something like eight copies. Known as the Oxford edition, it was worth a considerable fortune. The other edition, the 1926, also known as the Subscriber's edition, had been somewhat abridged by Lawrence, although not as much as the later 1927 version, published under the title *Revolt in the Desert*. Bernard Shaw had dismissed it as an "abridgment of an abridgement." Two editions of *Seven Pillars*, 1922 and 1926. The hair on the back of her neck stood up. *Twenty-six.*

Holden still had the book. The 1926 edition. Resisting the urge to snatch it from his hands, she held out one of hers. "May I?" When the DI handed it over, one eyebrow raised, she looked at Bryan. "What were the rest of those numbers? After 26, I mean?" Bryan turned to go back to the table where they had left the letter, but Ayesha put up a hand. "Never mind. I remember—327 and 15."

She put the book down on the nearest table and rapidly turned the pages, her fingers trembling slightly. She got to page 327 and glanced up at Holden and Bryan. Both detectives sensed her excitement and were staring from her to the book with wide eyes.

She looked down at the page once more and scanned the text— an amusing episode when Lawrence, returning to "civilization" in Egypt after much time in the desert, was mistaken by British military police for an Arab. She absorbed this subconsciously while she counted the line numbers till she got to 15. She read the line. Now that she had the answer, her heart slowed. She read it again.

"Come on," Holden demanded. "Spit it out."

"Line 15 contains a reference to Lawrence's gold head rope and dagger."

"That's it?" Holden's face fell. "That's the answer? Please tell me you're joking!"

"It's not the answer, sir." Bryan had gotten it. Again. "It's where we'll *find* the answer."

"You couldn't hide anything in a head rope," Ayesha explained before Holden could berate his subordinate for his own lack of understanding. "At least I don't think you could. But a dagger could be a good hiding place. In the hilt. Or engraved on the blade."

Holden grunted. "Say you're right. How on earth would we find Lawrence's dagger?"

"That's easy," Bryan said. Holden looked like he was going to explode, but the DS hurried on. "I've seen it. With all of Lawrence's things. His robes and so on. At the Imperial War Museum. You remember? Dr. Ryder found a newspaper article that referred to an exhibit there. I saw it when it was on, but they also have some of his things on permanent display. I'm pretty sure the gold dagger is one of them."

Holden glared, then checked his watch. "Right. The Imperial War Museum it is. I'll call ahead."

"Aren't we forgetting something?" Bryan asked. "Sir."

"Are we?"

"There was another line in Lawrence's letter."

"Of course!" she gasped. "'In passing, 25:10.'"

"Page 25, line 10?" Holden gestured at the book that lay open on the table.

She flipped back through the pages. There was nothing on page 25, other than the title of the book, repeated, before the introduction she had looked at earlier. Certainly there was no line 10.

"Could it be another biblical reference?"

"*In passing?*" Holden groaned. "How the devil do we find—"

But she was already running across the floor. She snatched a Bible from its place between a Koran and a Tanakh, opened it at the Book of Proverbs and skimmed the text. At 25:10 she read the lines, and her brow furrowed. "'Lest he that heareth it put thee to shame, and thine infamy turn not away.' Sounds like a warning."

"It looks like it follows on from 25:9," Bryan said.

"You're right," she said, looking at the line above. "'Debate thy cause with thy neighbor himself; and discover not a secret to another.'"

"What's that in English?" Holden sounded bewildered.

"Basically it's just an admonition to keep secrets secret," she said. "And a warning of what might happen if you don't."

"That doesn't make any sense," Holden complained. "Why would he put that in code?"

She stared at the page, puzzling over the words. Holden was

right. It didn't make sense. That the rest of the letter was in code spoke for itself.

"Perhaps it's not a reference to Proverbs," Bryan said.

She looked up. "What do you mean?"

"The first clue was a specific reference to the Book of Proverbs—proverbially speaking. Could 'in passing' be a reference to another book of the Bible?"

"In passing." She took up the Bible and flipped back to the contents page. "Genesis. Exodus." *Exodus!* "Exodus, from the Greek, *exodos*, meaning departure. What happens in Exodus? The first Passover. Passover. The Israelites pass out of Egypt. It must be Exodus." She turned pages until she came to the second book of the Old Testament, then skimmed to 25:10.

Holden was too impatient to wait. He eased the book out from under her hands. Aloud he read: "'And they shall make an ark of shittim wood: two cubits and a half shall be the length thereof, and a cubit and a half the breadth thereof, and a cubit and a half the height thereof.'" The DI looked up. "What the hell is shittim wood?"

"Tell you on the way to the War Museum," she said.

Outside the Walsingham Institute, in Seething Lane, the unmarked van was still parked opposite St. Olave's. In its dimly lit interior a red-haired man poured a cup of coffee from a thermos and turned a page in the book he was reading, Chris Hedges's *War Is a Force That Gives Us Meaning*. His companion, a heavyset man, munched on a cold hot dog and peered into the night. They had nothing to listen to—no one had known to bug the Walsingham Institute. All they could do was wait. The minutes ticked by. Then, after they had been there nearly an hour, the red-haired man's cellphone rang.

RYDER

"Yes?" he said.

The call was brief, lasting no more than ten seconds. When it ended, the red-haired man turned to his colleague. "They'll be coming out in a minute," he said. "Then we're off to the Imperial War Museum."

CHAPTER 13

"How does the Ark of the Covenant relate to the thing that was done and agreed upon that Winston had to tell MacDonald?" Holden demanded as Bryan turned their car into Lambeth Road.

"I've no idea." Ayesha had been racking her brain over that question since she'd read the words in Exodus. The Ark of the Covenant. Lawrence and the Ark. She knew he'd been fascinated by it. Could he have discovered what happened to it? Was it possible that the Ark still existed, hidden somewhere? Was this the secret Evelyn had stumbled on? Was that why he had been murdered? "Maybe it doesn't have anything to do with the thing that was agreed upon. Or only tangentially."

"How do you mean?"

"The 'in passing' reference led us to the Book of Exodus, right?"

Holden nodded.

"Maybe it has a double meaning. In passing. Like 'by the way,' or a postscript."

"Come on!" The DI shook his head. "You mean Lawrence was saying to Winston, the treaty is signed, tell RM, and by the way, the Ark of the Covenant?"

"I don't know." She shrugged. "Even if I'm right, what was Winston supposed to make of it? 'By the way, the Ark.' The Ark what?"

Holden grunted and sagged in his seat. "I've seen *Raiders of the Lost Ark*. A couple of times. But I thought that whole Ark business was just a legend."

"Not at all." She forced herself to answer. She didn't want to talk, would have preferred to mull over whatever lay behind the final clue in Lawrence's letter. "The Ark of the Covenant is extremely well documented, although a great deal of mythology has built up around it. Some of it because of that movie."

"So you mean you think it really exists? That it's not some fairy tale? What exactly is it?"

"The Ark was—is—the holiest object known to the Jewish people. It was thought to have been hidden somewhere below the Temple Mount in Jerusalem. One story says the Knights Templar removed it along with many other precious objects during their custodianship of the holy sites. At the time of the Crusades," she added, suspecting that Holden wasn't all that familiar with the story of the Knights.

"Hey." He leaned toward her, his expression serious. "There's no curse, is there?"

"Curse?" She recalled what she'd read of the Ark. "Not exactly. But it was supposedly an object of enormous power—the physical manifestation of God on earth. The means by which He would speak to His people. His voice emanating from the Mercy seat. You know that it's supposed to contain the tablets bearing the

Commandments given to Moses by God? The original, broken ones, too?"

"Sort of."

"According to the stories in the Bible, the mere presence of the Ark was considered enough to destroy armies, or cities. Like Jericho. Where the walls came tumbling down after the Ark was paraded around them."

Bryan pulled the car to the curb beside the gardens fronting the Imperial War Museum. "Even viewing the Ark improperly is said to have resulted in death," he said.

The massive Victorian pile that is home to the Imperial War Museum was formerly the Bethlem Royal Hospital—Bedlam to Londoners. *Meaning uproar and confusion*, Ayesha reflected as they walked toward the great fifteen-inch guns that guarded the entrance, reminders of an empire on which the sun never set. Once mounted on the battleships *Ramillies and Resolute*, the guns lowered overhead, casting inky shadows against the lighter darkness of the night.

A man emerged from the illuminated and pillared portico at the front of the museum, across which hung a huge banner that advertised the museum's special "Christmas Truce" exhibition, commemorating the amazing moment when, during Christmas 1914, to the disgust of their leaders, British, French, and German troops had stopped shooting each other, emerged from their trenches, and greeted one another with gifts of food and wine.

"DI James Holden, Metropolitan Police." Holden stepped forward, hand outstretched. "Sorry to drag you out of bed," he added.

"I wasn't in bed." Giles Ritchie shook his hand. The curator had salt-and-pepper hair and a heavy five o'clock shadow. He wore blue jeans and a tweed jacket with leather elbow patches. "I was here, working. Bit of a night owl. Which is why the chief rang me after he got your call. What can I do for Scotland Yard?" he asked, with a nod to Bryan and a curious glance in Ayesha's direction.

Holden introduced them. Everybody shook hands, then the curator ushered them inside. He waved them through security, then led them along a short hall and out onto the main exhibition floor.

Holden, with a boyish whoop, ran past Ayesha. He stopped at the edge of the floor, turned, and raised eyebrows on the curator, who grinned and nodded. With another whoop Holden was gone, disappearing behind a tank of the 1914–18 war.

It had not been that long since Ayesha had last visited the museum. Three years ago. With Evelyn. He'd wanted to look at a special exhibit on the war between the British and the French in Africa and the Middle East. Few people knew that, for much of the year and a half following the fall of France in June 1940, more Commonwealth soldiers and airmen had died fighting the forces of Vichy France than from fighting the Germans. Her memory of the visit had not prepared her for the sight that now met her eyes. On that occasion the main floor was flooded with light and crowded with people. Now the exhibits were only visible as dark shapes against the emergency lighting. And, of course, they were the only ones there.

She had to admit that the display, seen like this, was more than impressive. Tanks stood guardian at the edges of the floor, silent sentinels of another age. Interspersed were artillery pieces and assorted vehicles, including, incongruously, a World War I vintage London bus. Old Bill, it was called, after Bruce Bairnsfather's famous wartime cartoon character. The bus once formed part of a fleet requisitioned to help get British troops to the front—the army not having enough vehicles of its own for the purpose.

Dark shapes hung suspended from the ceiling overhead. As her eyes became accustomed to the gloom, she made out V-2 and Polaris missiles, weapons of mass destruction far greater—and more real—than anything Saddam Hussein ever possessed. Some of the famous aircraft that bore aloft the first aces were there as well, menacing in their stillness: a Sopwith Camel, its canvas, wood, and wire fragility belying the acrobatics of which it was capable, and nearby, its much deadlier progeny, the Supermarine Spitfire.

She dragged her gaze from the birds of prey overhead and turned to Ritchie. The curator leaned against a nearby pillar. Of Holden and Bryan there was no sign. Squinting into the gloom, she saw movement off to her right—Holden, clambering over the top of a Grant tank. Then she spotted Bryan, sitting in the driver's seat of Old Bill.

"Want to try something?" Ritchie asked her. "It's one of the reasons I love working here at night. I get to indulge all of my boyhood fantasies."

"No thanks. Where is the Lawrence exhibit?"

"Next level." Ritchie jerked his head and walked across the floor toward a broad staircase on the far side. She followed him. Holden and Bryan disengaged themselves reluctantly from their respective vehicles and tagged along behind.

At the top of the stairs Ritchie stood aside to allow his visitors a better view of the larger-than-life portrait mounted on the facing wall.

She had seen the original Augustus John portrait at the Tate, and many reproductions of it. But she was still stunned by how the vivid color of Lawrence's robes was eclipsed by the even more vivid blue of his eyes. She studied his handsome face. Not for the first time she thought there was something very appealing in his expression of calm certainty. T. E. Lawrence reminded her of Evelyn. Not that there was any resemblance, but something about him . . . Somehow, without ever having met him, she knew instinctively Lawrence was a man she would have trusted. She gazed into the intense blue eyes. *What happened in 1935?* she wondered. *What were you hiding?*

"You see what I see?" Holden broke the spell. He walked up close to the portrait. "Gold head rope. And that must be the dagger." He pointed to the golden hilt, and part of the haft visible beneath Lawrence's robe.

"That's right," Ritchie acknowledged. "We have them both, as well as some of his robes. The exhibition's through here." He stepped through the doorway and flicked a series of light switches on a wall panel.

Ayesha, Holden, and Bryan had taken only a couple of paces after him before they stopped, their collective gazes drawn to the object in the center of the exhibition space, surrounded by a low rope barrier. Spotlit from above, its polished chrome gleamed and sparkled. License number GW 2275. George VII, Lawrence's Brough Superior motorcycle, was every inch a thing of power and danger. The danger, she told herself, probably came from the knowledge he'd been killed while riding it. Thrown over its handlebars when swerving to avoid two boys on bicycles. So the story went.

"Care to try it?" Ritchie looked at Holden. "Not something you could do if you were here during the day." He laughed.

"Someone would probably shoot you. Joking," he added. His expression said not.

The DI took a pace forward, eagerness showing on his face, then something changed. He shook his head. "Doesn't seem right," he said, stepping back.

Ritchie looked at Bryan. He made no movement, and the curator was turning away, when Ayesha stepped over the rope barrier. Swiftly, she swung one long leg over the seat, sat down, brought her feet up to rest on the pegs, leaned forward to grip the handlebars, and lowered her head until she looked through the miniature windshield.

She couldn't resist the impulse. Just as the two detectives were fascinated by the machinery of war, she was drawn irresistibly to the great vintage motorcycle. The Brough had been known as the Rolls-Royce on two wheels because of its power and expense. She recalled the scene near the end of *The Mint* where Lawrence described, almost erotically, racing his motorcycle against a low-flying airplane. Now, sitting on it, bent over as Lawrence must have been on his last ride, she experienced a surge of . . . something. Power. Something more primal, too. The engine was not running, but she could almost feel it throbbing between her legs. Abruptly she let go of the handlebars, eased back, and swung herself off the seat. As she stepped back over the barrier she glanced at the three men, defying any of them to say anything. None of them did. All were looking at her, though. Holden with naked lust in his eyes. It paled, however, against the ferocity of desire she glimpsed, just for an instant, in Bryan's face.

She pushed between the men and strode toward a large upright glass display cabinet. It housed three mannequins, dressed in clothing once worn by T. E. Lawrence. An infantry officer's khaki uniform. An aviator's heavy leather flying jacket, circa World War I. And the centerpiece: the robes Lawrence wore when he sat for the portrait she'd just seen. His head cloth, complete with gold *agal*, or head rope, was mounted atop the robes. Projecting from the belt was his golden *jambiya*, the Arab word for dagger.

Ritchie opened the case and withdrew Lawrence's dagger from the display. He held the weapon carefully in two hands and walked to a low, flat-topped case that displayed a number of original documents and letters relating to the Arab Revolt. He hesitated. Bryan, understanding, slipped off his suit jacket and spread it over the surface of the display case.

"Thanks." Ritchie laid Lawrence's precious dagger on top of the cloth.

Four heads bent to peer at the curved golden sheath from which the hilt of the dagger protruded.

"Well," Holden said. "This is it. Now what?"

"You expected to find what, exactly?" Ritchie asked.

"Some sort of message left by Lawrence," the DI said.

"Hmm." Ritchie rubbed his chin. He picked up the weapon, took the sheath in one hand, grasped the hilt in the other, and pulled. The wicked-looking blade came out easily, glinting in the overhead light. He upended the sheath and shook it gently. Nothing fell out. "I'm not surprised," he said. "Too many people have looked at it over the years for anything concealed inside not to have been found." He put down the sheath, held up the blade, and considered it closely. "Mecca. Lovely workmanship," he commented. "Just as you'd expect, of course." He held the blade close up to his face, then moved it farther away. "Hello. Some sort of engraving along the blade."

Ayesha, whose hopes had crashed when nothing was found inside the sheath, felt the stir.

"What?" Holden demanded. "What is it?"

"I hardly think it's what you're looking for." The curator squinted at the blade. "It's a series of musical notes. You often find highly personalized inscriptions engraved on daggers like these. Lines of poetry. Dedications to lovers. That sort of thing. I can't say I've ever seen music. Lawrence was an odd bird, though." Ritchie groped in his trouser pockets with one hand. He produced a small folding magnifying glass, opened it, and held it against the blade. "Yes. It's really quite lovely work."

"May I?" Ayesha asked.

Ritchie handed over the blade, hilt first.

At first she saw nothing but the steel of the blade, honed to a razor thinness. She held the dagger close to her face, then farther away. She turned to the curator. He was already holding out the magnifying glass. She held it close to the blade. Now she saw the markings plainly. A treble clef, followed by the time—4/4. Sharp notation, then four notes. She tried to sound out the notes in her head. Nothing. It made no sense.

"Well?" Holden asked.

"I don't know if it means anything. But there's nothing else here. Perhaps if I could play the notes?" She looked at the curator. "I don't suppose you have a piano?"

"Actually we do. It hasn't been played for a while, but I happen to know it was tuned not all that long ago." The curator paused. "It's in a bit of an unusual location."

Ritchie's "unusual location" was something of an understatement. Leaving the Lawrence exhibition, he led them down two flights of stairs and into the "trench warfare experience." This was a permanent exhibit, one that, next to the "Blitz experience"—where visitors could sit in a World War II bomb shelter and submit themselves to the sound and fury of an air raid—was the most heavily visited attraction in the museum, he informed them. A segment of frontline trench from the 1914–18 war, surmounted by coils of barbed wire, was approached via a communications trench, just like the real thing. Museum visitors would be exposed to a cacophony of sound: machine guns, mortar and artillery shell explosions, whistles, and recorded commands urging soldiers "over the top."

She was standing on the fire step, peering through a periscope into "no man's land," when Ritchie's voice brought her back to the reason for their presence. "Down here," he called as he clattered along the wooden boards that floored the main trench. He ducked beneath a sacking curtain in its side wall and vanished. They followed him, bending to get through the low opening, then straightening up in the dugout on the other side.

"Mess." Ritchie swept a proprietorial arm around the cavelike space, dimly lit by fake oil lanterns. "Temporary. Officers, for the use of."

The wooden bunk beds and the deal table were much scuffed and bore the scars of numerous cigarette burns. The dugout was bedecked in military equipment: rifles, bayonets, canteens hung from nails thrust into the walls. A 1918 calendar featuring a colorful advertisement for Pebeco toothpaste hung from another nail. Helmets likewise. Plates, mugs, and utensils lay on the table, looking as if they had been in recent use. All of the ephemera of the British soldier at war. Plus a piano.

"It's original," Ritchie explained. "Looted—or salvaged rather—by the Royal Welch Fusiliers from an estaminet outside Amiens, after it was pretty much destroyed by shelling. They brought it back to Blighty after the Armistice. God knows how. It was at their regimental HQ for a long time. When they amalgamated with the Royal Regiment of Wales in '06, they donated it to us."

She sat down at the piano, on top of a wooden crate marked BEST JAFFA ORANGES. *Nineteen eighteen.* If everything in this re-creation was accurate, then the Jaffa oranges that had been in the crate would have been among the first to come from Palestine after its capture from the Turks by the British under General Allenby in December 1917. A Palestine soon to be a British mandate under the League of Nations. Until it wasn't any longer. Until it was Israel and the occupied territories. And Jaffa oranges, once Palestine's best known export, became Israel's.

She splayed her fingers and played a few notes to hear how the piano sounded. As Ritchie had said, it was well tuned, although it sounded odd in the confined space of the dugout. She'd mem-orized the notes on Lawrence's dagger. Now she played them. Deliberately. Slowly. Then faster. She played the notes again and again. Slow, faster, faster still. Finally she stopped and bowed her head, defeated. It meant nothing. How could it?

"Laughter." Bryan spoke into the sudden hush. "It sounds like laughter."

"Fuck laughter," Holden snapped. He kicked his foot against the wooden bunk bed, drawing a frown from Ritchie. "I've had enough of this." He turned to leave the dugout.

The echo of the notes still rang in Ayesha's head. It did sound like laughter. She turned to Holden, who was holding the sack-ing curtain to one side, bending under it. "Wait—" she said, breaking off as Ritchie stepped forward and clapped Bryan on the shoulder.

RYDER

"It *is* laughter!" the curator exclaimed. "And I think I know what it means. Have you ever heard of a word painting? A madrigalism?"

She shook her head. Madrigalism? The word meant nothing to her.

CHAPTER 14

Nazir grunted with satisfaction. Work on the pipe bomb was finished. He glanced at his watch. The man, code name Esh, should be here any minute to pick it up. Then all he had to worry about was what Ayesha Ryder was going to discover next. The last report he received said the woman was on her way to the Imperial War Museum to look at Lawrence of Arabia's dagger. He shook his head. His chief was not going to be happy when he heard that one.

He was halfway across the living room when he heard a knock at the front door of the Whitechapel safe house. He froze, his head cocked, listening. The knock came again. He relaxed. The pattern was correct. Esh.

At the front door he paused to withdraw a pistol from beneath his jacket. He flicked the safety off, undid the door latch, and stepped back and to the side. "Enter," he called, just loud enough to be heard.

The man who walked into the hallway held his hands out in front of him, palms upward.

Esh was medium height, in his mid-thirties, with dark hair cut short. Beneath his leather jacket it was clear he was powerfully built. An otherwise nondescript face was made memorable by the jagged scar that ran from under his left eye almost to his chin.

"Trouble?" Nazir asked.

"None."

"Followed?"

"No. I'm sure of it."

Nazir grunted. He slipped the safety back on, put his pistol away. Then, with a jerk of his head, he headed back into the house.

The bomb-making equipment had vanished from the kitchen, along with the bomb itself. The only thing on the table was a neatly wrapped brown paper package. One of his men was reading; the other leaned against the sink, drinking from a can of Pepsi.

Nazir ignored them. He turned to Esh. "You know what to do?"

Esh nodded. "Yes."

When Esh had gone, Nazir returned to the living room and picked up his cellphone.

Ayesha Ryder, he thought, as he thumbed the redial button. *Who the hell is she?*

CHAPTER 15

The MI5 duty officer approached his desk with a fresh cup of tea. He sat down, took a sip, and contemplated the blinking icon on his computer screen. He put down his cup, opened the message window, and scanned the text of another capture relevant to the ongoing investigation into the death of Sir Evelyn Montagu. The investigation was now officially deemed top priority with potential major implications for national security. The director-general had ordered him to stay on it.

The capture was a "partial" email. The software had not been able to retrieve everything. Sometimes a great deal was corrupted and unreadable. Crucial information was missing from this one. There was no way of telling who sent it. Or who received it.

The duty officer picked up a pen and began to jot down the salient facts, immediately intrigued by the reference to Lawrence of Arabia. The business of a message supposedly engraved on the great man's dagger made him sit up. At the next sentence, though, he nearly exclaimed out loud. Ayesha Ryder! He bit his lip. Coincidence? It couldn't be.

He read back over the email fragment, frowning at the connections someone had made to former prime minister Ramsay MacDonald. And to Churchill. Ryder? No, she was referred to in the third person. Whoever it was, their speculation about Lawrence's death was intriguing. He shook his head over the bit about the Nazis. That made no sense.

He came to the end of the fragment, clicked an icon on his computer screen, and opened a database. He entered terms into the search engine: "T.E. Lawrence," "Winston Churchill," and "Ramsay MacDonald." He wanted to see if the database would turn up anything with all three names. It did. One entry. A file on Thomas Edward Lawrence—Lawrence of Arabia. With cross-references to entries under John Hume Ross, and Thomas Edward Shaw. Aliases.

His practiced eye moved rapidly down the screens of text. There was a lot of information. Some of it was familiar. He'd seen *Lawrence of Arabia,* of course, and the Hollywood bits were there. The remarkable coup of capturing Aqaba from the Turks with Arab irregulars. The destruction of Turkish troop trains and railway lines. Lawrence's sabotage had wreaked havoc on the enemy's lines of communication and supply, greatly aiding the British advance on Jerusalem and Damascus.

Descriptions of Lawrence's relationships with prominent individuals took up many screens of text. His complex friendship with Prince Feisal, leader of the Arab troops in the field, was the subject of much analysis. Not surprising, given the prince's importance both during and after the war, when he became, first, king of Syria, then, after his expulsion by the French in 1920, king of the newly created country of Iraq.

Churchill was there, of course, and General Allenby. Lloyd

George and Clemenceau, the French Premier. Al-Husayni—the Grand Mufti of Jerusalem, a polarizing figure if ever there'd been one. Writers too—George Bernard Shaw, Robert Graves, E. M. Forster. Others. Lots of others. There was mention of possible homosexual relationships—an Arab servant named Dahoum figured prominently, but nothing was known for certain. The duty officer remembered reading about Lawrence's ambivalent sexuality. The rumored episodes of sadomasochism.

Another section of the file dealt with Lawrence's long friendship with Gertrude Bell, the renowned female Arabist and architect of the creation of Iraq. Bell had said that Lawrence could set a cold room afire with the force of his personality. There'd been rumors of a sexual relationship with her. With other women too. So much for the myth. The duty officer read the names. The wife of an RAF wing commander. Lady Astor. The wife of the American ambassador. One of the Mitford sisters. These were only rumors, though, and he knew what his service was like for collecting those.

In silent admiration, he read through the material about Lawrence's involvement in the 1919 Paris Peace Conference. Lawrence had made a real nuisance of himself lobbying on behalf of the Arabs, pretending to interpret for Prince Feisal, who merely recited passages of the Koran while Lawrence said whatever he wanted. The duty officer chuckled. Lloyd George, infuriated, had practically accused Lawrence of treason.

After the peace conference, Lawrence worked out of the Colonial Office, acting as advisor to Churchill on Middle East affairs. He was instrumental in the creation of the new Kingdom of Trans-Jordan. Then, suddenly and completely, in 1922, he dropped out of public life. That was when he enlisted under assumed names—the Ross and Shaw aliases—in the Tank Corps and the RAF. Supposedly because he couldn't take the attention. The duty officer shook his head. It just seemed wrong.

There was an account of Lawrence's motorcycle accident. He lost control of his machine when he swerved to avoid two boys on bicycles. His death several days later was described. The file included the report of the coroner's inquest, an account written by the surgeon who tried to save his life, and several newspaper reports and obituaries. That was it—only it wasn't. A frown creased the duty officer's forehead. There was a link to another file. Marked *Ultra Classified*.

Only certain senior personnel of the Security Service had clearance to access Ultra Classified files. He was one of them. He clicked on the link, swiped the ID card that hung on a thin chain around his neck through a reader attached to his computer, then entered a lengthy alphanumeric encrypted code from memory. A new file opened on his screen.

Eleven minutes later he finished reading. He'd skipped some parts and had to go back several times. His tea was cold and forgotten and one knee twitched. He'd started to make notes but stopped after reading the first paragraph. There was no way anyone wanted any record of this, no matter who made it or how soon it was to be shredded. Closing the connection to the file, he picked up his phone and thumbed the button for the director-general's office. This, he thought, was going to make her very unhappy.

On the far side of the room the woman with platinum blond hair raised her eyes from her computer screen and watched the duty officer get up hurriedly from his desk, buttoning his jacket as he did so. Her eyes flicked back to her computer screen. She could guess where he was going, who he was going to see. And she knew why.

CHAPTER 16

Ahmed Ali-Yaya switched his briefcase to his left hand and fumbled in his trouser pocket. He pushed away thoughts of the package that was tucked inside the briefcase and what he had promised he would do with it. *Tomorrow, when the Israeli and Palestinian leaders meet in Downing Street.*

He found what he was hunting for. His front door key. His hands shook so much it took him two attempts to get it in the lock, but before he could turn the key the door was wrenched open.

Reem stood in the doorway. Dressed in baggy tights and a dark blue sweatshirt stained with food and baby vomit, her long brown hair in disarray, his wife looked as if she'd been crying. "Where the fuck have you been?" she shrilled, with a glance over her shoulder toward their bedroom. Where Janine would be asleep in her cot. Her lip curled in a way Ahmed had come to know all too well during the past few months. "You're drunk," she accused. "Again."

"Just had a couple." He hadn't, but he couldn't tell her what he'd really been doing. He stepped past his wife into the small room that combined living, dining, and cooking functions. "At the pub," he lied, "with Tim and Ali. It's been a long day." He did not see the child's doll lying on the floor by the sofa. When he stepped on it, his foot twisted under him and he slipped. He scrabbled at thin air, slammed against the dining table, and knocked a china bowl flying. It smashed into a dozen pieces. The sound rang through the small apartment. A split second of silence, then another sound started up. Janine's crying turned into an earsplitting shriek.

Reem threw her husband a look of pure hatred, swung on her heel, and slammed out of the room.

He put his briefcase on the kitchen table, bent, and scooped up the fragments of the bowl. He dropped these into the kitchen trash bin, then realized he had blood on his hands. He'd cut his palm on the sharp edge of one of the pieces. He ran his hands under the tap, then wiped them on a filthy tea towel. Pots, pans, and dishes filled the sink. Reem had cooked something. Whatever it was, she hadn't left any for him. He opened the cupboard above the stove and peered in. Cans. The cupboard was filled with cans. Baked beans. Pasta. Baby food.

He took down a can of baked beans, put it on the countertop, and crossed to the fridge. He took out a pizza from the freezer compartment, opened it, and put it in the microwave. He went back to the fridge, found a can of Foster's, popped the ring pull, and downed a long swallow. He wiped his mouth with the back of his hand and stared at his briefcase. Could he really do it? he asked himself. Of course he would. He'd sworn a vow.

CHAPTER 17

Madrigalism, Ayesha murmured to herself, back once more in the library of the Walsingham Institute, seated before the same computer. What could it mean? She'd thought about nothing else since they left the re-created World War I trench dugout, ignoring Holden's dark mutterings. He'd made a couple of threats to call in Special Branch, but she persuaded him to return to the library and make a last attempt at solving Lawrence's riddle.

She mulled over what Ritchie had told them.

"When I was up at Cambridge," the curator had said, "I thought about making the history of music my specialization. Early English music, in particular."

The others had listened, Holden with growing impatience, as Ritchie explained.

"Word painting has ancient origins. It goes back to Gregorian chant, which takes its name from Pope Gregory I, at the end of the sixth century. The same kind of thing was often used in the composition of madrigals in the fifteenth and sixteenth centuries. Hence *madrigalism*."

Ayesha was sure this must be the clue Lawrence intended to convey in his coded letter. There simply wasn't anything else. But what did it mean? "What exactly *is* a madrigalism?" she'd asked Ritchie.

"Essentially it's a musical conceit." The curator had assumed a professorial air. "Notes are used to represent words. For example, a series of ascending notes might be used to represent climbing a hill. Or a series of dark notes might portray death." He paused. "Or a series of short, sharp staccato notes, like those engraved on Lawrence's dagger might"—Ritchie held up a hand, although no one had said anything—"*might*, represent laughter." He shrugged. "But that's really just a guess. It could be something completely different."

She glanced up from her computer screen as Holden launched a paper plane across the library in the direction of Bryan, hunched over one of the flat-screen computers. The paper plane veered away from the detective sergeant at the last second and fell into the fireplace.

"An exercise in futility," the DI grumbled. He glanced at his watch. "When I think I could be home in bed. Sleeping." A suggestive leer in her direction. "Or something."

When neither she nor Bryan responded, Holden tried again. "Have either of you two geeks come up with anything yet?"

She had read dozens of screens of information about madrigalisms and word painting, and felt none the wiser. In the sense of being any closer to understanding what Lawrence had meant by his clue, at any rate. "I've got nothing."

The DI walked over to her reading table and leaned his backside against it. "Is there anything else about his life that would make sense of this? Did he write music? Have a favorite composer? Was he known for anything musical?"

"He did have a keen appreciation for classical music," she said. "Oddly enough, he had a particular interest in German lieder. But that's all I know."

"Codes, then? Is music ever used to carry codes? Maybe that's where we should be looking. You said he was a spy."

"I've tried that." Bryan joined them. "There's not much on using music as a code-carrying medium. Some stuff with Morse code, that's about it. I've tried translating the notes on the Lawrence dagger using various algorithms—but nothing."

"Well done, Sergeant." For once Holden seemed impressed with Bryan. "I'd never have thought of that."

She was impressed, too. Bryan had an original mind, and he knew more about some things than Holden. The inspector knew it, too. She turned back to Holden. "I didn't say Lawrence was a spy. Just that there were rumors."

"No truth in them, then?"

She thought about the question. "The rumors started in the 1920s when the newspapers learned that he was serving in the RAF, under an assumed name, and that he was based near what would now be the Afghanistan-Pakistan border. You've heard of the Great Game?"

Bryan nodded.

Holden saw and scowled. "Something to do with Russia?" he hazarded.

"Yes. The Great Game refers to the secret duel fought between Britain and Russia to expand their spheres of influence in Asia in the nineteenth century. Russia was expanding west and south. That posed a potential threat to British India. Both empires vied for control of Afghanistan. Nothing really changed after the Russian Revolution. If anything, the perception of threat grew with the advent of the Soviets. That Lawrence—soldier, linguist, historian, diplomat—should be based at such a sensitive location, under an assumed name . . . It struck many people, when the fact came out, as simply too good to be true. It was rumored that what he'd really been doing was making secret journeys into Persia and Afghanistan. Spying for Britain."

"And was he?" Holden wanted to know.

"No one seems to know. When his cover was blown in the press Lawrence was transferred back to England. Ostensibly he was working on the development of new fast sea rescue craft to pick up downed airmen. He developed quite a reputation in the field." She thought about the great motorcycle at the museum. What was it with Lawrence and speed? Freud would say he was running away from something. "Then he retired from the service and was killed shortly afterward."

She stood up, stretched her arms high above her head, and arched her back to clear the kinks. "Was he a spy?" she continued, aware that Holden and Bryan had watched her exercise with interest. Not caring. "For some, or all of the time he *was* hiding out in the military?" She tilted her head back. "It's generally accepted that he was a sort of amateur spy when he was working on archaeological digs in the Middle East, before World War One, sending reports about the local situation for the Foreign Office. I'd never believed there was any substance to the later stories, though. But now, if we assume he was murdered, well there must have been a reason. Espionage is as good as any.

"I always thought it was such a waste. His life after the war, I mean. After all that he did during it. Well, maybe it wasn't a waste. Maybe he kept on . . . doing things. But in secret. Maybe I just want it to be true. For it not to have been a waste. What I'm really saying is that I want there to be some meaning to Evelyn's murder." She sighed. "And what if Lawrence *was* a spy? Does that help us? Does it?"

Neither man answered her.

"Tea," Holden decided. "We need more tea."

Bryan headed in the direction of the kitchen. *Probably relieved to be doing something constructive*, she thought. She sat down and pulled the computer keyboard toward her. Brought up another screen of Lawrence-related entries. She'd been mining the deep Web. Trying different search engines to probe the massive amount of documents that had been scanned and digitized in recent times, much of it material never before available to the researcher. She'd pulled up entry after obscure entry. Totally irrelevant, all of them. She clicked on the top one on the new screen, inadvertently hitting the IMAGES button. A screen full of thumbnails appeared.

She moved the cursor to backtrack, then stopped. One of the images caught her eye. She opened it up and enlarged it. Lawrence after a trial of a new high-speed sea rescue boat. He was smiling broadly, looking pleased with himself and life. A woman stood next to him. A young, very attractive woman, dressed in the height of fashion. Ayesha stared. One of the woman's arms was linked through one of Lawrence's. *Who was she?* Lawrence, as far as anyone knew, was totally uninterested in women. This photograph said otherwise.

The photograph was sourced. From the *Lincolnshire Herald*. She clicked on the link. A new screen opened. The original newspaper article. With the photograph. And its caption. Her skin turned to gooseflesh. *Lady Madrigal Carey photographed with Mr. T. E. Shaw.* She gasped.

"What have you got?" Holden demanded.

She pointed at her computer screen mutely. Moments before she was near despair. Now she felt as if a shot of pure adrenaline had been injected into her veins.

Holden and Bryan bent over the computer and peered at the image on the screen of the handsome, smiling man and the stunningly beautiful girl.

"Lady Madrigal Carey. *She's* our madrigalism?" Holden asked.

The tiniest smile twitched Ayesha's lips. "Must be. The coincidence of names is too incredible for it to be anything else."

"I thought he wasn't into women?"

"As far as anyone knows. Lawrence was an extremely private person, though. We have no definite information, and I've read all of the biographies, of a sexual relationship with anyone. Man or woman. Which doesn't mean there wasn't. Just that we don't know."

"Okay. Fine." Holden's expression darkened. "But if Lawrence's message was a clue leading to this Madrigal woman, we're at a dead end."

"Why do you say that?"

"It's obvious, isn't it? Lawrence must have entrusted his girlfriend, or whatever Lady Madrigal was, with his secret. The copy of the treaty he talks about in the letter? He was telling Winston that, if anything happened to him, he should go see Lady Madrigal. In 1935 that would have been doable." Holden looked back at the screen, at the black-and-white image of the smiling couple. "She was some babe," he remarked, with a touch of wistfulness, "but she's got to be long dead by now." He spread his hands. "Dead end," he repeated.

"How do we know Churchill didn't go and see her?" Bryan asked. "In 1935? What's to say he didn't get the treaty and destroy it?"

"Good point, Sergeant," Holden said. "Furthers *my* point that this whole thing is a damn wild-goose chase."

Ayesha's jaw tightened. It was not a wild good chase, and she would not give up. *Evelyn*.

CHAPTER 18

S ir Norman Eldritch, Her Majesty's Home Secretary for the United Kingdom of Great Britain and Northern Ireland, opened the door to his apartment. Despite the hour he beamed at his visitor. When she'd rung him up he was in a deep sleep and inclined to be furious with whoever was disturbing him. These feelings vanished as soon as he heard the voice on the phone: Imogen Worsley, Director-General of MI5, the only woman he'd ever really loved. As soon as the call was ended he'd flung himself out of bed, showered, and put a pot of coffee on. He had no idea what she wanted to see him about other than that it must be important. He didn't care.

"Norman." Dame Imogen bussed him on the cheek. "Can you forgive me for getting you up at this ungodly hour?"

"Imogen, please." He helped his visitor out of her coat, surreptitiously admiring her legs as he did so — they were shown off to magnificent effect in a classic black Chanel suit with white cuffs and collar. It might be the early hours of a winter morning, and Imogen had likely been at the office since early the *previous* morning, but he had rarely seen her looking lovelier. Her auburn hair shone with a rich luster and her blue eyes sparkled. He knew what that meant.

"Disaster looms, I take it?" he asked, ushering her into the living room. A tray with coffee things sat on a low table centered on a Persian rug. A dark leather chesterfield and two matching chairs were arranged about it. The scene, illuminated by floor lamps, was made even cheerier by the glow from a gas fireplace and the obligatory Christmas tinsel, and by a vast decorated tree.

The head of the United Kingdom's domestic security service stood in front of the fireplace, warming her hands before the flickering flames. She turned and smiled at her host. "Yes, the game's afoot all right." She sat down on the chesterfield, opened a capacious leather handbag, and extracted a file folder. She put this on the table and waited while he poured coffee for them both.

Eldritch handed his guest a large mug emblazoned with the House of Commons logo. He knew she had no patience with delicate china. Imogen lived on coffee. How she slept he had no idea. Then again, he wasn't sure that she *did* sleep. He sat in an armchair facing her and glanced at the folder on the table. "So, what's it all about?"

"What do you know about T. E. Lawrence? Lawrence of Arabia?"

His eyebrows twitched. "The basics, of course. The revolt in the desert. Blowing up Turkish trains. Something about his involvement in the Paris Peace Conference. Like everyone, I've seen the movie. Peter O'Toole in Arab drag."

"Would it surprise you to know he worked for us? Or not *us* exactly—MI6."

"Not really. From what I know of Lawrence—languages, Arabist, something of a diplomat—I'd have thought he'd have been a first-class spy."

"He was. He started doing secret work in 1911 when he worked as an archaeologist in Syria. We recruited him properly in 1920. At the time we were actively engaged in countering Soviet espionage. All over the place, but particularly in the Middle East and the Subcontinent. Afghanistan and Iran—Persia, as it then was—were particular concerns. Lawrence's knowledge of the area, languages, customs, and so on was invaluable."

"Yes, I see that." He contemplated the extraordinary woman opposite—a view he'd give anything to make permanent. "I'm intrigued to hear where this is going."

Dame Imogen smiled. "The big problem with Lawrence was his fame. He was the hero of the hour. The press followed him everywhere. As Lawrence of Arabia he'd have been useless to us. So we arranged for him to disappear."

"Joined the Royal Air Force, didn't he?"

"That's right. MI6 had him join up as an ordinary aircraftsman. Name of John Hume Ross. That cover was blown, then he spent some time in the Tank Corps under the name T. E. Shaw before transferring back to the RAF. With him as a complete unknown in the armed services, a nobody of low rank, we could post him to wherever he was needed, and he could conduct secret activities without anyone being the wiser."

"Couldn't happen now." He chuckled. "You'd have all of his fellow servicemen snapping his picture on their cellphones and blogging and tweeting about him."

"Yes." Dame Imogen laughed. "There was something to be said for life before the Internet." They shared a look. She dropped her eyes first, picked up her coffee cup, took a sip, and continued her narrative. "In the mid-twenties Lawrence was based in northern India. While he was there he spent most of his time on secret missions into Persia and Afghanistan, dressed as a tribesman. I won't go into what he did, Norman. It's not relevant now. One day it'll come out, though, that he was single-handedly responsible for defeating a dozen or more Soviet schemes. Any one of which would have caused us serious problems if it had come off."

"I'd love to hear the whole story. But I'm guessing this doesn't involve the Soviets." He sighed. "Much as I wish we could go back to those days. Everything was a lot simpler then."

"You're right there." Dame Imogen smiled her agreement. "And no, this doesn't involve the Soviets. Lawrence's cover was blown in 1928, with a great deal of press speculation about him being a spy. Pooh-poohed by the government of the day, of course. We had no choice but to bring him back home, though. He was still extremely useful as an advisor on all sorts of Middle East matters, particularly Iraq and Palestine."

He grunted. "I'm guessing we didn't follow his advice."

"No, it doesn't seem we did." Dame Imogen gazed into the flames. "Not long after Lawrence was transferred home, things started to heat up in Germany."

"The Nazis?"

"Yes. Most of our very limited resources were focused on Hitler. Lawrence was a major asset."

"You surprise me. I'd have thought Hitler and the Nazis would have been outside his area of expertise."

"On one level, yes, of course. But remember who Lawrence was. He was still incredibly famous. Like one of today's movie stars, or rock stars. We used his fame to get him close to all sorts of people. He became great friends with Lady Nancy Astor. He often stayed at her country house, and met all of the Cliveden set. He got close to cabinet ministers who were suspected of Nazi sympathies. High Nazi officials too. People like Ribbentrop, Hitler's foreign minister, were completely starstruck by him. And here's the thing—they hoped to recruit him to their cause."

"Lawrence?" He snorted with disbelief. "Surely not."

"Of course not. But the Nazis didn't know that. All Lawrence—who spoke fluent German, by the way—had to do was drop the occasional hint. Mention admiration for something the Germans had done, and he had them hooked. Remember, he was renowned as a supporter of the Arab cause. Jewish immigration to Palestine was already causing a lot of problems with the local population, so the Nazis might well have assumed he'd sympathize with their anti-Jewish policies."

"So the idea was for Lawrence to work his reputation to get close to Nazis and possible Nazi sympathizers, pretend sympathy himself, and see what he could come up with?"

"Yes. And it worked quite well. Lawrence was able to obtain all sorts of insights into Nazi plans." Dame Imogen sighed. "Not that we used his information very well. But we were able to put tabs on a lot of people, some of whom later tried to spy for the Germans, others who'd have formed a fifth column here. The names of some of these people came as quite a shock. One of them more than the others, though." She handed Eldritch the folder.

He opened the cover and looked at the top sheet of the dossier within. It was densely covered in old-fashioned typescript. He read the first couple of paragraphs, then looked up, scowling. "So the stories are true."

"Yes. Edward, Prince of Wales, the future King Edward the

Eighth. And it gets worse," Dame Imogen said. She waited, sipping her coffee, as he went back to reading.

Finally he looked up. "He was really going to . . . I can hardly believe it." His voice was hoarse. "It's incredible. This is far worse than anything I've ever heard before. Far worse than anyone ever imagined."

"I'm afraid it is."

"I can hardly believe it," he repeated.

"Believe it."

"It never happened, though."

"No. Thanks to Lawrence. And Churchill. It was Churchill who first got onto the story, by the way. But Lawrence uncovered the whole plot and it got him killed."

"The Germans?"

Dame Imogen hesitated. "I'll come back to that. Just before Lawrence was killed, he convened a top-secret conference at Wareham, in Dorset. Malcolm Bullivant, the head of MI6, attended, along with the prime minister's principal private secretary, Peter Ashgrove. The conference was held in Wareham because Lawrence's cottage at Clouds Hill was nearby. In case anyone got wind of the meeting, we leaked a cover story that Lawrence was conducting secret negotiations with the Grand Mufti of Jerusalem, at the behest of Prime Minister Ramsay MacDonald. Over independence for Palestine. The idea had come up a number of times in the twenties and thirties."

"That makes sense. Given Lawrence's background. So what happened? Obviously Edward's plot failed."

"That's right. And he abdicated. Because of Mrs. Simpson."

He snorted. "I never believed that. Always thought there was more to it."

"I agree with you." Dame Imogen shrugged. "But if there was another reason I've never come across anything about it, although this . . ." She nodded toward the folder. "As to why the plot failed, I don't know that, either. If I had to guess I'd say Churchill had a hand in it. This file tells us what Lawrence was investigating. But that's as far as it goes. All we know for sure is he was killed, supposedly as the result of a motorcycle accident, right after the Wareham conference. The head of MI6 and Peter Ashgrove were also killed, in separate accidents, within days afterward."

"The implication being they were all murdered. By the Germans?"

"I forgot to add that Prime Minister MacDonald resigned from office before the month was out. For reasons of ill health."

"The old excuse. It must have been connected. Too coincidental to be anything else." He cocked an eyebrow. "I asked you if it was the Germans?"

"That's the obvious conclusion. But there were rumors that another party was involved."

"I give up. Who?"

"I told you the cover story for Lawrence's meeting. That it was a conference to negotiate independence for Palestine. With rumors about the Grand Mufti being in attendance."

"Ye-es."

"What if someone believed that cover story? Someone with a vital interest in ensuring those supposed negotiations did not succeed? Someone willing to do anything to make sure that Palestine—an *Arab* Palestine—never got independence?"

"Someone?" Then it clicked. He felt the muscles clench in his gut. "Oh, no . . ." "There's no proof."

"Thank God for that! If that idea ever got out there'd be hell to pay. Hell." He cupped his chin in his hand. "This business about Edward's plot, though. If *that* gets out, the fallout will be nuclear." He shuddered, picturing all too easily the stories the media would publish. People's reactions. Consequences. "Is that what you've come to tell me? That this is all about to hit the fan?"

Dame Imogen nodded.

He rose and walked across the room to an antique sideboard. He picked up a Waterford decanter and two tumblers. "In that case," he said, "I think we need something stronger."

A quarter of an hour, and a whiskey each later, Dame Imogen finished telling him about the torture and murder of Sir Evelyn Montagu, and what her people had learned about Scotland Yard's investigation into his death. The involvement of Ayesha Ryder, researcher with the Walsingham Institute, Montagu's lover and former member of the Palestinian *Fedayeen*, took the most explanation.

Eldritch splashed more whiskey into their glasses. He raised his, took a long swallow. "So. Lawrence may have hidden papers that reveal everything about Edward's collaboration with the Nazis, and his proposed coup. That the Prince of Wales was a traitor." He stared hard at Dame Imogen. "If such papers *do* exist, we must find them. *Must*. At all costs. Do you realize what's at stake?"

Dame Imogen returned his stare. "Yes."

"The monarchy itself. I don't think it could survive a scandal of such proportions."

She nodded.

"The two Scotland Yard detectives are one thing. We can shut them up. Ryder scares me, though. She's Palestinian. She'll have her own agenda. Especially if she gets hold of the cover story about the Palestinian conference."

"If our friends find out about her past, they'll go ballistic."

"You think they murdered Montagu?"

"Not them. At least . . . No. *Shamir*, though. If they got hold of the cover story it's the sort of thing they'd do."

"Hmm. Yes. Do we have any information on who their leader is yet?"

"No. Six have tried to infiltrate. So far all they have to show is two dead officers."

"If it's *Shamir*, they must really think—"

"Yes."

"But we could let them know. Leak the information somehow. That it was just a cover story . . ." He broke off. "They wouldn't believe us, would they?"

"Unlikely."

"Right. Imogen." He leaned forward in his chair. "Do whatever you have to do. On my authority. The PM will back me up. Find these documents, papers, whatever exists. Make damn sure no one else gets to them first. Not Scotland Yard and for certain not Ryder." He held her gaze. "Do whatever you have to do," he repeated.

"Whatever it takes?" Dame Imogen did not blink.

"Whatever it takes."

As her car pulled away from the curb in front of Eldritch's building, Imogen Worsley picked up a secure phone. She thought for a moment, then placed a call to Peta Harrison, one of her most trusted officers. The call was answered immediately. In clipped tones, the director-general fired off a series of instructions.

CHAPTER 19

Ahmed Ali-Yaya gazed at the television set—the lead story, eclipsing the usual Christmas hype, was the peace conference at the Tower of London between Israel's prime minister, Judah Ben David, and the Palestinian leader, Sayyed Khalidi. His heart lifted. Maybe there was no need for him to do what he'd promised to do on the morrow. He'd made a solemn vow, though. He fully intended to honor it.

He'd turned the TV on after Reem gave up on the idea of getting the baby back to sleep. He'd showered, forced down some of the pizza he'd heated up. He'd tucked his briefcase beneath the sofa. There was no reason Reem would look there tonight. It was churning his insides, what he was going to do with the package inside it, making it nearly impossible to swallow his food.

"Do you think there's any chance?" he asked his wife. "Of peace, I mean."

"No way." Reem cradled baby Janine in one arm while she watched the TV. "The Israelis are just stalling. Again."

He saw how tired his wife was. She worked as a nurse at Guy's

Hospital. She wasn't working the hours he was, but she was on her feet for hours. And she was still breast-feeding. Janine saw to it that she got little sleep.

He looked past the TV at the mantel over the long-ago blocked-up fireplace. In addition to a trio of Christmas stockings, a few greeting cards, and a layer of tinsel, the mantel held a collection of mementos and framed photographs. A history in miniature of his and Reem's families. His gaze went to the old brass key, mounted and framed, that hung in pride of place above the photographs. The key was a symbol. It made him angry, but it was unlikely it would ever be anything more. Like it used to be for the Jews who talked about "next year in Jerusalem," without ever really believing it, the "return to Palestine" had become a refrain with little meaning. For those who'd made lives elsewhere, the idea of returning to some old house and orange orchard outside Jaffa had become part of their mythology. One day Janine would have the key. A lump rose in his throat at the thought.

He tried to think of something to say. Something normal. Take his mind off things. "What about their new PM? Ben David?"

"He seems better than the others. Like he wants to do something." Reem shrugged. "So did Rabin. Look at what happened to him. The right-wingers will never let him succeed." There was no bitterness in her voice, just acceptance of a state of affairs that had existed since long before she was born.

He looked back at the television. The story was now about an unseasonal hurricane that threatened Haiti. He closed his eyes. Tried to focus on something else. Opened his eyes as his wife spoke again.

"Will you see them tomorrow?"

"Hmm?"

RYDER

"The Israeli PM. And Sayyed Khalidi."

"Yes," he said. "I'll see them." *Tomorrow.* There would be no peace agreement, he knew that. There never would be. He would fulfill his vow.

CHAPTER 20

Ayesha refused to believe that they were at a dead end. She accepted that Lady Madrigal Carey must have died long since, but there had to be something else. "Her papers," she insisted. "We have to find out what happened to her estate. And there's another thing," she said before Holden could interject. "I don't think Churchill ever received Lawrence's coded letter. If he had, how would Evelyn have ever gotten hold of it? If Churchill had received it, he would have acted on it, then probably destroyed it. Or else it would have been with his archived papers."

She took three paces away from the table, then turned. "I think the letter is why Evelyn was tortured. Someone wanted it, or what it might lead to, badly enough to do those things to him. Someone believes the treaty is still out there."

Bryan placed a large volume on the table next to Holden. "What have you got here, Sergeant?" the DI asked. "Oh right, Debrett. Let's have a look at her then." He opened the book, *Debrett's Peerage and Baronetage*, the bible of the British aristocracy since 1769, flipped pages until he reached the C's, and located the entry for Lady Madrigal Carey. "'Born, 1916.'" He nodded at the computer screen. "So, when that photo with Lawrence was taken she couldn't have been much more than seventeen or eighteen."

Holden turned back to *Debrett's*. "'Only daughter of Henry Carey, 11th Earl of Wolverhampton, diplomat, Ambassador to Spain, et cetera. Engaged, 1939, to Peter Latimer, Squadron Leader, RAF, DFC, DSO. Battle of Britain ace with 11 confirmed kills. Killed in action, 1943.'" He looked up. "'Wartime service in SOE.'"

SOE. The Special Operations Executive. Created by Churchill after the fall of France in 1940, with the mandate to set Europe alight. SOE was responsible for dropping agents into German-occupied Europe charged with organizing resistance and carrying out acts of sabotage. The men and women in its ranks were the bravest of the brave.

"Lady Madrigal was a spy." Holden's voice was hoarse with excitement. "Apparently a successful one. She was awarded the George Cross. As well as an MBE, the Croix de Guerre, and the Médaille de la Résistance."

"What did she do?" Ayesha asked. The George Cross was the highest honor bestowed on civilians for bravery, the equivalent of the Victoria Cross for a member of the armed forces.

"All it says here is she was captured by the Gestapo in France in 1944. Then she was held in Ravensbrück concentration camp until it was liberated in 1945."

"Anything else?" Her calm voice belied the sudden tightening in her gut. Lady Madrigal had been tortured.

"Just that she was in the Civil Service after the war. Home Office. Retired in 1979. Never married. No children."

"When did she die?"

"Doesn't say."

"When was it published?" She put a hand out to the book.

"Hmm? Oh, right." Holden flipped open the front cover. "Nineteen ninety-one. I guess she was still alive then."

Ayesha entered "Madrigal Carey" into the Google search engine. The Wikipedia entry was a long one, and included photographs. Mostly of Lady Madrigal during wartime. Dark curling hair in the style of the forties, strong eyebrows slanted upward, high cheekbones, and a full mouth gave her a striking resemblance to the young Lauren Bacall.

The entry had several paragraphs about Lady Madrigal's wartime service with SOE. Most of it was in occupied France, until she was betrayed and captured. Somehow she survived interrogation and torture by the Gestapo, and was hours away from execution when Ravensbrück was liberated by the Russians on April 30, 1945.

"So when did she die?" Holden was reading the entry over her shoulder.

"Uh . . ." She frowned. "It says Lady Madrigal lives in London's Mayfair."

"'Lives!' Come on! How old is that entry?"

She scrolled to the bottom, a nerve twitching in her temple, not daring to believe. "It was last updated three days ago."

"Bugger me!" Holden exclaimed. "That would make her, what? Close on one hundred years old?"

"She's still alive. Living in London." Her heart was pounding. "Perhaps it's time someone asked her about Lawrence's papers."

"Fucking incredible," Holden muttered.

"I'll get her address." Boiling with elation, she turned back to the computer. "Then we can go."

RYDER

"A bit late to call on an old lady, isn't it?" Holden objected.

"People her age hardly sleep," she replied, hitting the ENTER key. "She's bound to have live-in help. We have to try. It'd be too awful if she died before we got to her." She bit her lip in frustration. "The Internet seems to be down."

"This one's down, too," Bryan said, trying another computer. He pulled out his cellphone, looked at the screen, thumbed buttons. "No signal."

Holden drew his phone and held it up. "Nothing. Maybe your router or whatever is down."

She frowned. She knew little enough about computers and wireless technology, but was fairly certain that cellphones and the Internet used different communications systems.

"Phone book?" Bryan asked, looking in the direction of the reference shelves.

"The library doesn't keep them in print anymore."

"There'll be a signal outside," Holden said. "Or we can call the Yard from the car." He headed toward the exit. "Come on, Scooby gang. Let's roll."

They left the Victorian building that housed the library and walked quickly back across the enclosed courtyard to the main house. A heavy frost muffled the sound of their footsteps. This close the old mansion eclipsed any view of the modern city. A shiver coursed through Ayesha's body that had nothing to do with the cold. With little difficulty she could imagine herself transported back to the England of Elizabeth I.

"I'm going to re-arm the security system," she said as they entered the entry hall of the main building. "I'll join you outside."

Her thoughts were on Lady Madrigal Carey as she entered the office, her hand reaching for the alarm panel. The room was darker than it should have been but she did not stop to think why. Then she glanced toward the window and the fog vanished from her brain. The office was dark because the window was blocked. By a man. His face, distorted by the thick goggles he wore, was pressed against the glass.

The reflexes drilled into her when she was a teenager kicked in. Adrenaline surged through her body. She sprinted across the hallway to the front door, flung herself at Holden, grabbed his arm just as he was turning the brass latch, and hauled him roughly backward, nearly knocking over Bryan, who gaped at her in astonishment. "Someone's out there," she rasped.

"What—" Holden broke off as the beam of a powerful flashlight pierced the gloom of the dining hall. It came through one of the front windows and swept across the room, dancing along the surface of the massive refectory table. Another light joined it, spearing through the window on the far side of the room's broad stone fireplace. Holden pulled away from her grip on his arm, took a step toward the doorway. Something struck the wall where he had been standing with a dull *thunk*. A large piece of plaster fell to the floor. All three ducked beneath the refectory table.

She peered sideways at the heap of debris on the floor. Something lay amid the fallen plaster.

Holden saw it, too. "What's that?" he asked.

"Tranquilizer dart." Her reply was flat-voiced. Her heart was racing, but she felt oddly calm. She raised her head just above the level of the table and looked toward the nearest window. A spiderweb of cracks surrounded a hole in the glass. Someone was a very good shot.

Bryan, crouched behind a chair, peered at the projectile on the floor, then at her.

RYDER

"What the fuck is going on?" Holden snarled. He jerked out his phone, dropped it, picked it up again, and snapped it open. Stabbed buttons. With a curse he held it up and waved it around. "Fuck!" he growled. "Nothing. Sergeant?"

Bryan had his phone out, too. He was already shaking his head.

"Landline?" Holden jerked the word at her.

"Nearest one's in the office." They all looked toward the hallway. Just as the front doorknob was rattled by someone outside.

Conflicting emotions chased each other across Holden's face. Anger. Confusion. "Who the fuck is out there? And what the hell do they want?"

"Evelyn," she answered. "Whoever tortured him to death hasn't given up. They followed us." She rose in a single lithe movement and dived through the doorway. "Come on," she flung over her shoulder. "There's another way out."

She charged down the passage, past a flight of stairs that led to the upper floor, then twisted left into another passage. This one headed toward the back of the building. As she ran, with Holden and Bryan pounding the ancient floorboards behind her, her mind raced. Whoever these people were, they were responsible for Evelyn's death. She was sure of it. And she was running away from them. *Shit.* But they were armed, and she wasn't. Neither, of course, were Holden or Bryan—unlike their North American cousins, British police detectives did not routinely carry firearms.

The passage ended in a large kitchen. Although the staff of the institute used it, it was designed to serve the caterers who supplied the food and drink for the events hosted in the great dining hall. A door on the far side opened onto a delivery area. The kitchen was in darkness, but a light outside illuminated the opaque glass panels in the service door. It also silhouetted the man who stood on the other side. She stopped dead, just as one of the glass panels in the service door shattered inward. The butt of a pistol was used to clear away the remaining glass fragments. Then a black-gloved hand thrust through the opening, groping for the latch.

CHAPTER 21

In the living room of the Whitechapel safe house, Nazir closed his phone and stared into the empty fireplace. Ayesha Ryder and the two Scotland Yard men were still inside the Walsingham Institute. The lights had gone off shortly after two military-type Land Rovers had pulled up in front of the old building. Six men clad in black fatigues, carrying weapons, had vanished into the grounds. Nazir's man hadn't been able to see much, but he identified an MP5K—the submachine gun favored by many of the world's special operations forces. Whoever these people were, they were serious.

His phone buzzed again. He flipped it open and looked at the screen, half expecting to see that his man had called back. It was not him. It was someone else entirely.

He answered the call with a grunt. For two minutes he listened to the rapid-fire speech that crackled through the phone from his superior. Now he understood what was happening at the Walsingham Institute. The unknown gunmen were unknown no longer. Their identity raised things to a whole new level of complexity, however. The voice on the phone stopped speaking.

"It's too late," Nazir said.

A torrent of words responded to this statement. He held the phone away and paced the room while his interlocutor vented his fury, trying to come up with a course of action he could take to redress the situation.

His two men in the van outside the Walsingham Institute had surprise on their side, but they were outnumbered. He had other men. The two in the kitchen for a start. They could get there quickly—the safe house was only minutes from the institute. He could hardly start a full-scale battle in the heart of London, though. That's what it would be if he intervened with force, and the other side had far more in the way of reinforcements to call upon.

The invective on the phone ceased. "No," Nazir said into the sudden silence. "That is not possible. . . . No . . . You hired me for a reason, is that not so? . . . Good, then trust me to get the job done. . . . Yes . . . Yes, of course, as soon as I know something."

He ended the call. He had persuaded his superior to leave things with him. He just didn't have the first idea what he was going to do next.

CHAPTER 22

Ayesha slammed through the doors into the library and raced across the reading room, the two detectives right behind her, weaving between furniture red-lit by the glow of the exit signs. When the armed man broke through the kitchen door she knew there was only one way out. It was one she didn't want to take, but she was certain their pursuers, whoever they were, would have no knowledge of it.

Hurtling through a doorway on the far side of the reading room, she braked her momentum against a large table. Holden collapsed beside her, panting for breath. Out of shape. One part of her brain recorded the fact, while noting that Bryan was in superb form. Another part of her brain reacted to their predicament. Pushing away from the table, she moved into the deeper recesses of the room, one of several that opened off the main reading room. There was a particular reason why she chose this one. "Follow me," she said.

"Where?" Holden wheezed.

She put a hand out to touch the bookshelves with which the

walls of the room were lined, keeping them on her right as she paced forward into the dark. After eight steps her hand encountered empty space. Reaching behind her, she touched Holden's arm. "There's a doorway here," she told him. "There's a spiral staircase just inside. We're going down. Keep one hand on the railing. And be *quiet*." She stepped through the doorway. Into stygian darkness. A light switch was on the wall just inside the opening, but there was no way she was going to turn it on.

The colder air swirling up the staircase swept the bare flesh of her hands and face. The air brought something else with it. A smell. A stale smell, not unpleasant, but it spoke of great age. Maybe that was just her imagination. Maybe it was because she knew what lay below.

She glanced back just as a beam of light from a powerful flashlight swept across the room's entrance. Wasting no more time, she took a firm grip on the rail and descended the spiral staircase as quickly as she could, putting each foot down carefully to reduce the sound of her boots on the cast iron treads. She could hear Holden and Bryan moving down above her.

She had ventured down the staircase on many occasions since she discovered where it led, more than a year ago. It had never seemed a great distance before. Now, in complete darkness, it was as if she were journeying down to the earth's core. It came as a shock when she did finally reach the bottom. She nearly stumbled as her boots found the stone flooring. She took a couple of paces forward to give Holden and Bryan room. "Wait here," she whispered.

"Where are we?" Holden whispered, too, but she heard the irritation in his voice. Probably because he was having to rely on a woman, she thought. Not something he was used to.

RYDER

"The cellars. Wait here," she repeated as she moved to her left, one hand outstretched. She found the wall almost immediately. The smooth stone was dank to the touch. Now that she had her bearings, she stepped forward more confidently. After she'd gone several feet, her hand knocked against a metal cabinet. It took only moments to open its doors and reach inside. Relief flooded over her as her fingers brushed one of the cylindrical rubber-coated objects she was seeking. A flashlight. She clicked it on and aimed it at the floor, keeping the illumination to a minimum. She swept it over the ground between her and the two detectives, showing them the way. When they joined her, she directed her flashlight into the cabinet. Old stationery and office supplies, including inkwells, boxes of iron nibs, and typewriter ribbons, filled it. One shelf held a collection of flashlights. As Holden and Bryan each took one, she cocked her head and listened. No sound. They were not being pursued. Not yet. She gestured behind her, in the opposite direction from the spiral staircase. "This way," she told them. "Keep your lights off, for now. One's enough."

"What is this place?" Holden's voice was hushed but he sounded confident again.

"Storeroom." She picked her way between two metal shelving units that could have dated from any time in the past century, then squeezed along a passage that doglegged between piled wooden boxes and chests of all sizes. "Books," she said, playing her flashlight over the boxes. "All sorts of stuff. Some of it junk. Much of it rare."

"What's it doing down here?"

"No one's got around to sorting it." She waited on the far side of the boxes for the two men to join her. When she turned her light to illuminate the way ahead, Holden gasped.

"A cannon?" He leaned over the squat black iron tube mounted on a wooden carriage with solid wheels. He ran his hand over the escutcheon. "George the Second," he said. For the moment he seemed to have forgotten their predicament.

She heaved a sigh. This was going to be a repeat of the Imperial War Museum. "It's part of the armory." She shifted her flashlight to the right.

Holden gaped. Bryan gave a low whistle of appreciation. Another time she would have taken some pleasure in showing them the collection housed on shelves and in dusty cabinets. "It was started by Walsingham," she explained. "Some of them"—she waved the light across a stand of swords—"are definitely his. We have documentation. Most of the weapons postdate his death in 1590. Obviously." Her light illuminated the cabinets, their glass-fronted doors, cracked and dirt-streaked though they were, doing little to conceal the array of historic armaments stored within.

"Now you're talking!" Holden exclaimed, lunging forward. "We can take on those bastards upstairs."

"Holden! No!" She glanced back toward the staircase. She thought she'd heard something. She shone her light on the DI, causing him to shield his eyes. "The most advanced gun in the collection predates the Crimean War. Even if you matched up the ammunition you'd blow a hand off trying to fire it."

Holden made a face, then eyed the stand of swords.

"Leave it!" she snapped.

The DI, one hand on the gilded basket hilt of a sword, scowled and let it drop back. As he moved away, his sleeve caught on the hilt. He jerked it free, but in the process the whole stand teetered. Holden tried desperately to stop it, but the thing was too heavy, too unwieldy. With a tremendous metallic clatter that seemed to echo on forever, the entire collection cascaded over the stone floor.

Three pairs of eyes stared in the direction of the staircase. For an eternity there was nothing, and she dared to hope. Then the staircase shaft lit up. Booted feet crashed on the cast iron treads.

She jerked around, aimed her light into the darkness, and ran. Holden and Bryan needed no invitation to follow her. She threw herself over a pile of rolled-up carpets, thick with the dust of ages, dived beneath a collection of old tables and chairs, eeled between their legs, and then, with the two men coughing on the dust, she scrambled upright in front of an ancient wardrobe. Both its doors were wide open, revealing what looked like a collection of old barristers' robes hanging within. She pulled the left-hand door of the cupboard toward her. Behind it, deeply recessed in the stone wall of the cellar, was a solid wooden door.

The door looked old. Far older than the Victorian building above. A big iron key, pitted with age, projected from the lock below the equally aged handle. She twisted the key from the lock, flung open the door, and stepped through to the other side. When the two men followed her, she slammed the door shut and used the key to lock it. "That should stop them for a bit," she said, withdrawing the key and slipping it into one of several zippered pockets in her pant legs. She turned and played the beam of her flashlight over the new space.

"This is the way out?" Holden gasped, peering over the edge of the abyss before them. He eyed the narrow wooden steps. They seemed to be built into the side of the rock wall. Zigzagging out of sight into the depths below, they had the appearance of something from a crazy dream. Or a nightmare.

"It's safe," she told him.

Holden snorted his disbelief.

"You've been down there?" Bryan asked.

"Yes."

Holden turned back to the ancient door. He took a step in its direction, then stumbled backward as something crashed against it. The three exchanged glances, then, as one, they swung around and launched themselves down the stairs, Ayesha once more in the lead.

The new descent was better than the spiral staircase. At least they had light. It was far longer, though. The wall on their right was cut from the London bedrock long before machines made such work easy. Here and there the marks of the handheld tools that had done the job could be clearly seen. The stairs creaked ominously under their weight. The stairs were not as old as the shaft. Mid-Victorian, she thought. Likely constructed by the builders of London's Underground to replace whatever had been there before.

After they'd been descending for some time, a loud noise echoed in the shaft from above. She picked up her pace, ignoring Holden's muttered curse.

The bottom of the steps came into view. She jumped from the second last and, in two long strides, covered the ground to a metal door in the brick wall that faced the staircase. She turned a wheel that released the lock mechanism, eased the door open, and stepped over a foot-high coaming. Her flashlight illuminated a grimy tunnel lined with bricks the color of black coal. Heart trip-hammering, she pressed herself against the wall of the tunnel, bidding the two men do the same as they followed her through the opening.

"Where—"

Whatever else Holden said was drowned beneath the deafening sound from the train that exploded around a bend in the tunnel and roared past, inches from their faces.

CHAPTER 23

The powerful vortex of the train sucked at Ayesha's body. Evelyn. She only had to take a step forward. Obliteration in an instant. It would be so easy. She gritted her teeth. That would never be her way.

"We're in the fucking Underground!" Holden yelled, over-compensating for his partial deafness and the lingering noise of the train as the last carriage rumbled past, amplified and echoed by the tunnel walls.

She pushed herself away from the brick wall and checked her watch. "Three minutes before the next train," she said. *Maybe less till someone comes down those stairs*, she thought, eyeing the door-way through which they'd plunged. She turned away and jogged along the track in the direction the train had gone. Bryan loped after her.

"Fuck! Ryder! Fucking stop! Bryan!" Holden flung one more expletive after their retreating backs. Then he ran after them.

She ran with an easy athletic grace, Bryan next to her. As she ran, she listened for the first sound of an approaching train, straining to hear over the noise made by their boots crunching on the crushed stone ballast of the track bed. She also searched with her eyes. The tunnel lighting was enough to see by; she didn't need to use her flashlight.

"Where the fuck are we going, Ryder?" Holden caught up. "I need to get out of here and call for help," he added, panting.

She ran for another fifty yards, then stopped, drawing a curse from Holden, who had to jump to the side to avoid running into her. A shout echoed faintly behind them. She ignored it and stepped to the tunnel wall.

Anyone not looking for the opening would have missed it. As she had, the first time she came this way, more than a year before, after she discovered the passage into the Underground through the institute cellars. It was only on her return journey, when a rat ran across her path, that she found the entrance. Her eyes had followed the rodent as it scuttled into a shadow. A shadow where there should not have been one. She investigated and found that what at first appeared to be a crack in the brickwork of the tunnel wall was actually an opening wide enough for a slim person to squeeze through.

"Quick," she snapped, grabbing Holden by the arm and tugging him toward the wall.

The DI started to protest, then he saw the opening. He took a pace forward and pulled out his flashlight. She put a hand out to stop him, jerking her head in the direction of their pursuers. Holden grunted, nodded his understanding, then pushed through the entrance.

"It's straight going for about seventy-f-five yards," she whispered. "There's a left turn. You can turn your flashlight on then."

Bryan followed Holden. He was bigger, with broader shoulders, and it was a tight fit. He squeezed through after a brief struggle, then Ayesha stepped up to the wall. With half of her body already through the opening, she turned her head and looked back the way they had come. Three figures ran toward them, silhouetted in the light of the train rushing up behind them. The train driver spotted the trio in the same instant. A horn blared, enormously loud in the tunnel's confined space. Ayesha did not wait to see what happened.

Past the entrance, the passage widened out so two people could have walked side by side. It was, she concluded after her earlier explorations, originally an access tunnel for Underground staff engaged in maintenance work, although it had not been used in decades. The tunnel was damp and the floor was thick with rat drop-pings. No cobwebs, though—it was too dark and there was little in the way of insect life. The walls, lined with pipes and ducting, were filthy with the coal dust and Tube dirt of more than a hundred years.

She picked her way forward, one hand against the wall, moving as swiftly as she dared. She had covered perhaps thirty yards when she stopped, gasping from the sharp pain that lanced through her right thigh. She touched the spot. The cloth of her tight black pants was torn and her skin was wet. Blood. She ran a hand over the wall. Found the jagged edge of the projecting brick that caused the damage. With a mental shrug she kept on.

Her groping hand encountered another wall. The left turn. Three paces into the new passage she drew out her flashlight, turned it on, and shone it down at her leg. A six-inch ragged tear in the cloth along the top of her thigh exposed the pale flesh. A long gash oozed blood. Hardly serious, and there was nothing she could do about it now. Another forty yards and she saw light ahead. Holden and Bryan.

"Fenchurch Street Station," the DI said when she rejoined

them. He directed his light across the words picked out in dark tile against a background of white. Or what had once been white. The tile, like everything, was covered in a thick layer of grime. "I've never heard of a Fenchurch Street Station on the Underground."

"It was closed in 1945. At the end of the war. They usually stripped the platforms out when they closed a station," Bryan added.

"I know a lot about the Underground," he explained. "I don't think anyone knows this is still here," he went on. "Not with all this stuff." He shone his light over the platform wall.

"What stuff ?" Holden growled, still simmering over Bryan's earlier insubordination. "Oh!" he exclaimed a moment later, playing his own light over the posters that adhered to the curving platform wall. Faded, dirty and peeling, they were easy enough to read. "First-Aid Station This Way." "How to Tackle Fire-Bombs." "Air Raid Wardens Wanted." A movie poster: *Too Many Crooks* with Terry-Thomas, playing at the London Odeon.

Bryan moved along the platform, stopping to examine each poster, coming back to look at some he'd already checked out. Ayesha turned back to the narrow passage through which they had come. She listened. No sound. And no light. She was not surprised. If they had not been seen to enter the passage, then she didn't think their pursuers, assuming they hadn't been crushed to death by the train, would easily discover where they had gone. When they found no trace of their quarry they would come back and look more carefully. They would find the passage. It was just a matter of time.

When she turned back to the platform, Holden was walking up and down, holding his cellphone, the screen blinking, as he waved it this way and that. "No signal," he groused.

"We'll have to get out of here before you can get a signal," she said.

"How do we do that?" Holden raged. "I've got to report to the Yard. Get my people after these shitheads." He nodded toward the passageway. "Whoever the fuck they are."

"That's the way out." She gestured with her light. "Along the tracks."

Bryan jumped down from the platform and strode forward on the permanent way. The beam of his flashlight sliced through the inky darkness.

The DI opened his mouth to say something, then, with an angry shake of his head, lowered himself to the tracks. He put up a hand to help her. She ignored him. Instead, she sprang lightly down. She disturbed a cluster of rats that split, squeaking furiously, and vanished.

"It's cold," Holden observed, turning and jogging in Bryan's wake.

"We're a long way underground." She matched his pace. "This is one of the deep tunnels. It'll be colder near the surface."

"There are no exits?"

"They'll all have been sealed up." Bryan had stopped to wait for them. "We'll have to get out of this line before we can find a way out."

"I know a way out," Ayesha said. "It's quite a distance yet, though."

"Which direction are we headed?" Holden asked.

"West."

"Have you been down here much, Miss Ryder?" Bryan asked.

"Some."

"On your own? You weren't afraid?"

RYDER

"Why should I be?"

Holden muttered something she didn't catch. She glanced behind. Nothing—yet. She quickened her pace.

Bryan ran with ease beside her. Holden struggled in the beginning, but found his wind after a little and settled down to a steady pace, his breathing less labored. Their running feet crunched on the ballast. A low rumble came from somewhere behind the walls. Train noises were commonplace in London belowground, like the all-pervasive smell of sweat, hot metal, food, and rodent droppings. Nothing was visible. Just the beams of their flashlights bouncing along the black curving walls, sometimes catching the reflected gleam from beady eyes.

She thought hard as she ran. Who was chasing them? She had an idea, but no proof. Without proof she could do nothing. Her mind had turned back to Madrigal Carey and what help the old woman might be able to offer when an exclamation from Bryan dragged her back to the present. She stopped and rested her hands on her knees. The blood on her thigh had dried.

"Cornhill?" Bryan sounded perplexed. He shone his light over the station name. "I remember reading about it. But I thought it was dismantled decades ago."

"Glad to hear there's something you don't know, Sergeant." Holden's sarcasm lost some of its effect in his heavy panting. "What are those boxes?" He waved his light across the platform.

Bryan bounded up onto the platform and moved toward the mound of wooden boxes, tea chests mainly, that had caught Holden's attention. The boxes were stacked two high and filled most of the platform space. As Bryan peered at the nearest one, she said, "Don't get excited. They're just records."

"Records?"

"Yes. City of London. Property records. Financial statements. Budget papers. That sort of thing. From before the war." She put up a hand to shield her eyes when Holden swung his light toward her. She anticipated his question. "I've looked in quite a few of them. That's what I found. They must have been brought down here for safekeeping. Then forgotten."

"You really have got around," Holden commented. "How many times did you say you'd been down here?"

"I didn't." She levered herself up onto the platform.

Holden joined her. He stooped over one of the boxes. "Just city papers?" He sounded disappointed.

"Yes—" Whatever she was going to say was lost as a light speared from the tunnel and played over the permanent way. "Go!" she snapped at Holden, clicking off her flashlight and shoving him through an opening between two chests. She dived after him. Then, with a whispered "Follow me" to the DI, who'd had the presence of mind to turn his own light off, she grabbed his hand and led him behind the piled boxes, her other hand on the wall, feeling her way toward the far end of the platform. As they approached, she heaved a sigh of relief. Bryan had found and opened the door she was headed for.

She thrust through the doorway. Holden, right behind her, stumbled and nearly fell. She slammed the metal door, swung the wheel to lock it, clicked her flashlight on, and shone it around the room they had entered, adding her light to Bryan's.

"Fuck!" Holden exclaimed. "We're trapped."

The room was small and sparsely furnished with a row of metal lockers against one wall, a table, and three battered chairs. A filthy sink occupied one corner. An ancient hot plate and a rusty kettle sat on the cupboard next to it.

RYDER

She directed her light into the far corner. A metal ladder was bolted to the wall behind the lockers. She moved the beam up the wall to the ceiling. It revealed a covered opening, like a manhole. "The way out," she said, stepping toward it.

"Wait." Bryan put his flashlight down, picked up one of the chairs, and laid it on top of the table. He seized hold of the chair frame with both hands and heaved. The muscles in his back and shoulders tensed and bulged. For a moment nothing happened. Then a low cracking sound, inaudible more than a few feet away, was accompanied by a grunt of satisfaction from Bryan as the old wood broke apart and a leg came away. He jammed the leg between the spokes of the locking wheel on the door. She thrust her flashlight inside her jacket, grasped the sides of the metal ladder, and ran lightly up the steps. At the top she pushed aside the manhole cover and scrambled through the opening. Holden followed her with far less grace. She gave him a hand, then assisted Bryan.

"Fuck me!" gasped Holden. "Don't tell me *this* is an abandoned Underground tunnel." He shone his flashlight into a rectangular shelf hollowed out of the rock wall.

"God above!" Bryan whispered. There was real fear in his voice. He beamed his own flashlight into the darkness. Its light did not pierce far, but it provided enough illumination to show that the tunnel in which they now stood was ten or twelve feet high, with a ceiling and floor of rock. The walls, too, were rock, but had been carved, or hollowed out, into banks of shelves or niches. Each niche was five or six feet long, two or three feet in depth, and the same in height. The niches started at ground level and reached the height of the tunnel, with five niches in each bank. Some of the niches were empty, but most were not.

The word for the niches, as she knew from her research, conducted after she first ventured through the manhole six months before, was *loculi*, and they held bones—human bones. She directed her light ahead, along the tunnel, and walked forward. "Catacombs," she said. "They're Roman catacombs." She didn't tell them what lay ahead. If Bryan was afraid of old bones, he was going to be terrified of what came next.

CHAPTER 24

Dame Imogen Worsley looked up from her desk at the two people who had entered her office: the duty officer, Bill Jameson, and Peta Harrison, a senior officer with more than fifteen years of service. It was Peta she'd called as soon as she left Sir Norman Eldritch's apartment, ordering together a team immediately to find and bring in Ayesha Ryder. While Ryder and the two detectives might have come easily, as the result of a simple request, she couldn't afford to take any chances. Who knew what they'd discovered? Or who they might tell if they knew the security services wanted to question them?

Still, although she'd employed maximum precautions by sending in an armed team, she didn't really think they'd have any trouble. Ryder, Holden, and Bryan had no idea they were being sought by the security services. They hadn't even troubled to conceal their movements during the night, shuttling between Sir Evelyn Montagu's apartment, the Walsingham Institute, and the Imperial War Museum. Half an hour, Imogen decided, and they'd be secure. Another thirty minutes and all three would be nice and comfortable in an interview room back at Thames House.

She checked the time on her watch, then pushed a button to put her desk phone on speaker. "Michaels. Have you got them?"

A slight pause, then "Director-General, I regret, no. Not yet." The male voice on the other end of the phone was clipped, concise. Military.

"What seems to be the problem, Michaels?" Imogen spoke mildly, her tone belying the annoyance she felt. And the concern. Was this going to be harder than she'd thought?

Michaels did not respond. He was talking with someone. Snatches of conversation were audible, but the words were impossible to make out. "Dame Imogen? Ma'am? I'm sorry but it seems they have, uh . . . eluded us for the moment. There was a way out of the institute we weren't aware of. From the cellars. It wasn't on the plans. It led into a tunnel."

"Where does this tunnel go?" She ignored the defensive tone in his voice.

"Ah . . . when I said tunnel, I should have said the Underground. The Tube."

"They're in the Underground?"

"Not actually." Michaels sounded hesitant. "They were. But they seem to have got into a part that was shut down years ago. Some sort of abandoned section of the system. It's something of a rabbit warren down there. My people managed to locate them, but then they got away again. We're in pursuit."

"Very well, Michaels." She leaned back. "Keep me posted, would you please?"

"Of course, Director-General. Michaels out."

She turned off the speakerphone. She picked up a pen from

her desk, tapped it on the polished wooden surface. "If they're in an abandoned part of the Tube," she told her two officers, "then it stands to reason they'll find their way up before long. Assuming Michaels doesn't get to them first. What's the first thing they'll do?"

"DI Holden will call Scotland Yard," Peta Harrison answered.

Bill Jameson nodded his agreement.

"I concur." Imogen picked up the handset of her phone. She jabbed at the top button with the pen. Waited. A voice was faintly audible to the waiting officers. "Norman," she said. "Yes, sorry . . . Listen. I need your help. The matter we discussed earlier." She chose her words carefully, even though they were using a secure line.

When she ended the call she turned once more to her two officers. "The home secretary will take care of Scotland Yard," she told them. "They'll be in touch when Holden surfaces." She looked at the duty officer. "Bill, take point, would you? Take the team Peta put together and head up to the vicinity of the Walsingham Institute."

Jameson nodded and moved toward the door.

"Bill?" Imogen said.

Jameson stopped and looked back.

"Don't lose them."

CHAPTER 25

Ayesha ran, counting her steps, hearing the footfalls of the two men close behind her. These were the only sounds in the catacombs hidden below the surface of London. Other than their breathing. Bryan's was the loudest, a rasping rattle that had, she knew, nothing to do with his level of fitness, which was obviously superb. It was fear.

Distracted by her concern for Bryan, she failed to see a chunk of rock in the middle of the tunnel floor. She stumbled, her flashlight went flying, and she fell heavily. She allowed Holden to help her up, although she hastily pulled her arm from his grip. The fall had reopened the gash in her thigh. It oozed fresh blood. Bryan picked up her flashlight and handed it to her. Miraculously, it still worked.

"You okay?" Holden asked, concern in his voice.

She was surprised. Holden had never expressed any regard for her well-being. She didn't want him to start now. "I'm fine." She walked forward once more, beaming her light over the *loculi* carved into the walls of the catacomb. She was trying to recall how far she'd come when she'd found the opening. About a month before, on her last trip into the catacombs, she'd stumbled across her greatest find. And, at the same time, a way out. Trouble was, one bank of *loculi* looked very much like another, and the catacombs stretched for miles.

"I've never heard of Roman catacombs in London," Holden remarked.

"No one has," she replied. "These burials are definitely Roman, though. I found coins. Pottery, too. Some with inscriptions. After I stumbled across this place, I came across a collection of unpublished papers in the archives of the University of London. In 1939, an archaeologist named Jonathan Wright was employed by the London Underground to investigate a find made by their workmen. He identifies the catacombs and states they were in use from late in the first century until at least a hundred years after the end of the Roman occupation."

"So what happened?" Holden asked. "Why aren't there regular tours down here? Like in Paris and Rome?"

"Wright was killed in the Blitz. Cornhill Station was closed down. By the time the war ended, whatever the workmen found was long forgotten. Buried."

"This will be huge when it comes out." Bryan's voice sounded odd. Flat.

"Who have you told about it?" Holden asked Ayesha.

The silence drew out, became protracted, until the DI spoke again. "You haven't told anyone, have you?" he said accusingly.

"No." There'd only been one person she'd wanted to share her discovery with. Evelyn. Now it was too late. She fully intended to tell the proper authorities about the catacombs. And her other great discovery. Just . . . not yet. She wanted to be sure she'd found everything there was to be found first. Also, when she did tell, it would be an end to her solitary explorations in subterranean London.

"What are we looking for, anyway?" Holden asked. "An exit sign?"

"There's an opening. A doorway. Sort of. It's in one of the *loculi*—the grave niches."

Holden grunted. "*In* one?"

"Yes. You'll see what I mean when we find it."

"And that's the only way out?" Bryan asked.

"I haven't found any others."

By the time they'd walked for five more minutes, she was worried, thinking she'd missed it and would have to backtrack.

"Is this it?" Holden stepped through a low doorway that appeared out of the darkness on their right. She and Bryan stood behind the DI while his light illuminated a small chamber. Each wall was lined with *loculi*. All held bones, rotting grave clothes still visible on some of them.

"It's a *cubicula*," she explained. "A family tomb. Sort of a crypt. And no, it's not the way out. It's right next door, though."

At first glance the *loculus* appeared like all of the others they had passed on their flight through the catacombs. A simple stone shelf holding a forlorn collection of ancient bones. When she directed her flashlight beam into its interior it was apparent, however, that this one was different. Behind the shelf on which lay the bones of an ancient Roman Londoner a black hole could be glimpsed, an opening no more than two feet in height, and slightly more in width. "Through there," she told the two men. "That's the way out."

"You have to be kidding!" Holden exclaimed.

She glanced back the way they had come. What she saw triggered an oath and caused Holden and Bryan to swing round from the *loculus*.

"Ah." Holden observed the light in the distance. "Company."

"Lights out," she snapped, flicking off hers. Holden and Bryan obeyed. Except for the pinpricks of light that represented their pursuers, the darkness was now absolute. In her imagination she pictured the catacomb walls with their grim burdens closing in around her. She pushed away the thought, stretched out a hand, and found Bryan's arm. He jerked away from her touch. Whatever was eating him, there was no time to find out now. "Down," she snapped, pushing him toward the *loculus*.

Bryan was trembling, his breath coming in hoarse gasps, but he did as she said. She kept one hand on his body as he went, felt him grope his way forward through the grave niche. When his feet had disappeared, she found Holden and guided him in turn. He wasn't afraid, but his passage was accompanied by a great deal of grunting and muttering. Then it was her turn.

She had only taken the path through the *loculus* once before. If it was unpleasant wriggling through an ancient grave with her flashlight held before her, lighting the way, it was far worse in total blackness. Now, too, she knew what the chamber on the other side held. In her imagination the smell seemed stronger in the dark. Thick and musty. Old. And very dead.

Once through the opening, she stood up, pressed back against the rough stone wall, and waited. She couldn't see Holden and Bryan. But they were close. She could hear their breathing.

Perhaps two minutes went by before footsteps sounded in the tunnel. Light percolated through to the chamber in which they stood. She stared at the opening and tried to melt into the wall.

Every fiber in her body tensed and her heart hammered. Then adrenaline surged through her and she bit her lip to stop from crying out. The cause was not their pursuers, though. It was Holden. He had grabbed her arm at the elbow and squeezed, painfully hard. At the same moment a low moan broke the silence. Bryan.

Too late, she realized the detectives might react when they saw the horror that shared the chamber with them. Holden would be fine. Bryan was a different story, however. She cursed herself for not taking precautions, pulled free from Holden's grip, and took two careful steps sideways, past the DI.

Bryan was just visible in the fading light from the tunnel. His whole body shook, as though with a fever; she feared that at any moment he would run from the chamber. She couldn't let that happen. Their pursuers would not have gone far. She stepped forward and wrapped her arms tightly around him. At her first touch Bryan went rigid. Then he fought her. In total silence he strained and heaved with every effort of the powerful muscles she had discerned earlier when he broke the chair. She held on, exerting every ounce of strength in her own lean frame. Then, without warning, a shudder racked Bryan's body. He stopped heaving. At the same moment a low moan came from deep inside his throat. She placed a hand across his mouth. She held it there for what seemed an eternity. Slowly, his body relaxed. She dropped her hand.

"S-sorry," Bryan stammered.

She stepped back from the DS and retraced her steps, brushing past Holden, who had not moved. She groped her way to the opening. "Wait here," she whispered. Then, stopping and listening each time she made a movement, she eased herself through the opening, wriggled through the *loculus*, and stood upright in the catacomb. She strained her eyes and ears. "They've gone," she reported when she'd eeled back into the chamber. As she straightened up, she pulled her flashlight out of her jacket pocket and clicked it on. Bryan gasped.

She flashed her light over him. His face was beaded in sweat and the whites of his eyes showed huge. She turned it toward Holden. His face was pale, but nothing more. Shock, she thought. He'd soon get over it. She wasn't so sure about Bryan.

She played her beam over the chamber. It was perhaps twenty feet by thirty, and maybe eleven feet high. It was difficult to be sure. Except for a narrow passage along the near wall, in which they stood, the chamber was filled with the bones of the dead, brown with age. It was a charnel house. A sepulchre. A giant ossuary.

"In hell's name, Ryder!" Holden hissed. He'd recovered from the shock. Now he sounded angry.

She knew why. It had nothing to do with their predicament. It was because of what she'd done with Bryan. She gazed at the stark reminders of human mortality heaped in front of them. An image of Evelyn flashed into her mind. Cold and soon to be in the grave . . . It was a sharp, stabbing pain in her chest.

"Roman?" Holden sounded slightly calmer.

"No." She waved her light over the heaped bones. "This is something else."

"Okay. I give up. What?"

Bryan was silent, although he was breathing heavily. She suspected the detective sergeant guessed the significance of the bones. He seemed to have a great deal of knowledge about the city, and especially about the Underground. His reading and research had probably clued him in. Maybe it was the reason he'd acted like he did. "It's a Plague pit," she answered.

"Plague!" Holden exclaimed. "How the fuck do you know

that?" The fear in his voice was the unreasoning, illogical fear ingrained in the genes of Londoners. The same fear that will lead construction site workers, if they uncover a Plague burial pit, to throw down their tools and flee. No inducement will persuade them to remain.

She was not surprised at Holden's response. She had felt it herself, when she first realized what she'd found. Half to two-thirds of the population of Europe had died in the Black Death of the fourteenth century and an estimated one hundred thousand people, or 15 percent of London's population, were wiped out in the Great Plague of 1665. The fear was primal. She flicked her light in Bryan's direction once more. He had not reacted to her announcement, confirming her guess that he knew what it was.

He tore his gaze away from the bones and looked at her, jerked a nod, then, "I'm okay," he said.

She waited, listening to the sound of their breathing. Then she spoke again, her voice echoing in the tomblike silence. "Because of the manner of the burial. It's how I know this is a Plague pit. Only Plague victims were treated like this. Tossed into mass graves. With no regard to the niceties." Her light flickered over the deep eye sockets of a skull. Somewhere in the darkness, something skittered, then fell silent. "And because we're in the vicinity of a place known to have been used for the care of the sick and dying during the last London plague."

Holden stared at the bones. Stretched out a hand toward a femur that jutted out from the pile within inches of where he stood. His hand hovered for a moment, then he quickly withdrew it. "Can we get the hell out of here now?"

She directed her beam along the narrow passageway. At the far side of the chamber a low doorway was visible. "That way." She stepped toward it, touching Bryan on the arm as she passed him. His body was still tense, but at least the shaking had subsided.

The doorway led to another chamber, a near replica of the first. She strode across it and through yet another doorway. The new chamber was also a sepulchre, but here no bones were visible. Instead, a single tomb rested in the center of the stone-flagged floor. It stood about five feet high and swallowed up most of the small space, allowing only a few feet on each side. Tiled in an intricately laid mosaic, it had open, arched sides, through which a sandstone sarcophagus could be glimpsed.

She shone her light on a carved tablet mounted on the near wall, the proof of her second great find—she didn't count the Plague pits—recalling how she had trembled with emotion when she first read the words.

Holden stepped up close and peered at the tablet. "'Here lieth the body of King Ethelred,'" he read aloud. "'King of England, son of King Edgar.'"

"What?" Bryan ran to the tablet and examined the inscription himself. "Ethelred the Unready? I can't believe it!"

"It *is* hard to believe, isn't it?" she acknowledged, reliving her own excitement at having found the resting place of one of England's last Saxon kings.

"Incredible!" The detective sergeant crossed to the tomb and ran a hand over the old stone.

"You haven't told anyone about this, either. Have you?" Holden demanded.

"I'm going to."

"I thought Ethelred was buried in St. Paul's," Bryan said. "Old St. Paul's, that is. The original cathedral that was destroyed in the Great Fire. In 1666."

"He was," she said. "Two or three of the old Saxon kings were interred there. Their tombs were lost in the Great Fire, like so many others." She'd read that dozens, possibly hundreds of tombs were destroyed in the cataclysm that wiped most of old London off the map. Kings and queens, famous prelates and clergy. Nobles like John of Gaunt. John Donne, the great poet. Sir Francis Walsingham himself. They were all buried in Old St. Paul's. All of their tombs were believed lost. Until now. She had not explored more than a fraction of the labyrinthine catacombs. Now she wouldn't have the chance. She'd have to tell. If she didn't, Holden and Bryan would.

"So why was Ethelred Unready?" Holden asked with a chuckle.

"The word is actually *Unraed*," Bryan explained, spelling it. "And it didn't mean what unready means now, to us. It was more like he was ill-advised, ill-counseled. It was also a pun, like. On Ethelred. Which means 'noble counsel' in the Old Saxon."

"God save us," Holden muttered. "How do we get out of here?"

For answer, she walked past the tomb of Ethelred and shone her flashlight on the bottom of a narrow curving stone staircase. She put one booted foot on the first step and started up.

The staircase, worn down deeply by the feet of countless pilgrims to the royal tomb, wound tightly upward for perhaps thirty feet. It ended in what looked to be a solid linenfold wall. She knew otherwise. Lifting her right hand, she reached above her head, groping in the dark. Her fingers found a long chain made of iron. She grasped it firmly and pulled down. A sharp crack broke the silence; a sliver of light appeared in the wood paneling.

Holden, on the step behind her, grunted in surprise.

She gripped the panel by its now-exposed edge and slid it toward her. It moved easily enough, sliding on grooves at its top and bottom, like the lid of a pencil case. When she had a gap of a couple of feet, she stepped through. When Holden and Bryan joined her, she grasped the edge of the panel once more and slid it back into place. The entrance was once again concealed.

"Okay," Holden said. "So where are we now?" The space they had entered, a church or chapel, was well, if dimly, lit. Vaulted ceilings and thick heavy pillars said they were in a structure of considerable age. Plush carpeting, laid over a marble or polished stone flooring, white painted walls, the altarpiece, covered in crimson velvet, the odor of sanctity that hung in the air. These things spoke of an important place, well maintained and much visited.

"St. Faith's," Ayesha told him.

"St. Faith's?" Holden queried. "That's a new one on me."

Bryan knew. "Its full name is St. Faith's under St. Paul's," he explained. "We're in St. Paul's Cathedral."

CHAPTER 26

Holden's phone signal returned while they were still in St. Faith's under St. Paul's. The DI at once contacted Scotland Yard. He talked quickly, keeping the details to a minimum.

Ayesha listened, but, now they had successfully evaded their pursuers, her mind was revolving Lawrence's clues once more. She didn't want to go to Scotland Yard. She wanted to visit Lady Madrigal Carey. Clearly she wasn't going to be able to persuade Holden. Could she break away?

The West Porch of St. Paul's Cathedral, at the top of the stairway that leads up to the famous double columns and the Great West Door. That's where Scotland Yard told Holden they should wait. A car and officers would be sent to collect them. She decided to bide her time. Trouble was, if she did vanish Holden would know exactly where she'd gone.

Before they left the cathedral, she and the two detectives cleaned themselves up as best they could in the restrooms on the lower level, adjacent to the public cafeteria. She also cleaned and bandaged the wound on her right thigh, using a first-aid kit she found in a staff room behind the cafeteria. There was no time to do anything about the tear in her pants.

The cathedral was locked up for the night, but they found an exit through the stonemason's workshop. It opened onto St. Paul's Churchyard. The area, once famous as the domain of London's booksellers and favored haunt of Samuel Pepys, was deeply shadowed by the bulk of Sir Christopher Wren's masterpiece. She greedily breathed in the crisp winter air as they crossed the churchyard. She was thinking about what Holden had told her while they waited for Bryan.

"Don't let on I said anything," he said. "But I think I know what freaked Bryan out. Down below, in the Plague pit. When he was a little kid in Ethiopia, his family were Falasha. The dictator—Mengistu—he wanted them all dead. One night his soldiers came. They made the people dig a trench in the graveyard. Then they butchered everyone in Bryan's village with machetes and threw the bodies into the hole on top of the bones of their ancestors. Bryan's whole family was slaughtered. He was the only survivor." Holden grimaced. "It was three days before he was found, beneath the bodies of his mother and older sister."

Ayesha could picture the scene Holden had described, all too vividly. It more than explained the DS's behavior. As they reached the end of St. Paul's Churchyard she looked down Ludgate Hill, shaking her head to dispel the surreal feeling they had returned from a parallel universe. Abandoned Underground tunnels, Roman catacombs, and Plague pits. The massacre of Bryan's family in Ethiopia. None of these things belonged to the London she now beheld, of modern office towers and twinkling Christmas lights. The London where Evelyn had been murdered. They left the churchyard and stepped onto the paved area below the West Porch. And stopped dead.

"We'll stand out like a bunch of sore thumbs," Holden remarked, surveying the brilliantly lit cathedral.

"The porch is in shadow," Bryan observed, looking up the broad steps. "We can wait behind the columns."

"We still have to get up there," Ayesha reminded them. "In full of view of anyone." She nodded toward the traffic passing up and down Ludgate Hill. It was light, but constant. No pedestrians were in sight, not surprising given the time, but St. Paul's was one of the world's great tourist attractions. It wouldn't be long before someone came by.

Holden looked toward the statue that towered at the foot of the stone steps, behind a spiked iron railing. Queen Anne, Britain's monarch when the cathedral was being completed. It surmounted statues of "lesser" ladies, representing England, France, Ireland, and North America. He took a step toward it.

She put a hand on his sleeve, shook her head warningly. They would still be in full view from the south.

In the end they stayed where they were and lurked in the shadows at the corner of the north wall. While they watched for the car from Scotland Yard, the cold, kept at bay before by their exertions, seemed to deepen. Before long they were all hugging themselves and stamping their feet for warmth.

"Here they are," Holden said after perhaps ten minutes had gone by. Three simple words, but she heard relief, impatience, and excitement in his voice. Relief that their ordeal was over. Excitement that he could make a full report on what had happened. Impatience to get after whoever had pursued them into the darkness below London. The DI strode forward onto the brightly lit pavement in front of the West Porch and took up a position in front of the Queen Anne statue, arms folded. After a moment she and Bryan joined him. They watched as two black Jaguars pulled off the road and parked on the other side of the polished granite bollards that blocked vehicular access to the churchyard.

"Why two cars?" she heard Bryan ask.

Holden spared the DS an irritated look, then walked forward to greet whoever had come to collect them. He'd taken no more than two steps before doors were flung open and men emerged from the cars. One was balding and wore a dark suit. Three others wore nearly identical black leather jackets. All four men drew weapons and pointed them at the little group in front of the statue.

Bryan's question about the two cars had triggered an internal alarm and Ayesha's body was moving even before her conscious brain realized what was happening. She rose to her toes, was twisting away when something happened to the man closest to her. The balding one in the suit. A crimson rose flowered in the center of his forehead. At the same instant his head jerked violently forward. The man fell, his gun flying from his nerveless hand. The back of his skull made a sickening crack as it hit the pavement.

She'd heard nothing. No shot. But she'd seen the shocking death—she had no doubt he was dead—of the balding man in the suit.

The leather-jacketed men dived for cover behind their vehicles. A tinkle of cascading glass sounded from the nearer Jaguar as the driver's window disintegrated.

Of the three, Holden was closest to the cars. Unbelievably, he now took another step in the same direction. Mentally cursing his stupidity, she leaped forward. Hauling him backward, she shoved him to the ground behind the fence enclosing the statue. Bryan was already there. Something thumped against her left shoulder. Simultaneously a shock surged the length of her arm. She looked down. A small chunk of masonry lay on the ground beside her. She peered up at the statue. "France" was missing a finger. "Back!" she snapped. "We can't stay here."

Bryan did not need to be told twice. Holden gaped like a just-landed fish. She punched him hard on the shoulder. "Move!" she barked. Then, tensing her back for the expected shot, she dashed, bent low, for the shelter of the north wall.

The several yards to the corner were some of the longest she had ever covered. Every moment she expected to feel the impact of the bullet that would end her life. It never came, and she made it with Holden breathing hard behind her. She looked around desperately. They might be out of the line of fire. She hoped they were. But they wouldn't be for long. They couldn't go forward. Nor could they go back into St. Paul's. The door through which they had left was deadlocked. "Come on." She jerked her head back behind them, into the churchyard. "We have to get out of here."

Moses Litmann listened to Nazir's machinelike voice with a profound sense of relief. He'd been terrified that Ayesha Ryder would be brought in by MI5, and that she would tell whatever it was that she knew. "They got away?" he asked for the second time. "You're certain of it?"

His cellphone pressed to one ear, he absorbed the assurances Nazir communicated. "Yes," he said. "I want you to find Ryder. But I want to give her some more rope before you pick her up. . . . That's right, see if she comes up with anything else. . . . No. I'm not worried. Our sources will keep us informed."

RYDER

He crossed to the writing table, glanced down at the old Palestine Conference file. It was then he remembered the other information his aide, Denburg, had come up with—the possible link to the "madrigalism" that Ryder had discovered engraved on Lawrence's dagger, news of which Nazir's informant had passed on: the old woman, Lawrence's lover, who, miraculously, still lived.

"There's something else," he said. "I want you to put someone under surveillance. Her name is Lady Madrigal Carey. She lives here in London. Mayfair."

He ended the call. He sat down at the writing table, gazed at the old file for a moment, and opened a browser window on the Mac laptop Denburg had set up for him. He spent several minutes browsing the latest news stories on CNN, the BBC, *Ha'aretz* and Al Jazeera. All of them had pieces on the London conference. CNN had a positive spin. The others were uniformly gloomy in their prognostications.

He closed the browser and opened up a piece of highly illegal software that Denburg had installed, and which the young man had shown him how to use. In less than a minute he was looking at a file directory from another computer—the personal laptop of Judah Ben David, Israel's prime minister.

CHAPTER 27

Ayesha surveyed the dingy Internet café, one of several such establishments that lined the narrow street behind St. Bart's Hospital, along with backpacker hostels, laundromats, and greasy spoons. They had stumbled into it after dodging through a series of alleys north of St. Paul's Churchyard. It seemed like a good place to take stock of their situation. They were alone, except for the young man who sprawled at the front counter, earphones tuned to something that echoed tinnily in the otherwise silent café, and whose face was buried in a battered copy of *The Da Vinci Code*.

She was sure they hadn't been followed. Although with the ubiquitous CCTV cameras you could never be sure who was watching. Turning, she saw Holden thumbing buttons on his phone. She seized it from his grasp and, with swift motions, opened the panel on the back, levered out the chip, dropped it to the floor, and ground it to fragments under the heel of her boot. She tossed the phone carcass into a garbage bin.

"What the fuck?" Holden's face was brick red.

She turned to Bryan, her hand out. The DS nodded, drew out

his phone, and handed it over. "Who were you going to call?" she asked Holden, as Bryan's phone joined his.

"The Yard, of course."

"That's who you called before." She enunciated each word slowly, deliberately. Waiting for Holden to catch on.

It took a moment, but he got there. Understanding dawned in his eyes. The red faded from his cheeks, which now took on a slightly ashen complexion. "The Yard sent those men," he said.

"Whoever did the shooting. They knew about the rendezvous, too. They must be monitoring Scotland Yard's communications." She tapped the garbage bin with her boot. "You can't call again. I assume your phones are official issue?"

Both men nodded.

"That's why I got rid of them. They'll be traced. You should know that."

"But who? Why?" Holden sounded like a child who'd had a favorite toy snatched away. He was obviously struggling to comprehend the transition from his vision of hot cocoa and a debriefing at the Yard, to the knowledge that his own organization had betrayed him. Had sent armed men to apprehend him.

"Those are good questions," she said. "I wish I had the answers. What we've found out so far has stirred up a hornet's nest. And it involves our own government."

Holden opened his mouth, then closed it again. He knew she was right. She saw it in his eyes. Someone very high up had to have sent the killers in the black Jaguars. She held the DI's gaze for a moment, then sat down on a plastic chair in front of an ancient PC, one of several that were lined up on a stained Formica-topped counter. She'd paid a pound for half an hour's access when they entered the café. She clicked the Explorer icon, and, while the browser slowly booted up, she said, "The only thing I can think of is to keep following the clues. If we get some more answers maybe that will tell us who is chasing us, and what they're after. Do either of you have a better idea?"

Neither did, so she turned back to the computer. A siren could be heard not far away. She had no doubt where it was headed, but it was too late. She'd found Lady Madrigal Carey's address. "Come on." She jumped to her feet. "We have to get out of here."

CHAPTER 28

Dame Imogen Worsley put down her phone, a rock forming in her chest.

She'd thought the call would be Jameson. It was one of his team. The director-general could scarcely bring herself to believe the man's report. Things had gone from bad to disastrous. What had started as a simple operation to bring in a female academic researcher and two Scotland Yard detectives had inexplicably turned into a nightmare. Tears stung her eyes. She blinked them away. It had been decades since she'd given way to such emotion. She wasn't about to start now.

"Bill Jameson's dead," she said, outwardly calm, when she raised her eyes and looked at the blond-haired woman who stood just inside the door to her office. *Jameson,* she thought. Like the whiskey. They'd joked about it. How long had she known him? Eight, nine years? He wasn't married. Divorced a couple of years back. No kids. Thank God. At Christmas, too. That would have been too much. She shook her head. It was too much. Someone was going to pay for Bill's death.

Peta Harrison reacted to her words with a sharp intake of breath. "How? What happened?"

"I don't have details yet. He took a team to bring in Ryder and the . . . detectives. They got to the rendezvous. At St. Paul's. Bill was shot. Killed instantly."

"Ryder shot him?" Peta Harrison sat down in the chair in front of Dame Imogen's desk without waiting to be asked.

"Not her."

"One of the detectives?"

"Someone else. We don't know who." Imogen hesitated. "At least . . . No. We don't know who it was."

"Ryder? And the others?"

"They got away. After Bill was . . . shot. We traced them. To an Internet café near St. Bart's. They'd gone by the time we got there."

"What do you want me to do?"

She tried to think. Bill Jameson. He'd been here, in her office. Just a little while ago. Alive. Now he was dead. His body on its way to the morgue. *Norman,* she thought. *I need to speak to Norman.* She realized Peta Harrison was still waiting for an answer. "Find Ryder," she ordered. "And find out who shot Bill Jameson."

CHAPTER 29

Milton Hoenig leaned back in his chair at London's *Daily Herald* newspaper. His phone was clamped firmly to one ear, as it had been for most of the night. His feet, encased in gleaming black brogues, were crossed at the ankles and rested on the edge of his desk. His free hand was wrapped around the latest of the numerous cups of tea brought to him by the *Herald*'s tireless copyboy.

"Come on, Simon," he wheedled. "Give me something. You're the embassy's press secretary. You know everything. What's your boss going to tell the world on Wednesday?" He sighed. "I don't believe you. Look, if it's money you want, we can do something. This story's the big one. Trust me, we'll pay." He shook his head in disgust. "Fine, Simon. Fine. If that's the way you want to play it. I'm crossing you off my Hanukkah list."

He swung his feet off the desk, slid his chair forward, and dropped the phone back onto its base. He picked up a pen and crossed a name off a list written on a page torn from his notebook. He cursed softly. It was the last name. He'd called everyone on the list. And it was a long list.

The meeting between Judah Ben David and Sayyed Khalidi was *the* story. Half the journalists in the world had arrived in London to cover it. All of them knew something big was going to happen. The two leaders were going to make an announcement. A very important announcement, about some development toward resolution of the decades old Israeli/Palestinian crisis. Obviously. Whether it would be more platitudes, useless words that went nowhere—like the Oslo Accords, or the "Roadmap"—or something more concrete, no one knew. There had been no leak. Nothing. It was driving Milton Hoenig mad. He'd contacted all of his sources. Wheedled. Cajoled. Tried bribery. None of the usual methods had given him a thing. He wanted this story. Wanted it desperately. But he couldn't think of a single other person to talk to.

He glanced at the clock on the wall. Thought about bed. Thought about bacon and eggs. The thought of food reminded him that the two leaders were dining at Downing Street later that day. He was reaching for his Rolodex—he was old-fashioned—to see who he could call at Number 10, when his phone rang.

"Hoenig." He listened, then he shot up in his chair and reached for his pen. "Yes," he said. "I know who you are. Where do you want to meet?" He scribbled on a piece of paper. "I'll be there." He ended the call and punched the air. "Yes!" he cried, causing the copyboy to spill his next cup of tea.

CHAPTER 30

Ayesha heard a clock chime somewhere not far away. She counted. Four A.M. That couldn't be right. Surely more time had passed since DS Bryan had knocked on her door and dragged her to the scene of Evelyn's murder. The hunt for clues at the Walsingham and the War Museum. The mad chase through the Underground and the catacombs. The ambush at St. Paul's. All of that could not have been squeezed into a mere six hours.

Her breath frosted, hanging in the frigid air next to Bryan's. Both waited on the footpath while Holden paid off their cab. She had reminded the DI to use cash—credit cards, like cellphones, could be traced. They'd walked from the Internet café behind St. Bart's as far as Covent Garden, using side streets and lanes—well aware of just how well London was covered by CCTV cameras—then boarded the Tube to Victoria Station. A cab brought them to Upper Brook Street in Mayfair. All of them were tired, stressed from looking over their shoulders for the first glimpse of a flashing light.

She looked up at the imposing Edwardian building that was

their destination. Would they find any answers there? Or would it be another dead end? All of the floors were dark except for one: the fifth. The top floor. Her premonition that this was the place they sought was confirmed by the brass plate at the front entrance. She pressed the buzzer for apartment 501. After a brief wait, a woman's voice spoke over the intercom. "Yes?"

Holden replied. "Detective Inspector James Holden. Metropolitan Police. I apologize for the hour, but I'd very much like to speak with Lady Madrigal Carey."

A long silence followed. So long Ayesha knew there was not going to be a reply. She was going to suggest Holden try the button once more when the woman's voice came again. "Please come in. Take the elevator to the fifth floor." Her accent was clear. Russian.

When the elevator doors opened they were met by a tall, slim woman casually dressed in blue jeans and a black T-shirt. Fortyish and extremely attractive, with masses of ash-blond hair. The two detectives showed their identification and Ayesha introduced herself.

"My name is Tatiana," the woman informed them. "I am Lady Madrigal's companion. Please come into the living room." She gestured toward a doorway behind her. "Lady Madrigal will join you in a few minutes."

They entered a room soft-lit by floor and table lamps and warmed by an open fire. An early Axminster carpet covered a parquet floor, and overstuffed leather sofas and armchairs were arranged about the room in front of the fireplace and beside crowded bookcases. The fireplace mantel and a baby grand piano were covered in framed photographs. As was the only wall space not hidden by bookcases. There was only one thing missing, Ayesha realized: Christmas decorations.

RYDER

"What would you like to drink?" Tatiana asked. "Miss Ryder? Detectives?"

"Coffee. Please." The reply came, simultaneously, from all three.

"Of course." The Russian smiled and waved a hand over the room. "Please, sit down. I will bring coffee."

"Oh yes," Holden said as he dropped into the nearest armchair and stretched his legs out in front of him. "This is what I need."

Bryan turned to the bookcases.

Ayesha crossed to the piano. She surveyed the serried ranks of photographs, black-and-white, sepia-toned, and color. Some meant nothing to her. Others held familiar faces. She recognized Lady Madrigal Carey from the newspaper picture with Lawrence. There were many photographs of her. Older, but still recognizably the same extraordinarily beautiful woman. Although there were solitary poses, most showed her with other people. Famous men. Churchill. Eden, de Gaulle. Eisenhower, Harold Macmillan. The important men of the war years. And the postwar years. They were all there. And T. E. Lawrence. Lots of photographs with Lawrence. He was mostly in uniform, while Lady Madrigal wore a variety of fashionable dresses.

She picked up a silver-framed photograph that showed the pair on one of Lawrence's Brough Superior motorcycles. He wore a turtleneck jumper and tweed jacket, while Lady Madrigal sat behind him, her arms around his waist, skirt hiked up to show long and shapely legs. Ayesha was still looking at the photograph when she became aware of someone else in the room behind her.

Expecting to meet someone who was possibly senile, more than likely wheelchair-or bed-bound, she was stunned. The woman who leaned against the doorjamb was straight-backed and wearing a midnight blue velvet dressing gown, a rich contrast with her shoulder-length thick silver hair. Her gray eyes were bright, sparkling even, and her jaw was firm. In one hand she held a cocktail glass. In the other a cigarette in a long black holder. She drew on this, exhaled a thin line of smoke, then lifted her glass and drank. Ayesha would not have put Lady Madrigal at much more than seventy-five—a very well-preserved seventy-five at that.

"I hear you've asked for coffee." Her voice low and pleasant. "Are you sure I couldn't interest anyone in a martini instead?"

Holden, who had scrambled to his feet at the older woman's entrance, chuckled. "I have no idea if I'm officially on duty or not," he said, bowing from the waist, "but I'd love a martini."

Ayesha set the photograph back on the piano and stepped forward. "Ayesha Ryder. I'll pass on the martini, but I'd kill for a dash of brandy in my coffee."

Lady Madrigal took her martini glass in the hand that held the cigarette holder, accepted her hand, and squeezed it, firmly. As Ayesha released her grip, her glance took in the gold brooch pinned to the older lady's robe. A double clef. Her earrings were of the same design.

"Of course, m'dear," Lady Madrigal replied, as her companion swept through the doorway carrying a tray laden with a coffeepot, cups, milk, and sugar. "Tatiana," she said. "A martini for the inspector. Brandy for Miss Ryder. And"—she arched one pencil-thin eyebrow at Bryan—"Sergeant?"

"Just coffee, please."

Lady Madrigal lowered herself into an armchair by the fireplace. She sipped her martini and considered her visitors. "Happy as I am to receive callers at almost any time, I must admit that my curiosity is enormously aroused. Would someone please tell me the reason for your visit?" She looked at Ayesha.

She held Lady Madrigal's gaze for several heartbeats, then she nodded her head in the direction of the silver-framed photograph on the piano. The one of Lady Madrigal and Lawrence on his motorcycle. "You knew T. E. Lawrence. Lawrence of Arabia."

Lady Madrigal drew on her cigarette holder and said nothing. The statement clearly needed no acknowledgment.

Ayesha took a deep breath, then she told Lady Madrigal about Sir Evelyn Montagu's murder. She left out the part about her own relationship with him, although her voice wobbled when she first mentioned his name. "I knew Evelyn," the old lady acknowledged softly, with a look that spoke volumes. "I'm so sorry."

Ayesha waited, but Lady Madrigal said nothing more, and Tatiana returned to the room just then with a martini for Holden and a bottle of brandy.

Ayesha helped herself to coffee, adding brandy. The warmth flowed down her throat and into her stomach. She took another sip, then continued recounting their story to Lady Madrigal.

She described the finding of the word *Vincey*, how that led her to Rider Haggard's *She*. Again she was aware that Lady Madrigal was looking at her intensely. No doubt she was familiar with the novel. When Ayesha moved on to the discovery of Lawrence's letter behind the movie poster, however, Lady Madrigal sat up straight and put down her drink.

"A treaty, you said?" Ayesha nodded.

"Do you know anything about this treaty, Lady Madrigal?" Holden asked. "Did

Lawrence leave something with you? Papers?"

"Tell me the rest of the story first," Lady Madrigal said.

Ayesha glanced at Holden, who shrugged. She turned back to Lady Madrigal. The old lady was the very image of sophistication. Yet she had been to hell and back. Ayesha knew what that was like. She wondered whether, in another sixty years, she might display the same qualities. She hoped so. She drew breath, then told how they'd gone to the Walsingham Institute. How they'd worked out that the first part of the clue was a reference to *Seven Pillars of Wisdom*, which in turn led them to Lawrence's gold dagger. She paused, remembering the second part of Lawrence's letter. "Lady Madrigal," she said. "The 'in passing' reference. The numbers referred, we think, to a passage in the Book of Exodus that describes the Ark of the Covenant. Did Lawrence ever talk about it?"

"Often. Ned had a thing about the Ark. He was always delving into ancient writings that concerned it."

Bryan leaned forward. "Did he tell you where he thought the Ark might be?"

"No, he didn't. I'm sorry."

A brief silence followed, then Ayesha told how they'd gone to the Imperial War Museum and found the bars of music inscribed on Lawrence's dagger.

"It was the sort of thing Ned loved," Lady Madrigal said. "Ancient riddles. He was quite the show-off when it came to his erudition." She smiled. "That was good detective work on your part. Making the connection to me. You must have got a shock when you found I was still around."

Holden laughed, but Ayesha could contain herself no longer. "Lady Madrigal, did Lawrence send you any papers shortly before his death in 1935? For safe custody?"

Their hostess would have made a successful actress. Her timing was calculated impeccably. The old woman drew on her cigarette, turned her head, and stared into the fireplace. When she turned back she exhaled a trickle of smoke. A mischievous twinkle glittered in her gray eyes. "There are things you haven't told me." Her glance flickered over Ayesha's torn pants and bandaged thigh.

Ayesha started to reply but, to her surprise, Lady Madrigal waved her to silence. "Very well. Yes. Ned did send me something. Just before he was killed."

Ayesha held her breath, waiting, holding Lady Madrigal's eyes.

Lady Madrigal returned her gaze, unblinking. A smile twitched the edges of her lips. "Would you like to see it?" she asked them.

CHAPTER 31

"Thank you, Norman." Dame Imogen Worsley replaced the phone handset and gazed at the large-scale map of Great Britain that took up much of one wall of her office. Her mind raced. MI5 was compromised. The home secretary, Sir Norman Eldritch, had just assured her he'd spoken to nobody. So the leak came from *within*. One of their own was responsible for Bill Jameson's death. She'd told only Norman. And Peta Harrison. She put her head in her hands. Not Harrison. Not her. Imogen lifted her head, her brow clearing. The more likely explanation was that their communications had been monitored. That their supposedly ultrasecure systems might have been hacked was extremely disturbing. Still, that was something they were equipped to deal with. Far better than the alternative.

She pressed a button on her phone. Two minutes later Steve Watts, the officer in charge of IT, tapped on her open door and entered. Tall and gangly, with thick ginger hair and rimless spectacles he was always pushing back on a beaky nose, Watts was a brilliant recluse who ruled his domain with an iron fist. That said, his staff adored him. Imogen lived in constant fear he'd be lured away by Google or one of its numerous progeny. "We've got a problem," she said when Watts closed the door.

He nodded, waited for her to go on. Problems were nothing new in his department.

"I think we've been hacked."

Watts opened his mouth to protest, but she held up a hand. "Steve, I know what you're going to say. That you have a zillion programs constantly monitoring for any trace of an attempted hack."

Watts nodded emphatically. Again, he started to speak. Once more she cut him off. "Humor me, Steve. Because I really, really hope it *is* a hack."

"Huh?" The IT director's eyebrows shot up. Bewildered, he waited for her to explain.

She glanced at the door to her office. "Bill Jameson's computer. I want you to personally check all traffic that's gone through it tonight. His phone, too." She hesitated, then added, "And the same for Peta Harrison."

Watts said nothing, but there was a look of understanding in his eyes now. Sorrow, too.

"I don't have to tell you to be discreet."

"Don't worry, Director," Watts said. "No one will know."

When her IT head had departed, Imogen turned to her desktop computer. The immediate priority was to find Ryder and the two Scotland Yard men. The foiled rendezvous had not rendered the mission entrusted to her by the home secretary any less urgent. In fact, as Norman had not refrained from pointing out to her on the phone, it meant things had escalated. Whoever was behind Jameson's death knew Ryder was urgently pursuing a lead arising from Sir Evelyn Montagu's murder. The action at St. Paul's—and Imogen had no doubt it was connected—said they wanted to know what Ryder had found out, and to suppress it or use it for their own purposes. What they might do if they got hold of the story of the former Prince of Wales's plot with the Nazis was anyone's guess. She repressed a shudder.

She called up T. E. Lawrence's classified service file. The one Bill Jameson had alerted her to. *There has to be something more*, she thought. Something that would give her some indication of what motivated the people responsible for the murders of Montagu and Bill Jameson.

A quarter of an hour later she stopped reading. She'd been skimming, but she was a practiced speed-reader and knew she hadn't missed anything important. She was frowning, though. A note at the end of the file indicated there were other materials that had not yet been scanned and digitized for inclusion in the online file. She buzzed her secretary.

Expert at compartmentalizing, she dealt with several routine matters while her secretary visited the records department. When the woman returned and placed a cardboard bankers box on her desk, Imogen removed the lid from the box. She lifted out the various items contained within, all enclosed in transparent archival-quality document sleeves. She put several handwritten letters and documents to one side and concentrated on a collection of photographs.

The photographs were interesting historically, but that was all. She was putting them back in the box when, jammed into a corner near the bottom, she found another photograph. She held it up. T. E. Lawrence. Dressed in a suit, he stood between a bearded man who wore Arab robes and a turban, and a man in a dark suit with fair hair. It looked to be just a variation on many of the others in the box. Lawrence with an Arab dignitary and an official of some sort. The Arab seemed familiar. She turned the photo over to read the words on the back. *Clouds Hill.* Lawrence's cottage. *May 1935.* Right before his death. At the same time as the Palestine Conference. But the Palestine Conference was just a name. The cover story for the secret meeting about Edward, Prince of Wales. It wouldn't have involved any Arabs. So who was the man in the photograph?

She put down the photograph, her fingers beating a tattoo on the desktop. Between the death of Bill Jameson and the old mystery of Lawrence of Arabia, she felt she was floundering. It was a new sensation for the head of MI5, one she would not tolerate.

CHAPTER 32

Ayesha hardly dared to hope that, after all these years, Lady Madrigal would still have Lawrence's papers. Yet the old woman, who, the more time she spent in her company, seemed somehow not to be so very old, had asked her if she wanted to see them. "Yes, please," she replied.

"Tatiana," Lady Madrigal said. "Please bring Miss Ryder a robe, then take her pants and sew up that tear. And fetch me the Lawrence box."

"Please." A blush rose to her cheeks. "There's no need—"

"Of course there is." Lady Madrigal interrupted. "You don't want to go around looking like a tramp."

The Russian came back into the room. She had a white robe over one arm, and was using both of her hands to carry an obviously heavy metal box. Bryan stepped forward to help. He took the box from a grateful Tatiana, then looked around for somewhere to put it down.

"There." Lady Madrigal pointed to a leather ottoman. "Push that in front of me and put the box on top."

While Bryan was carrying out these maneuvers, Ayesha accepted the robe from Tatiana, slipped it on, and belted it up. She sat down in an armchair and removed her boots, then she stood up again and wriggled out of her pants. She glanced at Holden, who smirked and saluted her with his cocktail glass. She ignored him, handed her pants to Tatiana, picked up her coffee cup, and walked over to the piano. The robe was thick and comfortable, but she felt naked without her pants and boots. She glanced at Bryan. The detective sergeant, who had resumed his position by the fireplace, was looking away from her, but she had the distinct feeling that he'd missed nothing.

Lady Madrigal stubbed out her cigarette in an onyx ashtray that already held several butts. She leaned over, lifted the hinged lid of the metal box. "There's all manner of things in here," she said. She rummaged inside the box, then sat up straight. In her right hand was a gun, a German Luger. It was pointed at Holden.

The DI froze in his chair, his cocktail glass sagging in his hand. Ayesha held her breath until, with a delighted laugh, Lady Madrigal lowered the Luger.

"Don't worry." She placed it on the table. "It's not loaded." She frowned. "At least I don't think it is."

"How did you come to know Lawrence?" Ayesha asked, trying to repress a smile at the effect of Lady Madrigal's weapon on Holden.

The older woman gave her a knowing look. "You know I was in SOE during the war?"

"Yes. We've read your record. It's truly impressive."

Lady Madrigal frowned at the compliment. "I was recruited to MI6 long before that. When I was still in my teens."

"Is that how you met Lawrence?" Holden interjected, having

recovered from the shock of Lady Madrigal's gunplay. "He was a spook, too, wasn't he?"

"Do you know that for a fact?" Lady Madrigal looked at the DI, then back at Ayesha. "Or are you guessing?"

"It's a guess," Ayesha replied. "But I think it's a good one."

Lady Madrigal said nothing for a moment. Then, "Well, you're right. Ned was a spook. And that's how we met. From 1933 until he was killed, I was his liaison with MI6."

"So that's it," Holden said. "We came across a picture of the two of you. We wondered. . . ." He broke off.

"I can guess what you wondered." Lady Madrigal chuckled. "I'm much too old to care anymore, though. You were right. I was his contact. I was also his lover."

Ayesha held Lady Madrigal's gaze. Something passed between them. Ayesha wasn't sure what. But it was there.

Bryan broke the silence. "So you know what Lawrence was working on when he died?"

"I knew some of the things Ned was working on. But no one knew everything he was up to. A more secretive man never existed. It's one of the traits that made him the perfect spy." Lady Madrigal sighed. "It was also incredibly infuriating at times." She turned back to the metal box and withdrew several bundles of letters, tied with faded ribbon. A package of photographs. Notebooks. More notebooks. Finally, a faded brown envelope. "This is it," she said. "Ned sent this to me. It was contained in another envelope postmarked the day of his motorcycle accident." She paused at the word *accident*. "There was a note. He asked me to keep this." She tapped the envelope. "And give it to Winston if anything happened to him."

"Winston Churchill?" Bryan asked.

"Of course Churchill. Who else?"

"And why didn't you?" Holden wanted to know. "Give it to Churchill, I mean?"

"I tried to. Winston wasn't interested. He said there was no point anymore." Lady

Madrigal shrugged bony shoulders. "So I kept it."

"What's inside it?" Ayesha asked.

"I've no idea. I don't open other people's mail." Lady Madrigal's shoulders slumped. "But I suppose that hardly matters now, does it?" She held the envelope out.

Palestine Conference—Keep for Winston. In case.

Ayesha read the superscription, then, her heart beating faster, she took the ivory-handled paper knife Lady Madrigal held out to her and slit the envelope open. Then she tipped its contents onto the occasional table.

The tension coiled inside her. She glanced up. Holden and Bryan had come to stand next to her. Both of them were bending forward, staring intently at the little heap of items that had spilled from the envelope. She turned her head to look at Lady Madrigal. The old woman held her gaze, until the draw of the occasional table proved irresistible. Ayesha looked down at two sheets of writing paper.

She picked up the top sheet of paper with fingers that trembled a little. The sheet was flimsy, almost transparent, but it was easy enough to read the words written on it in Lawrence's distinctive hand:

The man who taught you to fly—his old address. Ross's number.

She handed the sheet of paper to Holden and picked up the second piece. This one held a series of musical notes. Three bars. Nothing else. She handed it, too, to Holden, who had passed the first sheet to Bryan.

"What's this?" the DI asked. "Another madrigalism?"

"May I?" Lady Madrigal asked, extending a hand for the paper. She considered it for nearly a minute, then shook her head. "I'm sorry. I'm sure it *is* a madrigalism. But this one doesn't mean anything to me. It seems to be a simple movement repeated more than once."

A small collection of photographs had fallen from the envelope. Ayesha picked up the top one. Her eyes widened.

"What is it?" Holden asked.

She held the photograph out to Lady Madrigal, looked into her gray eyes, almost certain she saw something impish lurking there, and asked: "Can you tell me why Lawrence would have had a photograph of Edward, Prince of Wales, shaking hands with Adolf Hitler?"

CHAPTER 33

Dame Imogen stared at the images on her computer screen, the ones she'd found after she'd got herself a fresh cup of tea, drawn several deep breaths, and summoned her stiff upper lip. She would pierce this mystery. Whatever it was.

The images showed the same Arab who appeared in the photograph with Lawrence of Arabia taken at his cottage in May 1935. The other man in the photograph, the bureaucrat, she'd already identified as Nigel Clarke-Kerr, a career diplomat and number-two man in the League of Nations. At the time of the photograph Clarke-Kerr was based at the League's headquarters in Geneva, where he had special responsibility for oversight of the Palestine Mandate. He died shortly after the photograph was taken, when the plane taking him back to Geneva crashed into the North Sea.

But it was the man in Arab dress Dame Imogen was focused on now. Some of the photographs on her screen showed him at a younger age, but most were from later years. Now she knew why she'd initially thought he looked familiar. He was, after all, quite notorious. Haj Mohammad Amin al-Husayni had been the Grand

Mufti of Jerusalem and in all of his photographs he wore the trim beard and the distinctive turban of his office. Even when he was shaking hands with Adolf Hitler, or Heinrich Himmler, or inspecting Muslim recruits to the SS.

Al-Husayni had been behind the bloody revolt against British rule in Palestine that started in 1936 and petered out only with the advent of the European war. He'd been forced to flee. First to Iraq. Later he went to Europe, where he sought to enlist the help of Mussolini and Hitler in ousting the Jews from Palestine. So what the devil was he doing with Lawrence? Dame Imogen pulled up the Security Service file on the Grand Mufti.

Al-Husayni, she read, came from one of Jerusalem's most important Arab families. His half brother was Grand Mufti before him, and, on his death, it was an easy decision to appoint him to the role. Successive British high commissioners considered him a friend. They had consulted him on any matter affecting the administration of Palestine, enlisting his support to calm Arab concerns over continuing Jewish immigration. Al-Husayni apparently believed British promises that this immigration would not be allowed to have an adverse effect on the Arab population. Events proved him wrong. He lost control, most notably at the time of the 1929 Hebron Massacre. Rising up in response to false rumors that Jews were massacring Arabs in Jerusalem, Arabs killed sixty-seven Jews, wounded scores, and attacked synagogues. Some Arabs were also killed, and many more Jews were saved by the Arab families who sheltered them. The event was a pivotal one in the Jewish psyche, leading to the creation of the Haganah, which became the nucleus of the Israel Defense Forces. After Hebron, things came to a head. Tensions boiled over and al-Husayni could no longer walk the tightrope between balancing the competing interests of the officially pro-Jewish British administration and those of his own countrymen.

So what was happening in 1935? Imogen read quickly on. Lord Passfield, the colonial secretary, recommended that severe limitations be placed on Jewish immigration to Palestine. That there be equality of treatment for Arabs and Jews. That a legislative council be established as an important step toward self-government. It would have meant annulling the Balfour Declaration and, more crucially, the end of the dream of a Jewish homeland in Palestine. So what happened?

Her brow furrowed. Chaim Weizmann. The Great Zionist. Weizmann's maneuverings somehow convinced the British cabinet, in the face of almost unanimous conviction that they ought to get out of Palestine, not only to stay, but to quash Lord Passfield's recommendations. The colonial secretary himself was vilified as having betrayed promises made by the British government to the Jewish people.

That was 1930, she noted. The start of the Great Depression. Before Hitler. Things got worse over the next few years. A lot worse. *What if we decided to try again?* If we did, we wouldn't want a repeat of what happened before. We'd keep it secret. Until everything was concluded. Who would we have negotiated with? The Grand Mufti. Obviously. He was the spiritual and political leader of the Palestinian Arabs. The League of Nations would have to be involved. A frisson of excitement tingled her spine. Nigel Clarke-Kerr. Who would've represented the British government? The hair rose on the back of her neck and her skin erupted into a rash of goose bumps.

She reached for her phone, intending to call the home secretary, Sir Norman Eldritch. As she did so her eye was caught by a name on her computer screen. It was bracketed with that of T. E. Lawrence. She was sure she'd seen it before. *Madrigal Carey.* She made a note of it on a scratch pad, then picked up the handset.

CHAPTER 34

"I have no idea what this means," Lady Madrigal told them. "I'm sure you've heard the stories of Edward's infatuation with the Nazis, but I can't imagine what Ned would have been doing with this photograph. What are the others?"

Three other photographs had fallen from the envelope. The second photograph was also of the Prince of Wales. Edward posed with the unmistakable figure of Hermann Goering, the head of Hitler's Luftwaffe, the air force. Both men held shotguns and a brace of dead birds—pheasants. The third photograph also showed the prince, this time with a man she did not recognize. He was handsome, with dark hair brushed back and a mustache. He looked a little like Clark Gable.

"Oswald Mosley," Lady Madrigal told them. "Leader of the Blackshirts—the British Union of Fascists. A thoroughly nasty piece of work. Mosley married a good friend of mine, Diana Mitford. Never understood what she saw in him."

The final picture showed a trio of men. T. E. Lawrence was one, dressed in a suit. Another man, also in a suit, had the look of a senior bureaucrat. The third was attired in Arab dress. "The Grand Mufti of Jerusalem," Ayesha said.

"And that's Nigel Clarke-Kerr," Lady Madrigal said, pointing at the bureaucrat. "He was with the League of Nations."

A line of writing was scrawled across the bottom of the photograph. "'Clouds Hill. Tenth of May, 1935,'" Ayesha read aloud.

"Just before Lawrence's death," Bryan said.

"Nigel was killed at almost the same time," Lady Madrigal reminded them. "His plane went down over the North Sea. Tragic. He was a lovely man."

Ayesha's mind raced. Lawrence, al-Husayni, and Nigel Clarke-Kerr met only days before Lawrence's death in May 1935. The Grand Mufti represented Arab Palestine at the time and Clarke-Kerr was with the League of Nations, the governing body ultimately responsible for Palestine. Lawrence was working for MI6. What connection could there be between Lawrence and Palestine on one hand, and the Prince of Wales and the Nazis on the other? On the face of it, none. Other than the fact that photos of them all were contained in an envelope marked *Palestine Conference*.

Nineteen thirty-five. A lot was happening in Europe, but it was still several years before the war and the Grand Mufti's disastrous involvement with the Nazis. The Arab uprising in Palestine began a few months *after* Lawrence's death, though, and the Grand Mufti would lead it.

"Lady Madrigal," Ayesha said, "you said when you tried to give Churchill the Palestine Conference envelope he wasn't interested. He said there was no point anymore."

Lady Madrigal nodded, her gaze locked on Ayesha's. "That's right. It was a week or so after Ned's funeral. I was devastated.

And Winston was extremely busy. Ramsay MacDonald had just resigned and things were in a tizzy."

Lady Madrigal's last words had provided another link in the chain. "So," Ayesha said, "in 1935, Lawrence meets with the Grand Mufti and Nigel Clarke-Kerr. Lawrence and Clarke-Kerr are killed, and Ramsay MacDonald resigns from office. Then Churchill tells you there's no point in . . ." She gazed at Lady Madrigal, thinking. "What was happening in 1935? And how do the Prince of Wales and the Nazis come into it? I know the stories about Edward's Nazi sympathies. Everyone does. But Lawrence?"

"Would it have involved the Jews?" Holden asked.

Ayesha swung on the DI. "How do you mean?"

"Well, Palestine. Arabs. Presumably the Jews were involved. And we know how the Nazis felt about them."

She shook her head. "It doesn't make any sense. How would the Prince of Wales be involved? No. If it wasn't for the Nazi photographs I'd say the Palestine Conference was a negotiation being undertaken by Lawrence on behalf of the British govern-ment with the Grand Mufti. Given the timing, with war on the horizon, that likely meant they were talking about pulling out of Palestine."

"Where does the chap from the League of Nations come in?" Holden asked.

"The British derived their authority for the Palestine Mandate directly from the League. If they were going to do anything to alter things, the League would have to approve." She spoke faster, both hands tightly balled in the pockets of her borrowed robe. "I'm sure that's it! The British wanted out of Palestine. And that meant grant-ing independence — to the Arabs. If the British pulled out, Palestine would have become an independent Arab state. Any proposal like that would have been tremendously sensitive. It would have meant reneging on the Balfour Declaration, hence the immense secrecy. But the Nazis?" She shook her head, bewildered.

"Say you're right," Holden mused. "About this Palestine business. Why would any of that matter now?"

She glanced at Holden, then turned to look at Bryan, who had resumed his position behind Lady Madrigal's armchair. His face was impassive. Lastly, she looked at Lady Madrigal. The twinkle was back in her eyes. She was certain the old woman knew something.

"Clearly it does matter," she answered. "The last few hours ought to be proof enough of that. As to why now? A major conference is about to take place, right here in London, between the Israeli and Palestinian leaders. Presumably they're trying once more for a permanent peace settlement. And these two men have a better chance than anyone who's gone before." She turned her gaze on Lady Madrigal. "What if this treaty of Lawrence's was found? What effect would it have on the prospects for peace?" The hairs rose on the back of her neck as another thought occurred. "Imagine a treaty signed by the British government and representatives of the Palestinians, approved by the League of Nations, granting independence to Palestine!"

"So what?" Holden objected. "That was 1935. Before Israel was even created."

"Exactly. And that's why Evelyn was murdered." Ayesha's heart hammered with excitement. She was sure she was right.

"Huh?" Holden had finished his drink, but he didn't seem to have noticed.

"Think about it, Holden. If a treaty existed giving independence to Palestine, approved by the League of Nations, *before* Israel was created, what legitimacy does Israel have now? There couldn't have been a UN vote in 1947 to create Israel if that was the case. Don't you think certain people would kill to stop something like that coming out?"

"All right, all right, I get it. So we're still following Lawrence's trail of bread crumbs. Does anyone have any idea about the latest clues?"

Ayesha, her mind buzzing with the implications of the connections she'd made, picked up the two sheets of writing paper. "The writing must be addressed to Churchill. 'The man who taught you to fly.' We need to know who that was. 'His old address. Ross's number.' Ross was the name Lawrence adopted when he first joined the RAF. His number, though?"

"I suspect you'll find it means his service number," Lady Madrigal interposed.

Holden snorted. "How on earth do we find that?"

"Over there." Lady Madrigal gestured toward the bookcases. "Third shelf down. There's a copy of *The Mint*, Ned's book about the RAF."

Bryan crossed to the indicated shelf and found the book. He held it up for the others to see. The book jacket bore the title in bold print, and, below it, the author's name: *352087 A/c Ross*.

"Fabulous," Holden said. "Now, who taught Churchill to fly? I didn't know he could," he added.

"Winnie was a first-class pilot," Lady Madrigal stated. "He was flying from the beginning. Well, from the Great War at any rate. I can't remember who taught him, though. There," she said. "Second shelf. There's one of his autobiographies. Bring it to me."

Bryan located the fat volume. Lady Madrigal took it, opened

the book at the index. "Here it is," she said. "Winston's instructor was a Cornishman named Jack Trelawney."

"Cool," Holden said. "But how do we find the address of someone who must have died decades ago?"

"Luckily Winston believed in footnotes." Lady Madrigal held up Churchill's autobiography and smirked at the DI. "It says here that after the war Trelawney returned to Bodmin to resume his position as postmaster."

"His number!" A frisson of pure certainty erupted upward from the base of Ayesha's spine. "Ross's number!"

Three pairs of eyes turned to stare at her. "Don't you see? Trelawney's old address. Lawrence mailed the papers to himself, but used Ross's service number instead of his own name as the addressee. He mailed the papers to Bodmin post office to be held *poste restante*. To be held in safe custody until he, or someone else using his service number, came to collect it."

"Holy shit!" A blush rose to Holden's cheeks. "Sorry, Lady Madrigal."

"I may be old, but I'm not fragile," Lady Madrigal said crisply. "Miss Ryder, I believe you've hit the nail on the head. That's just the sort of thing Ned would have done."

"Bodmin's in Cornwall," Ayesha said. "How will we get there?"

"Have to be train. I can hardly call the Yard for a car. We can't hire one, either—that'd leave a trail anyone could follow."

"Why can't you call the Yard, Mr. Holden?" Lady Madrigal asked the DI. "And just who is following you?"

Holden was caught. "Ah," he said. He raised his eyebrows at Ayesha. When she nodded, he turned back to Lady Madrigal. "It's like this: We were at the Walsingham Institute. We'd just worked out that the madrigalism probably referred to you and that you were still alive." He grinned at their hostess, who nodded impatiently for him to go on. "We were leaving when these armed men turned up. . . ."

When the DI finished speaking Lady Madrigal leaned her head back against the armchair headrest and stared at the ceiling. "Government is involved," she said, lowering her gaze. "And someone pretty high up, too, to have got to Scotland Yard. If your suppositions about the true meaning of the Palestine Conference are correct, then MI5 has been brought in. As to who the other party is—whoever did the shooting at St. Paul's—I think perhaps you've made up your mind who it is?" This last was said with a shrewd look at Ayesha.

She nodded. "The Israelis killed Evelyn. I think it was them, too, who shot at us at St. Paul's."

Bryan grunted at this. She turned to look at him. He opened his mouth to say something, then closed it and shook his head.

"What really worries me is that this is somehow connected with the meeting between Ben David and Khalidi," Ayesha continued. "It starts tomorrow. At the Tower of London. If this treaty of Lawrence's does still exist, and someone wants it badly enough to kill . . ." She broke off. "We have to go to Bodmin."

"Bodmin is about three hours away by train," Lady Madrigal said. "It's plain that you're all exhausted. Are you sure you wouldn't rather rest up here for a while?"

"Thank you for your offer, Lady Madrigal," Ayesha replied, "but I think it's best that we keep moving. By any chance do you have a railway timetable?"

"I don't. I have something better, though. Tatiana, bring me my Mac, would you?"

A short while later Lady Madrigal had her Mac open on her lap. "You'd best hurry," she said, looking up from the National

Rail website. "The next train to Bodmin leaves from Paddington in forty minutes."

Dame Imogen Worsley finished rereading the file on Lady Madrigal Carey. *What an incredible woman*, she thought. *The stories she could tell.* She looked to see when Lady Madrigal had died.

A moment later she picked up her phone. "Harrison?" she said. "Lady Madrigal Carey. Lives on Upper Brook Street. I want a watch put on her apartment. Immediately."

CHAPTER 35

"**P**rime Minister?"

The familiar voice of Judah Ben David's personal assistant cut through a very pleasant dream about a blonde he'd met at the embassy reception. A dream he instantly pushed from his mind. Long years in the military had imbued him with the ability to be alert on waking. He sat up in bed and looked at the time on the electronic clock on the bedside table: 6:25. He found the switch for the lamp and turned it on. "What is it?" he asked.

Rachel Singer did not beat about the bush. "Sir Evelyn Montagu is dead."

Ben David was human. His first emotion was enormous disappointment. He had expected to see Evelyn first thing that morning, was frustrated not to have met with his old friend the night before. He fully intended to pump him dry over breakfast and hear all about what Evelyn thought really happened in 1935. And about the other thing. So badly did he want to know about that, he'd had trouble sleeping. He'd finally given in and taken a sleeping pill. Now he'd never know.

He threw back the bedclothes and swung his legs out of bed, his mind grappling with the news, unconscious that he was naked. As his assistant, with a degree of sangfroid that would have been remarked only by those who did not know her, hurried to bring him a robe, he spoke distractedly. "What was it? Heart attack?"

"He was murdered."

He stopped in the act of tying his robe. "Murdered! You're sure?"

"Yes. It's all over the news. He was found in his apartment last night. They're saying it was Palestinian terrorists."

Palestinians. No. That made no sense. Not Evelyn. Sure he was Jewish, but he'd never been a Zionist. He was a vocal opponent of Israel on so many issues—the occupation of the West Bank, theft of Palestinian land and water resources, demolition of their houses, the prevention of Palestinian fishermen from going to sea, the arrest and detention of their children for throwing stones at Israeli soldiers. He'd sailed on the *Mavi Marmara*, for heaven's sake.

While Rachel Singer went to fetch coffee, he grabbed the telephone. "Get me the Palestinian delegation," he said to the embassy operator. "Sayyed Khalidi." Less than a minute went by, then, "Sayyed? . . . Yes, it's me. Have you heard the news about Evelyn? They're saying Palestinians. Rubbish, of course." He listened to his friend. "I know. It's heartbreaking. I hoped he'd found something we might have been able to use. . . .

"I agree. The coincidence is suspicious. But who would have killed him?" A knot formed in the pit of his stomach. "You think so?" He heaved a deep sigh. "Sayyed, if it's *Shamir* it means they're on to our plans. . . . I hope you're wrong, my friend. I pray you're wrong."

RYDER

CHAPTER 36

The bedside alarm clock made a low buzzing noise. Ahmed Ali-Yaya opened his eyes and blinked in the darkness. It seemed only seconds since they'd turned off the television and gone to bed after watching the late news. He couldn't think what day it was. Then everything flooded back. The peace conference. The leaders of Israel and Palestine meeting at Downing Street. The package in his briefcase. What he'd promised to do with it this day.

He groaned and pushed himself up in bed. Had to. He couldn't afford to fall back to sleep. He eased out of bed, trying not to wake Reem, or the baby. He padded naked across the bedroom and into the bathroom, closing the door quietly behind him before he turned the light on.

He grimaced at the sight in the mirror. Red, bleary eyes. Sickly skin. He looked pasty. Ill. Scared.

He showered, then shaved, on autopilot. His thoughts were focused on the coming few hours. He checked his watch. The Israeli and Palestinian leaders were due at Downing Street shortly before noon. Again he went over the best approach. He glanced at his jacket, hanging on the back of the bathroom door so the steam from the shower would rid it of wrinkles. He put his razor down on the sink, washed and dried his face, then went into the living room and retrieved his briefcase from beneath the sofa. His stomach churned.

He dressed and tiptoed into the kitchen. Made a cup of coffee. His hand shook as he lifted the mug to his lips. He stopped, steadied himself. Didn't want to spill it. He only had the one clean shirt; Reem hadn't been keeping up with the laundry, not that it was her job.

Five minutes later he fastened the last gleaming brass button on his jacket, collected his helmet and briefcase, and walked as quietly as he could to the front door. He paused and looked back along the hall to where his wife and baby daughter still slept. *I wonder if they'll be proud of me*, was his last thought as he closed the door behind him.

CHAPTER 37

D ame Imogen Worsley closed Prime Minister Ramsay MacDonald's private diary for 1935 and placed it on her desk. She rubbed her eyes and stared into space, shaken to the core.

After giving orders for surveillance to be put on Lady Madrigal Carey's apartment, she'd taken a last look in the box of Lawrence's materials. Tucked in the middle of a sheaf of letters, held together with a frayed rubber band, she found a leather-bound book. The former prime minister's name was inscribed on the flyleaf. The pages were crowded with entries for the first half of 1935.

She was puzzled. What was the diary, which should have been in the National Archives, doing in the box of classified material relating to T. E. Lawrence? That mystery, however, was nothing to her curiosity to read the words of the prime minister who'd ordered Lawrence to resolve the question of Palestine. An hour later, her eyes bleary and her head aching from interpreting MacDonald's copperplate scrawl, she came to the last entry: June 7, 1935. The day MacDonald resigned from office, citing ill health as his reason. She still did not understand why the diary had been included with Lawrence's effects, but now she more than understood why it had never seen the light of day.

MacDonald's resignation had nothing to do with his health. It did decline rapidly thereafter, though, and he died in November 1937.

She paged back and reread the first important entry: Tuesday, April 22. *Met with T.E.L. today. Shocking news. Wales is involved with the Nazis. Plotting coup to remove KGV (murder?) and place self on throne with full dictatorial powers. Aided by the Fascists. Mosley to be PM. Intends to ally the Empire with Hitler, break pact with France. Adopt Nazi racial policies and establish concentration camps in Scotland.*

This entry came as no surprise. She'd read much the same information in Lawrence's classified service file. Fascinating to see it confirmed in the prime minister's own hand, though. Horrible, too, to see the confirmation of the Prince of Wales's plot to replace his own father—King George V—on the throne. Regicide, too, and concentration camps. She shuddered at the thought. What followed was coldly prosaic. *Options,* she read. *1. Confront Wales. 2. Allow plot to proceed and arrest all concerned. 3. Elimination.*

The last of the possible options was heavily underscored. Whether that meant MacDonald favored it, and whether it referred to the Prince of Wales, were impossible to know. He'd added no other commentary.

Ramsay MacDonald's diary entry for April 29 held more. Much more.

Broached with T.E.L. idea of revisiting Passfield recommendations. Need to quit Palestine. No strategic value in coming war. Spending huge sums maintaining garrisons, etc. Alienation of Arabs. Continuing conflict between Arabs and Jews with no resolution in sight. T.E.L. to draw up treaty, liaise with Clarke-Kerr over League approval. Grand Mufti coming to England. T.E.L. to conduct negotiations. Secret. Report only to me.

T.E.L. suggested meeting in Dorset. Wareham. Same time as meeting to discuss Wales affair (with Bullivant and Ashgrove). 2 birds 1 stone. Anything gets out, people will assume Palestine only subject talks. Take to Cabinet soon in any case.

There followed a brief summary outlining the nature of the proposed future Palestinian state that was to be embodied in the treaty. The idea was breathtaking in its simplicity. The plan would have received widespread support, she thought, saddened it had not come to fruition. She was astounded, too, to have confirmed the suspicion she'd half formed when she found the photograph of Lawrence with the Grand Mufti and Clarke-Kerr. At the same time he was meeting with Bullivant and Ashgrove to discuss what to do about the treachery of the Prince of Wales, Lawrence was *also* conducting secret negotiations over independence for Palestine with the Grand Mufti and the League of Nations.

MacDonald and Lawrence had concocted a stunning double bluff. Intending to reveal the results of the negotiations over Palestine before long, MacDonald believed it would be an effective way to divert suspicion from Lawrence's investigation of the Prince of Wales. Important as Palestine was, its significance paled in comparison with the evil plot by the heir to the throne.

May 13 was the next entry with anything relevant. The day of Lawrence's accident. *Treaty finalized*, she read. *Grand Mufti has agreed and Clarke-Kerr has signed for the League. I have signed for HMG. T.E.L. will meet again tomorrow with Grand Mufti to pursue arrangements. Take to Cabinet next week. T.E.L. also has plan re Wales affair. Meet with him Friday to discuss.*

On the day of Lawrence's motorcycle crash, everything had been ready to move forward on independence for Palestine. MacDonald had signed the treaty for Britain, and the League of Nations, in the person of Nigel Clarke-Kerr, had approved it. And the business of the Prince of Wales. It looked like some sort of resolution had been decided upon. Lawrence was to have met with MacDonald later that same week. But he couldn't. He was lying in a hospital bed, in a coma. The next entry was brief: *Doctors despair of T.E.L.'s life. I, too, am in despair.*

The nineteenth, the day Lawrence died, had no entry. MacDonald must have been too upset to write. In fact there was nothing further until May 27, a week after Lawrence's death. She read the entry, then read it again while a pulse throbbed in her temples. *Weizmann came to No. 10 today. His people killed T.E.L. and Clarke-Kerr. Bullivant and Ashgrove too. Aim, divert suspicion to Nazis. W learned about T.E.L. meeting Grand Mufti and Clarke-Kerr with view Palestine independence. Couldn't take chance of stopping it second time.*

Chaim Weizmann. The leader of the world Zionist movement and future first president of Israel. Weizmann was almost single-handedly responsible for getting the British government to declare their support for a Jewish national home in Palestine through the 1917 Balfour Declaration. The Zionists had come close to total failure in 1930. Brilliant strategizing on Weizmann's part, combined with pressure, artfully applied, allowed him to pull off an amazing coup. Passfield's recommendations for granting independence to Palestine were quashed and he was virtually pilloried in the press for his "betrayal" of the Jews.

By 1935, Weizmann knew things would be different. European war was approaching and the British Empire was overextended. It was the height of the Great Depression. The British were spending vast amounts of treasure each year on maintaining troops in Palestine for no good reason that anyone was able to offer. Strategically, the place had no value at all. But if the British pulled out and granted independence to Palestine there would never be a Jewish state.

MacDonald and Lawrence had been too clever by half. They'd underestimated, fatally, how the Zionists would react when word of the supposed cover story reached them. Lawrence was murdered, his death made to look like an accident, with suspicion thrown on the Nazis if anyone looked harder. Clarke-Kerr had to die, too, although there was much less interest in the death of a diplomat. But Weizmann's plan did not end with the murders of Lawrence and Clarke-Kerr. He had to put MacDonald out of the picture, too. The next passage in the former PM's diary described how that was achieved. *W said I must resign. Give any reason I want. Or he will reveal my relationship with S. I agreed. Alternative inconceivable. Baldwin will be PM. Zionist sympathies.*

Weizmann had blackmailed a British prime minister into resigning! But how? Stunned, Imogen had called up the file on MacDonald. It didn't take long before she understood. MacDonald's wife had died years before, in 1911, of blood poisoning. He never remarried, but there was a woman in his life. Had been for many years. She was married, though. To someone very close to the throne. The file didn't say who she was. Neither did MacDonald, even in his private diary. He referred to her only as S. Somehow Weizmann found out about S. He threatened to reveal all if MacDonald did not resign. MacDonald believed him. He had no reason not to. The woman's reputation would have been ruined—they were different times, and people cared much more about that sort of thing. MacDonald also likely believed, given who S was—"very close to the throne"—irreparable damage might be done to the Crown.

Stanley Baldwin had followed MacDonald as prime minister. Baldwin was a Zionist sympathizer. Presumably Weizmann was convinced he could count on Baldwin to bury anything to do with Lawrence's work on independence for Palestine.

The Palestine Conference was real. What staggered her, despite everything she had seen in her time in the Security Service, was the enormity of the actions that had been taken to make sure that MacDonald's plan failed and that the treaty never saw the light of day. If he and Lawrence had succeeded, there would certainly have been an independent Palestine in 1935, or soon after. The whole history of the Middle East—of the world—would have been very different.

She put her head in her hands and closed her eyes, massaging her forehead. When she'd come—not to terms—but to some degree of acceptance with the horror she'd dredged up from the past, she focused on the present.

The Palestine treaty, signed by Ramsay MacDonald on behalf of the British government and Nigel Clarke-Kerr for the League of Nations. She'd searched the record, official and unofficial. No such treaty was known to exist. Had Ryder somehow uncovered it?

She gazed unseeing at the map of Great Britain on her wall. Ayesha Ryder was out there, somewhere, on the run. MI5 and the police were hunting her. So were others. Not one for prayer, she nevertheless sent up a silent one that her people would win the race.

RYDER

CHAPTER 38

Moses Litmann sat at the back of a nondescript café off Soho Square, trying to tune out the background blare of Bing Crosby crooning "White Christmas" for the umpteenth time. He'd waited until Judah Ben David departed for his meeting with the British prime minister before slipping out of the Israeli embassy. Everything he'd downloaded from Ben David's computer was saved to a memory stick now in an inside pocket of his overcoat. Every few minutes he touched it to be sure it was still there. When he wasn't checking for the memory stick, he was glancing at his watch. The Americano he'd ordered sat on the table in front of him, ignored and cold.

"Mr. Smith?"

He looked up from the newspaper he was pretending to read. The man who pulled out a chair opposite him was nothing like his idea of a British tabloid journalist. He'd expected someone scruffier. Disreputable looking, in a cheap raincoat. Milton Hoenig was anything but scruffy. Mid-forties with dark hair just going gray, he wore a Brioni suit that must have set him back at least £1,500.

He glanced down. Shoes by John Lobb. "Yes," Litmann acknow-ledged. Smith was the alias he'd chosen for the meeting. His tweed cap and dark glasses were an attempt to disguise his well-known features.

A waitress placed a cup of coffee in front of Hoenig. "Anything else?" she asked Litmann.

"Hmm?" For a moment he had no idea what she was talking about. "No. Thank you." He checked his Rolex as she left.

"So, Mr. Smith," Hoenig said. "You have something for me?"

Litmann studied the journalist. The man had been carefully vetted. Hoenig was good at his job. The best. He'd know the value of what he was about to give him. Would have no qualms about writing the story. His newspaper, the *Daily Herald*, would tell the world and be happy to do so. Litmann reached into his pocket. Placed the memory stick on the table, then slid it beneath his newspaper. "It's all on here," he said. "Everything you need to ver-ify what I'm about to tell you."

"Fine." Hoenig dumped sugar in his coffee. "Let's hear it."

Litmann glanced around. No one was near. He checked his watch once more, then leaned forward in his chair and spoke in a low voice. "Mr. Hoenig. As you are no doubt aware, my prime minister is shortly to meet with Sayyed Khalidi, the Palestinian leader."

Hoenig nodded.

"They've been planning something for some time now. They're going to make a joint announcement about it. Here in London. Tomorrow at the Tower."

"I've heard that. But nobody knows what it's about. Believe me, I've tried to find out."

"It's all in here," Litmann repeated, tapping the newspaper

that concealed the memory stick. Then he told the journalist what Judah Ben David and Sayyed Khalidi intended to do.

Hoenig, whose eyebrows shot up at Litmann's opening sentence, scribbled notes as he spoke—Litmann had forbidden Hoenig from recording. When the Israeli stopped, the journalist folded his notebook, put it away, then slid the newspaper toward him and palmed the memory stick. "You don't want money?"

"All I want is for you to publish that story. Attributed to an anonymous source."

"No problem." Hoenig pushed his chair back and stood. He turned to go, then paused. "You keep looking at your watch. Are you waiting for something?"

"Hmm? No. I've got a meeting, that's all."

Hoenig left.

Litmann, sweating heavily under his armpits, glanced at his watch. It was almost time. If everything went according to plan. Would it?

CHAPTER 39

Bodmin's town hall was an eighteenth-century stone and slate building listed by the National Trust. An icy wind stirred the snow that adhered to its roof and the pavement in front of it. Ayesha shivered as the wind sliced through her thin clothes, and adjusted the head scarf and dark glasses she'd purchased from a Boots in Paddington Station. They'd seen her image prominently displayed on the overhead monitors at Paddington as a person of interest to the police. The rudimentary disguise served its purpose—they'd boarded the train for Cornwall without attracting any attention. It wasn't till the train had pulled out of the station that she began to relax, however. It took another half hour before she managed to doze off.

Bodmin was a typical English country town. Sleepy, with narrow, winding streets, and buildings from the past three or four centuries, currently tastefully decorated—there were exceptions—for the seasonal festivities. A nice place to live, she decided. If you wanted a quiet life. She looked along the street that branched to the left, off the little plaza in front of the town hall. "There," she said, pointing.

She pushed her sunglasses into place and set off, leading the way. No one had looked at her with anything more than ordinary curiosity since they left London, but Holden was paranoid that she'd be spotted. He kept looking over his shoulder. No one would be interested in him or Bryan, of course. There'd been no announcement about the two detectives. Scotland Yard could hardly announce it had misplaced two of its own.

They'd no idea what to expect in Bodmin. All of them were skeptical of finding Lawrence's papers. If there was nothing, it was the end of the road. They'd have to contact the Yard again. So Holden said. Ayesha had her own ideas on that. And if there *was* something, what then? Who could they approach? Who could they trust?

The post office was housed in a Georgian building with a slate roof and white-framed windows, a red pillar box on the footpath in front. A bell tinkled as Ayesha pushed through the front door. She stepped inside and breathed in air that reeked of the past, redolent of paper and stamps and ink. A warm, dusty smell that spoke of reading Dickens or Conan Doyle beside a crackling fire and journeys to distant places. The paraphernalia of a modern post office were there, too. Displays of new stamps to tempt the philatelist. Card readers on the counter for payment with plastic. But the counter surfaces and the display cases were old wood, oiled by time. The clock on the wall bore the words *Bristol 1821*. It also said it was just short of noon.

One customer, a middle-aged man, accepted change from the cheerful-looking woman with gray hair pulled back in a bun who stood behind the counter. "Thank you, Ruth," he said as he left.

"Hello. How can I help you?" The gray-haired woman spoke with a distinctive Cornish drawl.

Holden drew out his wallet and showed the woman his credentials. Bryan did likewise. Not having any official identification, Ayesha stayed where she was.

"Good morning," Holden said. "Detective Inspector Holden, Scotland Yard. These are my associates."

"Goodness," the woman said. "I put in a report about vandals painting graffiti on the side wall, but I didn't expect Scotland Yard to investigate!"

Holden snorted a laugh. He opened his mouth to respond, but the woman waved him down. "Joke," she said. "What can I do for you, Inspector?"

The DI looked at Ayesha. She stepped forward to the counter. "Would you be related to Jack Trelawney?" she asked, smiling.

The woman's dark eyebrows slanted upward. "Jack Trelawney was my grandpa. I'm Ruth Trelawney. Postmistress. Until he died, Grandpa was the postmaster here. Like his father before him."

"Did he teach Winston Churchill to fly?" Holden asked.

"Fancy you knowing that!" Ruth Trelawney exclaimed. "I get historians and such asking about it now and again. But never the police."

"It's not actually what we've come about," Ayesha said. "We're searching for some lost documents."

"Yes," Holden said. "They may have been sent here. *Poste restante*. It's . . . um . . . possible they have a bearing on a case."

"I see." The postmistress nodded. "We do get the occasional letter or package *poste restante*. Not many these days, though. It's gone out of fashion. How long ago was this?"

"Nineteen thirty-five," Bryan said.

Ayesha stared at Ruth Trelawney, hardly daring to breathe. If she'd been superstitious she would have crossed her fingers.

RYDER

The postmistress showed no surprise. Instead she turned to a board on the wall behind the counter. Keys hung there on brass hooks. She selected one. "Nineteen thirty-five," she told them. "That'll be in the storeroom. It's this way," she added, lifting a flap in the counter and walking toward a door in the far wall. When her visitors made no move to follow her, she turned back. "Come on," she said. "I'm not as young as I used to be and I'm going to need some help."

Ayesha followed Ruth Trelawney down the narrow wooden staircase, the two detectives behind her. A single naked bulb lighted the way. At the bottom of the stairs the postmistress used her key to open a heavy oak door. She stepped through the doorway and clicked a switch on the wall. An ancient fluorescent light flickered to life.

The cellar was a smallish room that seemed even smaller because of the metal shelves with which it was lined, all of them filled to capacity and sagging under the weight of their contents: boxes, some covered in faded brown paper, tins, even a couple of trunks. And parcels, packages, and envelopes of all shapes and sizes. These last were heaped in containers—cardboard boxes, plastic laundry baskets, shoe boxes. Ayesha surveyed the shelves and her heart sank. Maybe there was some sort of order to the collection.

"Heaven knows what's here," Ruth Trelawney said. "Love letters, long-lost wills, manuscripts of great novels, overdue library books. We've never thrown anything away. If it was sent here *poste restante* and not collected, it's still here."

"Incredible," Holden said, running a hand through his hair.

"You say people don't use the service much anymore?" Ayesha asked.

"No, the post office doesn't advertise it, and I don't think young people have any idea *poste restante* exists. Most of them hardly even use the ordinary post these days." She laughed.

Ruth Trelawney used her foot to push a wooden stool toward the shelves in the far corner. "Inspector, would you mind?"

"Hmm? Oh, right. Of course."

"Up there." Ruth Trelawney pointed. "That large black tin box on the top shelf. If you could lift it down."

Holden stepped up onto the stool and lifted the box. He grunted and swayed slightly from the weight. "Sergeant," he said.

Bryan lifted his arms and accepted the box. He looked round, then, as Holden got down, placed the box on top of the stool.

"I'm sure it was in here." Ruth Trelawney lifted off the lid. "You said the addressee was a series of numbers?"

"That's right: 352087."

"I know I've seen that before. Mind you, we've got all sorts of names here. Letters addressed to Rumpelstiltskin and the Dalai Lama. Santa Claus, of course. And we have so many John Smiths you wouldn't believe."

Ruth Trelawney rummaged through the box for some moments, then, with an exclamation of triumph, she straightened up, holding a bulky parcel wrapped in brown paper and tied with dusty string.

Ayesha accepted the parcel with hands that trembled. Her heart beat faster and a bead of perspiration ran down her spine. Was it possible Lawrence's papers had been sitting here, waiting for collection for more than seventy-five years? She looked at the words written on the brown paper. *Poste Restante Bodmin, 352087.* Lawrence's handwriting.

"I'll take that," Bryan said.

Ayesha heard him speak, but his words failed to register. Her whole attention was on the parcel. Then something in his tone penetrated her consciousness. She looked up. The pistol he pointed at her was a Browning Hi-Power, a weapon with which she was very familiar.

"Sergeant!" Holden took a step forward, one hand outstretched as if to take the pistol. "What the fuck—"

Bryan's pistol barked once. Its roar was deafening in the confined space of the cellar. Holden made a sort of grunting sound, stared at his sergeant, tried to form a word. He looked down at the blood that spurted from the ugly wound in his chest. Then his hand dropped. He slumped to the floor like a puppet whose strings had been cut.

Bryan's pistol roared again. Ayesha staggered, sure she'd been shot. But it was Ruth Trelawney whom Bryan had aimed at. The postmistress lay facedown in the doorway, an ugly dark hole in the back of her skull.

Ayesha dragged her eyes away from the dead woman and looked at Bryan. The tall black man raised his pistol to her face. For the first time since she'd met him, he smiled.

CHAPTER 40

"Judah, it is good to see you again!"

Susannah Armstrong, prime minister of the United Kingdom of Great Britain and Northern Ireland, gripped Ben David's hand in a firm clasp, then, once they were safely out of view behind the doors of Number 10 Downing Street, she gave him a warm hug and kissed him on the cheek. They held the embrace for a few moments, then Armstrong pulled back. The tall, attractive brunette, a divorcee who had been Britain's prime minister for less than a year, glanced upward at the mistletoe that hung over their heads, then smiled into her visitor's eyes. "The Americans have been on the phone," she said. "They've been trying to wheedle an invitation for the secretary of state to join us. You've no idea how badly they want to know what you and Sayyed are up to."

"And *you* don't?" Ben David laughed, relaxing in Susannah's familiar company. It felt so good to be with her, to know that he could tell her anything. Almost anything.

"Of course I do. Don't think I'm not going to exercise all my womanly wiles to drag it out of you."

"Susannah."

Armstrong nodded in understanding. "Come on." She touched him on the arm, then led the way to the elegant wood-paneled Small Dining Room. Where Sayyed Khalidi stood waiting.

"Judah, my friend." The Palestinian came forward, hand outstretched in greeting. "I was so sorry to hear about your friend Sir Montagu."

"You knew Evelyn Montagu?" Susannah Armstrong asked as a dark-suited waiter entered carrying a silver tray laden with drinks. Another followed with hors d'oeuvres.

"We've been friends since university." Ben David shook his head. "I still can't believe he's dead. Murdered. Tortured, from what the police tell me."

"Judah, I'm so sorry." Susannah Armstrong sympathized. "I had the report this morning myself. The commissioner tells me the police suspect terrorists. They think there might be a link to your meeting here in London. MI5 are looking into it."

"I've had the same information." He frowned. "But I cannot believe that terrorists had anything to do with Evelyn's death. At least . . . not Palestinians anyway."

"What do you mean?" Armstrong asked. "It sounds like you have some ideas of your own, Judah."

Instead of replying, Ben David looked at the Palestinian leader.

Khalidi held his gaze. "I think, Judah, we should tell Susannah."

"Let's sit down." Their hostess gestured to the polished oak table. "We'll get some food and you can tell me about it."

Once plates of salad were placed in front of them, Ben David turned to Susannah Armstrong. "Did you know your government once agreed to give independence to Palestine?"

Britain's prime minister put down the fork she had just lifted to her lips. "That's a new one on me. When was this?"

"Nineteen thirty-five."

"MacDonald or Baldwin?"

"Ramsay MacDonald. The story is, he asked T. E. Lawrence to undertake secret negotiations with al-Husayni, the Grand Mufti of Jerusalem, under the auspices of the League of Nations."

"Lawrence of Arabia?" Susannah Armstrong stared at Ben David. "You're kidding! Hold on, didn't he die about then?"

"That's right," Sayyed Khalidi answered. "At about the same time he supposedly negotiated a treaty on behalf of the British government."

"Supposedly?" Susannah Armstrong frowned. "Judah, you said 'the story.' Is this true or not?"

"Until very recently it was just that—a story with no foundation. Evelyn had a real bug about it. Years ago he really went into it, but he couldn't find a shred of evidence that it happened."

"Well then?"

"Until very recently," he repeated. "Quite by chance Evelyn got hold of some letters written by Lawrence. He called me yesterday. He said he'd finally found proof the negotiations actually did take place. He was going to tell me all about it last night."

CHAPTER 41

Ayesha stared up at the ceiling. It was very old, very dirty, and very cracked. A light fixture dangled precariously. It was not turned on. The room was small. Much of the plaster had fallen from its walls, exposing the lath construction. It stank. Of mold, rotten wood, and stale urine. Dim light filtered through a window so caked with filth she could not see what lay beyond.

She shivered with cold and struggled for comprehension, as if she had woken abruptly from a deep sleep. What day was it? She concentrated. Tuesday. When she remembered that, everything else flooded back. Evelyn's murder. Lawrence. Lady Madrigal. Bodmin. Lawrence's parcel. Bryan. Bryan shooting Holden. The postmistress, too. Then what? He'd aimed his pistol at her. She'd been sure he was going to shoot. Braced herself for the impact. It didn't come, though. Instead he'd ordered her to walk back up the stairs.

No one was in the post office. Bryan kept his pistol on her and peered out of the window. He unlocked the door. A man waited outside, a heavyset man in a dark trench coat. He stood next to a red SUV. It idled in front of the post office, its near-side rear door open. Bryan gestured for her to get in. What happened then? A prick in her neck. She'd been drugged.

She struggled to sit up. She couldn't. Only then did she realize she was naked. Every article of clothing had been removed from her body, even the bandage from the gash on her thigh. She craned her neck. Nylon rope bound her arms and legs to the posts of the old wooden bed. Her nose wrinkled. The mattress on which she lay was the source of the urine stench.

Alert now, she strained her legs and arms, testing her bonds. Her legs were tightly secured. She pulled, hard. First with her left arm, then with her right. One of the posts, the one on her right side, creaked slightly. Summoning every ounce of strength she possessed, she pulled. The wood held firm. Footsteps sounded on the other side of the bedroom door. She froze. A key scraped in the lock.

Bryan rested his hands on the rail at the foot of the bed and looked down at her. He smiled, his teeth white in the shadows. His tongue flicked over his lips. What she saw in his eyes did not surprise her. She'd glimpsed it before. Only now Bryan didn't hide it. She wasn't afraid; she'd been raped before. The man who'd done it would never rape again. She returned Bryan's stare and let the hate consume her, raised her head, and spat in his face.

Bryan wiped the spittle away. His expression did not change. Then he stepped to the side and another man came into view.

Ayesha's brain was unable to grasp what her eyes beheld. It could not be the same man. It was, though. He'd hardly changed. The same chubby, oddly childlike face. Round, rimless glasses perched on a snub of a nose. Innocuous. You'd never give this man a second glance, never imagine the vicious sadism that lurked below his harmless visage.

RYDER

She had not known his name at the time. Long afterward, she learned it. *Nazir.* The man who had tortured her, raped her, scarred and disfigured her body. She had marked him, too. In a way no man could ever get over. And now, once again, she was at his mercy.

CHAPTER 42

Judah Ben David rose from his chair as the tall, striking-looking woman summoned by Susannah Armstrong was ushered into the Small Dining Room. Mid-fifties, he thought. The head of MI5 must be at least that to hold the position she did, although she looked younger. Dame Imogen Worsley smiled as Susannah Armstrong performed the introductions, but he could see the stress and weariness in her eyes. He knew the look. Dame Imogen was running on adrenaline and caffeine, and little else.

Briefly, Susannah Armstrong recapped what she knew, and what he and Khalidi had told her: of Evelyn Montagu's search for a lost treaty by which the British granted independence to Palestine. Finished, she looked from Ben David to Khalidi, then back to Dame Imogen. "Is there anything you can add?"

The head of MI5 turned to Ben David. "Mr. Prime Minister. You've heard about certain events that might have happened in 1935. A meeting supposedly convened by T. E. Lawrence." He nodded, and she turned her gaze on Khalidi. "Mr. President.

You know the supposed meeting was to negotiate a treaty giving independence to Palestine. You've assumed, of course, it would have been an independent *Arab* Palestine."

Khalidi nodded.

The head of MI5 spoke for ten minutes without interruption. What she told them was a revelation to her astonished listeners. She began by explaining why MacDonald would have asked Lawrence to handle secret negotiations over independence for Palestine. She recounted what she knew of the discussions between Lawrence, the Grand Mufti, and the League of Nations' Nigel Clarke-Kerr.

"Is there proof of this?" Ben David interrupted, unable to contain himself any longer.

"Of a sort," Dame Imogen replied. "What I'm telling you comes from Ramsay MacDonald's private diary. Lawrence drafted a treaty for the establishment of an independent Palestine. MacDonald signed on behalf of the British government, the Grand Mufti for the Palestinians, and Nigel Clarke-Kerr for the League. MacDonald intended to take the treaty to his cabinet. He was confident of getting it ratified."

"How is it that the contents of this diary have not been known before this?" Excitement threaded Khalidi's voice.

Dame Imogen shook her head. "It wasn't with MacDonald's papers in the National Archives. That's all I can tell you."

"I think we can guess why," Ben David put in. "I'd like to see this diary," he added.

"Hmm." Dame Imogen glanced at her prime minister. "There's more," she went on. "In his diary MacDonald outlines how an independent Palestine would have been constituted."

She sipped coffee, then told them what the former British prime minister had written. She barely spoke two sentences before Ben David slammed his cup down with a crash.

"*Eben ahbe!*" Khalidi jumped up and strode to the fireplace. "Can this be true?" he demanded, whirling to face the table. His eyes glittered.

"It's what Ramsay MacDonald wrote," Dame Imogen replied. "He'd have no reason to lie."

"This is incredible!" Ben David exclaimed. "Truly incredible. This treaty must be what Evelyn was looking for."

"I've found no record of such a treaty, but clearly it did exist." Dame Imogen answered impassively. "I do believe it's what Montagu was looking for."

"What happened? In 1935? To stop this going forward?"

"It was all suppressed. Lawrence was murdered. Clarke-Kerr, too." Susannah Armstrong gasped aloud at this statement. Dame Imogen glanced at her, then went on. "So were others. The whole thing was covered up and buried."

"Who?" Khalidi demanded tersely.

"I think I can guess—" Ben David started.

The Palestinian held up a hand. "Judah. Whatever happened in the past is past. We have so much terrible history, your people and mine. We are here in London to bury that evil for good. I will not allow any ancient horror to deter me from that purpose."

"Thank you, my friend." Ben David grasped Khalidi's arm. "Thank you for telling us this, Dame Imogen. Is there any hope this treaty can be found?"

"We don't know," she answered bluntly. "Some people clearly believe there's a possibility it still exists. They murdered Montagu and one of my men. Chances are they'll kill again."

"Who are *they*?" Susannah Armstrong demanded. She had gone very pale.

"*Shamir*," Ben David answered before Dame Imogen could respond.

"Yes." Dame Imogen said. "I believe it's likely."

"They're here? In England?"

"I'm afraid so. There's someone else looking for the treaty, though. It's possible—if she's still alive—she may get to it first." Briefly Dame Imogen explained about the involvement of Ayesha Ryder and the two detectives who were, presumably, still with her.

"Ryder was *Fedayeen*?" Ben David shot a worried glance at Khalidi.

"I know who she is." The Palestinian nodded. "I met her once. Many years ago. She had a reputation for causing your people a great deal of trouble." His lips twitched in a smile.

"Then she must be good. We have to hope so, at any rate. Where is this Ryder woman now?"

"I'm sorry, Mr. Prime Minister," Dame Imogen said. "At this point, we just don't know."

"Find her, Dame Imogen," Susannah Armstrong said urgently. "Find Ayesha Ryder. And *find* Lawrence's treaty."

When the head of MI5 left them, Ben David reached into his pocket. He brought out a small, flat box, finely crafted in cedarwood, and held it out to Khalidi. "Sayyed. This is for you. It is a token of my friendship. I would like you to have it before our meeting begins tomorrow. It is symbolic, I think, of the future hopes of our two peoples."

Sayyed Khalidi, a puzzled smile on his face, accepted the box and lifted the lid. Inside, nestled on top of a bed of cotton wool, was a large, old-fashioned key made of some metal. Brass. It was pitted with age. Khalidi stared at it for a long time. When he looked up, his eyes were filled with tears. "Judah, is this what I think it is?"

"Yes, my friend. It is the key to the door of your family's farmhouse outside Jaffa." Ben David reached inside his coat once more. "And here are the papers, signed by me, that officially return the house and all of your family's property to you. The day, God willing, that you use that key will be the happiest of my life."

CHAPTER 43

Police Constable Ahmed Ali-Yaya's nerves were stretched to the breaking point as he paced behind the black steel gates that barred access to Downing Street. For centuries it was possible for members of the public to walk right past the famous front door to Number 10, home to British prime ministers since 1733. An IRA terrorist attack in 1989 led to the closing of the street and the erection of the gates. Armed police were now a constant security feature. Today, because of heightened security over the visit of the Israeli and Palestinian leaders, the normal police presence was doubled.

Ahmed, who had been on special duty as a patrol leader at Downing Street for a month now, was troubled by the increased security. It was going to make it harder for him to get close to Israel's prime minister without one or more of his fellow officers seeing what he was doing. His timing had to be just right; he'd only get the one chance. Was it worth it? For the thousandth time he asked himself the question. For the thousandth time he gave the same answer. *Yes.* It was something he could do for his people. He slid a hand beneath his body armor, felt again for the package he'd removed from his briefcase. It was still there.

His personal radio crackled and he heard the familiar voice of the police liaison inside Number 10 calling him. "Go ahead," he replied. Ahmed's voice shook; he hoped it wouldn't be noticed over the staticky radio.

"The leaders will be heading out shortly," the liaison said. *"Go ahead and call up their cars."*

He acknowledged the order and adjusted the Heckler & Koch MP5 submachine gun slung from his shoulder. It was part of the armament that, along with a Glock 26 pistol, he was issued as a member of the Downing Street protection detail. His hands free, he pulled out his cellphone from one of several pouches on his belt and entered the number for Judah Ben David's chauffeur. He waited ten rapid heartbeats, then entered the number for the Palestinian president's driver. He instructed each man to bring their cars up to the gates, where they would be allowed through. For security reasons they were not permitted to wait in the narrow street outside Number 10.

"I heard they'll be out soon. Is that right?"

Ahmed swung around to find himself face-to-face with a young woman in a very short skirt. He frowned, started to ask what the hell she was doing there, then remembered she had clearance. Ben David's personal assistant. One part of his brain, the tiny part that was not totally preoccupied with what he was going to do, registered that the Israeli was a real looker. He realized she was waiting for a reply, impatiently tapping her clipboard. "Yes. I've just called up their cars."

The young woman did not reply. She swiveled on one high heel and click-clacked along the street in the direction of the door to Number 10. Waiting for her boss. Ahmed frowned. One of her jobs was probably to run interference for Ben David. Stop anyone getting close to him. The frown faded. Even a woman like her would give way to the authority of his uniform.

CHAPTER 44

"Remember me?" Nazir spoke in a low rasp. The voice of a heavy smoker.

It was the same voice that had haunted Ayesha's nightmares for twenty years. She stared up at him. Disbelieving at first, she accepted that he was really there, knew what she faced.

Nazir's eyes flicked over her naked body, lashed hand and foot to the bed, before returning to her face. Unlike Bryan, there was no lust in his gaze. Just intense, dark hatred.

She said nothing, waited for whatever she would have to endure.

Bryan entered the room. He carried a loosely wrapped package.

Nazir took it, lifted it up over the bed, and started dropping bits of something—paper—onto her body. "Know what this is?" Not waiting for a reply, he continued, "Newspapers. Old newspapers. From 1935."

She said nothing.

"They were in that parcel. The one you came here to Cornwall to find. The one sent by your oh-so-famous Lawrence of Arabia. The one Mr. Bryan here collected and brought to me. Along with you."

"Newspaper?" Her overwhelming need to know demanded she speak.

Nazir leaned over. He pinched a scrap of newspaper between his fingers. "The *Daily Mirror*. May 1935. Think it's a *clue?*"

She glared at him, her emotions in turmoil. Evelyn dead. Holden dead. Ruth Trelawney. *For nothing?*

"Bryan here tells me you're a great one for solving puzzles," Nazir continued. "So was your lover. Montagu. I would have got what I wanted from him, but Bryan was a bit . . . overenthusiastic. And I didn't know the old guy had a weak heart." He yanked on the cord that secured her left leg to the bedpost. She bit back a grimace. "You don't have a weak heart, do you, Dr. Ryder?"

She turned her head to look at Bryan. The hours they'd been together. If she'd known. She would have killed him. Without the slightest hesitation. The hate and fury welling up inside her were so strong that tears leaked from her eyes. She *would* kill him. Him and Nazir. Both of them. It didn't matter what they did to her. She would survive. And she would kill them.

Nazir smiled at her tears. She saw the sadistic gleam in his eyes and tensed. Slowly, deliberately, he reached into an inside pocket and drew out a gold cigarette case. He opened it. Extracted a cigarette and placed it between his lips, then he turned to Bryan. Who produced a lighter and clicked it into life. Nazir bent to the flame. When the end of the cigarette glowed red Nazir walked around to the side of the bed and bent over her. She smelled the familiar pungent odor of the burning tobacco—Gauloises—felt its heat.

Nazir's fingers touched her neck. She shuddered as he traced the outline of the scar he put there two decades before. His hand moved. He caressed her right breast, fingering the scars—his handi-work. Her skin crawled. He withdrew the cigarette from between his lips, blew smoke in her face, then spoke. "It's time we matched the set, don't you think?" Then he ground the burning end of the cigarette into the skin of her left breast.

RYDER

CHAPTER 45

As the Downing Street gates swung open, three of Ahmed's fellow police officers stepped forward and began to shepherd the crowd of tourists and onlookers to the sides, allowing the official cars room to enter.

The Israeli car was first through the gate, its headlights blazing against the dark of the short winter day. His heart hammering, Ahmed walked back along the street toward Number 10. His submachine gun was cradled in his hands, its cold metal slick with the sweat that seemed to ooze from his every pore.

He covered the short distance to the world's most famous front door, currently decorated in a beribboned wreath as befitted the season, and nodded to the constable on duty. He nodded, too, to the young Israeli woman in the short skirt. She waited off to the side next to the journalists and photographers, shivering as an icy wind found her bare legs. She ignored him. Ahmed's head jerked to the front door. Which had started to open.

A man in a dark suit stepped through the doorway. He wore an earpiece. He cast a searching look around the street. Satisfied, he spoke to someone behind him. The prime minister, Susannah Armstrong, emerged, smiling, followed by her two distinguished visitors.

Ahmed had seen the British leader on numerous occasions since being posted to the special Downing Street protection unit. He admired the policies her party stood for. Had even voted for it in the general election. But he did not like her. Something about the way she was always so elegantly poised. Confident. She seemed artificial. Then, too, there was the fact she was a divorcee. She had not remarried. There were rumors. Nothing definite. But you could tell she enjoyed the company of men. Like the two who stood next to her now. Israel's prime minister. Tall, handsome, commanding. The Israeli couldn't take his eyes off her. But neither could the slighter, dark-haired Palestinian. Ahmed felt betrayed by this. He'd expected more of Sayyed Khalidi. His lip curled. The man was a Palestinian, but he was, after all, just another politician.

The Israeli and Palestinian leaders posed for photographs on the front step of Number 10 with Susannah Armstrong. Questions flew from the assembled journalists, but the dignitaries politely refused them.

"Tomorrow, ladies and gentlemen," Ben David called. "Tomorrow at the Tower of London. We'll answer all of your questions then."

Khalidi waved and gave a thumbs-up. The two men shook hands a final time and Ahmed braced himself for what he was going to do.

The short-skirted Israeli woman stepped forward. She flicked a hand to her boss and nodded her head toward their car, a gleaming black Jaguar. It had nosed its way up Downing Street and had come to a stop a few feet away. Its chauffeur, a man with a jagged scar on his left cheek, emerged and stood ready to open the door.

Ahmed slipped his hand inside his jacket and gripped the package. As he drew it out, he glanced toward the Israeli car. He froze. Something was wrong. The chauffeur. The man with the scarred face. He was no longer standing by the Jaguar. Then Ahmed saw him. He was ten feet away, pushing frantically through the crowd of journalists and photographers, heading for the other end of Downing Street. Alarm bells went off in Ahmed's brain. "*Back!*" he screamed as he flung himself toward the national leaders in front of Number 10. Then the bomb exploded.

CHAPTER 46

Ayesha picked olives in her family's grove. The sun warmed her bare arms and neck while she worked. Her family were proud of their olives. Many said they were the best in the region.

Her bucket full, she climbed down the wooden ladder propped against the trunk of the tree she was harvesting. As she reached the ground she became aware of a rumbling noise from the roadway. She heard shouting. Peering through the branches she caught a flash of yellow. She dropped her bucket. Olives spilled over the ground, but she didn't see. She was running between the trees, following her sister Ghayda's small shape toward the road.

The yellow bulldozer had arrived without warning. There'd been no notice. It wasn't required. Not under the regulation the Israeli captain quoted while his heavily armed soldiers fanned out across the olive grove. The decision had been made. The farm was a threat. A place from which terrorists could operate. It was declared a closed military zone. There was no appeal.

Ayesha's parents and their workers tried to stand in the way of the bulldozer as it plowed into the first row of trees, its teeth biting into the ancient, gnarled trunks, scarring them so the raw wood showed bright through the bark. One worker was shot with a rubber bullet. Others were cuffed and dragged away. A soldier punched her mother in the stomach. When her husband rushed to protect her, he was knocked to the ground, punched and kicked in the head. Screaming and unable to restrain her tears, Ayesha kicked a soldier in the shins. He laughed and shoved her aside. A twelve-year-old girl was no threat to the Israeli army.

"What is your name?" The captain grabbed her arm, twisting it. "Who are your friends? Where do they live?"

She shook her head. The captain persisted. She frowned. *Not the captain.* The Voice. *Nazir.* "What is your name? Tell me what I want to know. If you do, the pain will stop."

She fought the pain. I am *Fedayeen*, she told herself. I will not talk. She opened her eyes. She was back in Gaza. In the tiny hovel her family had been forced into after the destruction of their farm. They had very little, and what they did have had to go a long way. Relatives helped. Her aunt sent money from England. Her father tried to find work. Her mother cried all of the time. Somehow, through it all, Ayesha found ways to continue her schooling. It gave her hope of something better. Then her sister was killed.

Collateral damage, the Israelis claimed. Ghayda was nearby, with a group of young friends, when they took out a known bomb maker, a killer of Israelis. Ghayda's death, the awful wounds suffered by three of her friends, were regrettable. There would be no compensation. But the action was a legitimate act of war against terror.

At Ghayda's funeral Ayesha met a man from the PFLP, the Popular Front for the Liberation of Palestine. The next week she started at a new school. One where she was taught new things. Things that would enable her to fight back.

Full dark. A moonless night. She clambered from the black rubber Zodiac boat. Laden with weapons, she struggled through the receding surf and onto the wet sand, her senses keenly alert for any sign they'd been spotted. Without warning her hair was grasped and her head was yanked back. She gasped aloud and opened her eyes. She was no longer on the beach. She was in the old fort outside Beersheba, bound, on a table in the underground room.

"What is your name?"

Nazir.

Steel pressed against her skin. A blade. Nazir held the point to her throat. She was going to die. Sixteen, and already she had been *Fedayeen* for two years—surviving longer than many of those who had trained with her. Now she had outlived her entire cell, all of them killed in the ambush. Now it was over for her, too. She was glad. She had lived to strike blows against the hated Israeli army and against colonists who stole Palestinian land. Avenged some, at least, of her comrades. Tears stung her eyes. Her parents. More than anything, she regretted the pain the news of her death would bring them. Leila, her mother, especially. She closed her eyes. Held her breath. The blade moved.

A searing pain pierced her neck. She felt the sting of the cut. The smell of blood, wet on her skin. A blow slammed into the side of her head, knocking her to the floor. Her hair was seized again. She was lifted bodily and flung facedown over the wooden table, which, apart from a pile of empty wine and beer bottles, was the only thing in the room.

One hand still gripping her hair, Nazir slammed her head against the tabletop. He forced her legs apart with his knees.

She refused to believe what was happening. She tried to

scream, but her cries were choked off as Nazir ground her face into the table. She bit through her lip, threw up, and nearly choked on her own vomit.

The pain and horror of the rape mixed with the pain from the burns on her breast until her whole body was an open, throbbing wound. Worse than the pain was the humiliation.

For two years she had trained and fought. Had become a finely tuned instrument of violence. She was used to control. To command. To the respect of her comrades. She gritted her teeth and drew on the hard core of steel inside her, the steel that was born with the murder of her sister. She had formed and shaped it. It had sustained her. Now it gave her the strength to put from her mind what was happening to her body and to fight back. She could not, would not, let this stand. She was *Fedayeen*.

Nazir grunted like a rutting pig. He finished and pulled out of her.

Her head released from his grip, she turned her face to the side.

Nazir murmured something indistinct close to her ear. It sounded like an endearment. He touched her cheek, caressing it almost, a gesture that sent a shudder of disgust surging through her veins. She heard him move away, intending, probably, to clean himself off and zip up his pants. It was a mistake. Naked, defenseless, tortured—that his victim had any kind of fight left in her was the last thing Nazir expected. It was then the young Palestinian woman rolled off the table, swept up a bottle, smashed it against the stone floor, and rammed it upward into his scrotum. While he shrieked and doubled over in purest agony, she twisted and ground the jagged edges of the bottle through skin and gristle.

~

A bucket of icy water was emptied over her naked body. The shock pushed back the darkness and she emerged into the light, blinking and shaking her head, knowing she'd been dreaming. Her mind had gone back to that other time. When she was sixteen. The ambush. When she was captured and tortured. By this same man. The Voice. Nazir.

"What do you know?" Nazir demanded. "Where is the treaty? Tell me, and the pain will stop."

She was dizzy. Part of her was still in the past. Her eyes hurt, too, with the light. Bryan stood there, holding a Coleman gas lamp and watching her intently, an expression of greedy anticipation on his face. Behind him she could see the window. The glass was black. Night had fallen. She twisted her head back to her tormentor, her body tensing as Nazir bent over her again, a glowing cigarette in one hand. His eyes bored into her from behind his rimless glasses, and his mouth was smiling. She felt the heat of the cigarette, then the searing, burning agony as it pressed into her skin.

Four times now Nazir had ground a lighted cigarette into the skin of her left breast, holding it there until she could smell her own burning flesh. Three of those times she had passed out. Each time Bryan had brought her round by dousing her with icy water. Every time Nazir burned her she screamed. It helped to counter the pain. That was the only sound she made. She'd said nothing. Given no answers. She felt the darkness closing in once more. But this time she remembered who she was. *Fedayeen.* Cold heat burned in her heart. *Evelyn.* She pictured his broken body and mangled flesh. Hatred and rage surged through her body, giving her strength.

"Anything to say?" Nazir asked, peering into her face. He sighed. "I'd be sorry if you did talk. Not yet, anyway." He drew out his cigarette case, opened it, and extracted a fresh Gauloises. "I'm making such good progress here."

"Fuck you," she croaked. Then she smiled up at her tormentor. "Oh, sorry. I forgot. You can't fuck anymore. Can you?"

Nazir moved with the speed of light. Before she could draw breath he was on top of her, straddling her, his hands around her throat, squeezing with an animal-like strength.

She did not struggle. There was no point. Her chest and lungs were being crushed under his weight and she couldn't breathe. She stared into the eyes of the man who was killing her, determined to defy him to the last. He returned her stare, his eyes blazing, his lips flecked with foam. Then, with a roar of fury, he let go and rolled off her. Air flooded into her lungs and she gasped aloud with the sweet pain of it.

"Too easy," Nazir said, calm once more. "I've waited too long to kill you so quickly. Besides, my friend here"—he glanced at Bryan—"hasn't had any fun yet. And I promised him some fun. Didn't I?"

Bryan grunted his assent.

Nazir took Bryan's lighter and ignited a fresh cigarette. He drew on it until the tip glowed red. "Where is the treaty?" he asked calmly.

"Fuck you!" Her throat was raw with pain and it was an effort to get the words out but she snarled them gladly. As the lighted cigarette touched the skin of her breast in a new place, the pain sliced into her, and once more the darkness descended. This time, her mind a kaleidoscope of images from the past and present, she clung on to consciousness long enough to realize that she did indeed know the whereabouts of Lawrence's treaty.

CHAPTER 47

Sayyed Khalidi woke to total silence. He raised his head. Winced. Put up a hand and touched his forehead. He drew it back, saw the blood on his fingers. He turned his head slightly and a high-pitched ringing started in his ears, echoing in his skull. He closed his eyes. Reopened them, looked at the bottoms of a woman's stocking feet. They were splayed in the open doorway in front of him. The feet moved. The owner of the feet crawled toward him. Her long dark hair was snarled and matted. Blood ran from a gash on her forehead and others on her legs and arms. Her clothes were spattered with gore. Her eyebrows were singed and she was almost unrecognizable.

"Susannah!" he gasped, just as his hearing returned, stunning him with an avalanche of sound. Screams. Moans. Shouts. Sobs. A cacophony over which could be heard the rising wail of sirens.

The British prime minister stared at him through eyes wide with shock. "Wh-where's Judah?"

Khalidi twisted around to look behind him. His brain refused to register what his eyes were seeing. Downing Street was like

Beirut at the height of the civil war. The Israeli limousine was a blazing, shattered wreck. Bits of it were strewn everywhere, tangled with wreckage from his own vehicle, which had been parked behind it. Shards of broken glass carpeted the roadway, sparkling like new-fallen hailstones. Bodies lay contorted amid the glass and wreckage. A woman's open-toed shoe lay nearby. Manolo Blahnik. Expensive. The owner's foot, toenails beautifully manicured and painted, neatly severed above the ankle, was still inside it.

He tore his eyes from the small pool of blood that surrounded the shoe. There was more blood. So much blood. It looked as if someone had used a giant machine to spray it over the road and the adjacent buildings. . . . He could smell it, taste it in his mouth. Its harsh iron tang mingled with the acrid odor of human organs and excrement, spilled violently from their fragile casings. Sayyed Khalidi was familiar with such odors. The last time he'd smelled them was in Gaza. When he'd visited an apartment building that had received a direct hit from an Israeli missile. This was no missile. One look at the remains of the Jaguar and he knew it was a car bomb. He'd seen the results of enough of them. How it had got past Israeli and British security was beyond his understanding.

The sirens wailed louder, closer. He concentrated. Struggled to focus. Then he saw Ben David. Israel's prime minister lay face-down to the left of the open doorway to Number 10. The back of his suit coat was on fire. Sayyed forced himself to his knees, grunting as a fierce pain lanced through his left ankle. He ignored it, scrabbled forward in a crablike motion, and threw himself across his friend. Heat seared his face and neck, then his body smothered the flames. He lay still, his head sunk against the Israeli's shoulder. He felt movement beneath him. "*Alham dulillah,*" Sayyed murmured. As gently as possible he eased himself off Ben David and lurched to his feet. Again the pain in his ankle. Remembering the blood on his head, he put his hand up, probed gingerly. There was a long gash across his forehead. He'd had worse wounds.

Police and emergency service workers were streaming through the Downing Street gates. Others were scrambling to reestablish a security perimeter. No way yet to tell how many had died in the carnage wrought by the car bomb, and how many were injured. Two bodies lay on the ground by the door to Number 10. Hardened as he was to death, the sight of the nearest caused him to blanch. A young woman—Judah's assistant. Rachel Singer. A piece of metal from the exploding car had sliced her body in half at the waist. The other body was that of a policeman, recognizable as such by his uniform, although this was shredded and burned, soaked with blood. Sayyed remembered. The man had flung himself forward at the last second, shielding the little group in front of the door from the full brunt of the explosion. Something was gripped in the man's right hand. A clutch of papers. Sayyed bent down and gently freed them. The papers were torn and charred, but he could make out the words. It was a petition. Addressed to Ben David. On behalf of Palestinians living in exile in Britain. Sayyed Khalidi let the papers drop. The ash-laden wind picked them up and scattered them.

CHAPTER 48

The knowledge Ayesha had won from the darkness slipped away. Just in time, she caught a thread and yanked it back. She had the answer. Holden. Ruth Trelawney. Evelyn. Their deaths had not been for nothing. Lawrence had laid a false trail, but she knew where his treaty really was.

She stared up at Nazir. He lit another cigarette and every muscle in her body froze. Nazir inhaled, then grimaced as the insistent buzz of a phone sounded from his jacket pocket. He dropped the cigarette and reached for his phone.

"Yes?" he said, his eyes on her face.

She made out the sound of an agitated voice, speaking urgently.

Nazir scowled. He turned away and walked to the window. "Calm down," he said. "The bomb went off? . . . Hmm. When? . . . You're sure? . . . He was injured, though? How bad? . . . Right. Listen. We have a backup plan, Sagheer. . . . Yes . . . Tomorrow." He swung round, his eyes on her once more. "Stay calm. Be outraged. Give interviews. You know what to do . . . Fine. If I leave now I'll be back in London in an hour or so. . . . Yes, I have her. . . . No. No treaty. Not yet . . . Do not worry. If she knows where it is, I will know. Soon."

Nazir ended the call. He stood without moving, staring at her. "I have to return to London," he told Bryan. "You stay here. I'll be back tomorrow. Possibly not till late. Do whatever you want with her. But don't kill her. I want that pleasure myself."

Bryan nodded, his eyes glittering with anticipation. "Come with me." Nazir walked toward the doorway.

The two men left the room. She heard the key turn in the lock, then receding footsteps. She pulled and twisted at the ropes that held her, groaning as her muscles bunched and flexed, igniting her burned skin and damaged nerve endings. An engine started up somewhere and she heard the distinctive whine of rotor blades. She gritted her teeth and fought the bedposts, channeling her pain into anger, using the anger to fuel her strength.

She concentrated on the post that secured her right arm. She strained, almost blacking out with the pain from the burns. The thin nylon ropes bit into her wrists. A keening sound burst from her throat as she bucked and heaved. Still she pulled and the pain became something else, something that was near to pleasure. The post snapped in two and she fell back.

She wanted to lie on the stinking water-sodden mattress and relish the sweet relief that washed over her. *No time*, she told herself. *Move*. She lifted her right arm, now free, worked off the rope that secured her left arm to the other post, and hauled herself upright. It took several attempts before she managed to untie the other ends from her wrists. Her limbs shook and her fingers were numb. The flesh of her lower arms was slick with blood from the deep cuts made by the ropes.

RYDER

When her arms were free she turned to the ropes that bound her legs. Not being slick with her own blood, these were easier. She swung her legs off the bed, took a ragged breath, then stood. The room whirled. Her legs turned to jelly and she fell to the floor. Darkness swallowed her again. Then a loud thumping roar penetrated her consciousness. *Helicopter.* She kept her eyes closed and forced herself to lie still.

When she opened her eyes once more she felt better. Not a lot. Her limbs still shook. But she knew what she must do. And there were her clothes and boots in a heap at the foot of the bed. She reached up, grasped the mattress, and hauled herself upright, a single loud moan escaping her lips as fresh pain exploded through her body. She clung desperately to the bed. Darkness threatened, but she closed her eyes and allowed it to roll over her. When she opened them again, the battle was won.

Move. She let go of the bed, found she could stand without falling. She looked at her clothes. No time to put them on. She picked up her jacket, wrapped it around her right arm, crossed to the window, and swung it hard against the glass. Broken glass cascaded onto the floor. She knocked out the remaining shards from the frame and peered through the opening.

Night. How many hours had she lain on the filthy bed while Nazir tortured her? And where was she? The ruins of a kitchen garden were visible in the moonlight. A child's swing set, rusted and broken, sagged against a high brick wall. Windblown trees and shrubs formed a border on the far side of the garden.

The fresh cold air cleared her brain. Whatever happened now, she knew she would not pass out.

The sound of the helicopter was very loud. She scooped up the rest of her clothes and her boots, returned to the window, swung over the sill, and dropped to the ground, cursing softly as the numbness in her legs wore off and circulation returned. She pushed across the remains of the garden into a clump of bushes next to a sagging shed. She dressed quickly, not bothering with bra or panties, swallowing a low moan at the sharp arrows of pain that lanced through her at every movement. Whatever she did caused the hurt to blossom anew. Worst was pulling on her boots. First she had to stop and pry a shard of window glass from the sole of her right foot. She hadn't felt it, but the wound had bled profusely. She managed to get both boots on. Then, as the helicopter pounded into the sky on the other side of the building, she left the cover of the shadows and ran into the night.

CHAPTER 49

Ayesha looked across the desolate landscape, her breath frosting in the frigid air. The moon, waxing gibbous, provided more than enough light for her to see that she was alone in an area of rough hills, sprinkled with dark patches—tors, massive slabs of granite that rose up from the earth, heaped on top of each other, as if scattered carelessly there by some ancient giant race. Stunted trees and shrubs. Little cover. And no lights. Not from passing cars. Not from houses. She looked behind her. Except for the derelict farmhouse from which she had escaped. Light glowed from two of its windows.

She looked up at the only light in the sky, other than the moon. It came from the helicopter now swiftly disappearing—toward London presumably. So that was the way she ran. She was cold. Her body was a whirlwind of pain. Pain she could cope with. She was free. She'd find a road. Flag down a passing motorist. Again she glanced back. Just as a light detached itself from the farmhouse. A flashlight. It moved and dipped in her direction. She scowled, then cursed herself for a fool. She was running along the top of a ridgeline, fully silhouetted in the moonlight.

Furious with herself for making such a basic error, she dived down the rough slope in front of her, careful where she put her feet—a twisted ankle or fracture would be fatal. She headed toward the dark mass of a granite tor that loomed up a hundred yards away at the bottom of the slope. It would provide cover. And hopefully it would allow her to head off in a different direction without being spotted by Bryan.

She reached the tor and leaned against one of the great slabs, winded, one hand cupped to her damaged breast. She looked back, saw the light bobbing along the crest line behind her. She worked her way around the tor, one hand on the weathered stone. The ground dropped away steeply on the far side. A narrow gully offered the best way down, its rocky, moss-covered sides providing concealment as well as plenty of places for her to put her feet. It was slippery going, though—there was a trickle of water from somewhere, and a tiny stream ran at the bottom of the gully. It was also in deep shadow and she had to use great care if she was not to miss her footing. Twice she slipped, saving herself from nasty falls by gashing both of her hands and her shins on the rocks. It was all she could do not to cry out with the pain. She refrained, knowing the sound would carry on the still night air.

At one point, after she'd been working her way down for what seemed an eternity, she stopped at a gap where water was running freely. She heard a noise. An owl. Then something else. She froze. Listened. Nothing. Then it came again. Small rocks or pebbles falling somewhere above and behind her. She moved on as rapidly as she could and reached the bottom of the gully, her boots, pants, and jacket wet and streaked with mud. She was going on pure adrenaline, but the cold was seeping into her bones. Her bleeding palms throbbed. She had to find shelter. She scrambled out of the gully, mounted a rough track that angled past another tor, and breathed a sigh of relief. A familiar shape loomed ahead of her: the solid stone walls, sloping leaded roof, and bell tower of an English country church.

A low wall surrounded the church. As she climbed over it, a chunk of stone broke away from the wall beneath her and she fell, landing on her hands and knees on soft earth. She rose to her feet in a graveyard. Ancient, lichen-covered tombstones leaned at crazy angles. She ducked around the nearest, a tall monument to some local notable, found a gravel path, and broke into a jog. She ran past the silent church, moonlight glimmering off stained-glass windows, and through the yew gate on the far side. The gravel path turned to hard-beaten earth and kept on across a broad sward of rough grass before disappearing into a thicket of spindly hawthorn trees.

One arm held in front of her face to ward off the low branches, she worked her way through the thicket. Emerging from the trees, she climbed an upward-sloping shelf of granite. At the crest she caught her breath at the sight of a little cluster of lights nestled in the valley below. She took a step forward, intending to climb down, then froze, startled by a shout from somewhere behind her. She listened. It came again.

"Help! Help me!" The cry ended in a choking sob.

She turned, made her way quickly back through the thicket, and stopped at the tree line.

"Help!"

She glided across the sward in the direction from which the cry had come, the opposite side of the church from the graveyard through which she had passed. She came to a wire fence. A large metal sign was attached to it. She read the words and understood. There didn't appear to be a gate. She climbed the fence and stepped carefully forward. She came to a dip, a sort of dell. The grass there seemed much thicker, higher and tufted. She moved slowly into the dell, testing each sod before she put her feet down firmly. She stopped.

Detective Sergeant Kaleb Bryan was sunk up to his armpits in the bog. "Help me," he pleaded, waving his arms at her.

She said nothing. Bryan had tortured Evelyn. Murdered James Holden. Ruth Trelawney, too. He'd watched and savored her agony while Nazir tortured her. Had intended to rape her. No doubt a psychiatrist could provide excuses, rationalizations—the horror Bryan endured as a child in Ethiopia. That horror, she realized, had been his undoing. His fear of the bones of the dead, of graveyards, had caused him to circle around the churchyard rather than take the direct route through the tombstones.

"I'll help you," she said.

"Thank you," Bryan croaked. His eyes, huge in the moonlight, seemed to start from his head.

She whirled and raced back to the thicket. Grabbing one of the spindly hawthorn trees that looked deader than the rest, she wrestled with it until it came out by the roots. Then she broke off branches to expose the main trunk. The activity ignited a fresh burst of pain, which she ignored. She ran back to the bog, dragging the tree trunk behind her.

Bryan had sunk lower in the short time she'd been gone. "Hurry. Please." He jerked out the plea, panic-stricken.

She lowered the tree and pushed it forward over the surface of the bog. Bryan tried to reach for it, but she kept thrusting, pushing it into his chest. "Stop," he begged. "Let me grab hold of it."

Ayesha did not stop. She kept on pushing. Forcing the tree into Bryan's face and chest. Pushing him down into the bog. The black man struggled, whimpering with fear. He tried to move away, but he was stuck and his struggles only made things worse. She leaned on the tree and pushed hard. Kept pushing Bryan down into the muck until his face, with its shocked, disbelieving eyes, disappeared. A mud-spattered hand fluttered feebly, then it slid from view. She pulled the tree back and let it drop. Her gaze swept across the surface of the bog. It looked solid, undisturbed. Calmly, she turned away and began to trot across the moor, to the lights in the valley below.

CHAPTER 50

Everything hit the fan after the explosion in Downing Street. None of the government leaders was seriously hurt. But many others were. Four police officers were dead. Judah Ben David's personal assistant. Three journalists, and one photographer. Others had injuries, some life-threatening. Politicians of all political persuasions were screaming for heads to roll. Naturally. So were the media, who'd already labeled it the Christmas Bombing. They were howling for blood, calling for investigations. Dame Imogen Worsley sighed. Heaven knew how many of those she'd eventually have to answer to. She sat up straight in her chair at the long table in the home secretary's conference room and focused on what the commissioner of the Metropolitan Police was saying.

"This is the bomber," the chief said. A photograph appeared on the screen behind him. A man in his thirties with a long scar down his cheek. "Jacob Steiner. Employed by the Israeli embassy as the ambassador's personal chauffeur." The chief paused while shocked murmurs ran around the table. "Former Israeli special forces. Outstanding record. Decorated for bravery. Steiner was seen running from Downing Street just after the bomb exploded. CCTV cameras had him in St. James's Park, then getting into a cab. Then he disappeared. His apartment's been emptied of personal belongings. Bank account cleared out."

Dame Imogen already knew this. She only half listened while the chief detailed the steps being taken to find Steiner. Surveillance of known associates. Watches on airports, seaports, the Eurostar. She thought about the conversation she'd had with Steve Watts, her head of IT, before leaving for this meeting. He'd tapped on her door while she was pulling on her overcoat.

"I asked you to find out if we've been hacked," she said. That had been what, days ago? No, hours, surely.

"Yes, Director. I've done a thorough check and everything seems to be in order. I've found no trace of a breach." Watts hesitated.

"Yes? What is it?"

"You also asked me to check all communications traffic to and from Bill Jameson and Peta Harrison."

Bill Jameson. It seemed a week since he'd been shot dead in front of St. Paul's. How long was it? A day? "What have you found?"

"Jameson seems to have made and received several calls from a number I haven't been able to identify."

A knot formed in her stomach. She couldn't believe Jameson had been a mole. A traitor. He was dead, though. If it was him, the problem was removed. Except for the witch hunt that would start once she made her report. Watts was waiting to say something else. "What is it, Steve?"

"I checked further. It wasn't Jameson."

"Tell me." She felt suddenly old.

"It only seemed as if the calls were made through Jameson's

phone. Someone used a very clever workaround to route calls to and from their phone through Jameson's network."

"Who?"

"Peta Harrison."

"Could it be another workaround?" She kept her face impassive. "To make it appear as if it's Harrison?"

"It could be," Watts replied, the doubt plain in his voice. "That's why I'm going to keep on it. It will take a while before I know for sure, though. I just wanted to keep you informed."

"Dame Imogen?"

She started out of her reverie, stared at the home secretary.

"Ideas?" Sir Norman Eldritch asked her. "As to who Steiner was working for?"

She looked around the room at the assembled security chiefs and heads of department. They looked back at her. Waiting. "Jacob Steiner," she answered. "Code name Esh—meaning 'fire' in Hebrew. He worked for *Shamir*." A collective sigh, like wind through the trees.

"Proof?" Eldritch pressed.

"Not yet. But it's the most likely explanation. Given the target, Judah Ben David's friendship with the Palestinian leader and his known liberal policies. And Steiner's known activities."

The meeting continued for another half hour of inconclusive speculation. When it broke up, Eldritch drew her into his private office. Poured them both scotch. "Sit down, Immy," he instructed. "Before you fall down."

Immy. How long had it been since he'd called her that? She sat in one of his leather armchairs and contemplated her dearest friend. He was still trim, despite the exigencies of his high office that called for a great deal of wining and dining. He ran every morning and was a daily habitué of the House of Commons gym. His hair was gray but otherwise he had altered remarkably little since she first knew him at Oxford. He loved her. Had since the beginning. As she loved him. But Norman never spoke, and Martin did. A feeling had been growing inside her over the past weeks, though, that he was going to speak this time. Not now. But soon. In any case, she'd made up her mind. If he didn't, she would. Life was too short to spend it alone. "Thank you, Norman," she told him. "I needed this."

They both drank. Sat without speaking, comfortably, as only close friends can. Eldritch broke the silence. "What about the other business? Any progress?"

"We've lost track of Ryder." She forced herself to think. "She was last seen early this morning at Paddington Station. CCTV cameras caught her and the two Scotland Yard detectives. No record of ticket purchases, though. They haven't shown up anywhere yet." Then she remembered. She rose abruptly and nearly spilled her drink. "Please forgive me, Norman, but there's someone I need to see."

Six minutes later she was sitting in the back of her official car. "Upper Brook Street," she said to her driver. As her car pulled away from the Home Office, she leaned back against the cushions thinking about the woman she was going to visit. The woman who once worked with Lawrence of Arabia. Who had been dropped behind enemy lines by SOE. Who had been tortured by the Gestapo, and who'd been held captive in Ravensbrück concentration camp. What did Lady Madrigal Carey know?

CHAPTER 51

"Kremlyovskaya?" Dame Imogen asked.

"You know your vodka." Lady Madrigal Carey, seated on the opposite side of the fireplace, nodded approvingly.

Silence followed this exchange. The only sound was the crackle of the flames. Imogen was wondering where to begin, when Lady Madrigal spoke again. "She was here. Early this morning."

"I'm sorry. Who was here?"

Lady Madrigal took a long sip of her own martini. "You've read my file."

The head of MI5 nodded.

"You realize I could have had your job? If times had been different?"

Another nod.

"Then you know I'm not stupid. Neither am I senile."

"I . . ."

"You've had a watch on my apartment. Since early this morning. They got here just a moment too late to see Ayesha Ryder and those two Scotland Yard men leave."

"How did you know?" For one of the very few times in her career Dame Imogen felt out of her depth.

"They're not very good. Also, Tatiana, as well as knowing where to find good vodka, was trained by the KGB."

A flush rose to Dame Imogen's cheeks. She raised her glass to her lips to hide it. She'd read Lady Madrigal's file. Knew she was regarded as the most brilliant recruit of her generation. One of the best field operatives they'd ever had. During the war she'd performed amazing feats of heroism. Survived the Gestapo.

Despite everything she'd read about Lady Madrigal, she had fallen into the error of thinking her great age made her somehow . . . less. It was not a mistake she'd make twice. "I'm sorry," she said. "Will you tell me where they are?"

Lady Madrigal considered her visitor. "I know what they're looking for," she said, ignoring the question. "Do you?"

"Proof Lawrence of Arabia secretly negotiated a treaty on behalf of the government granting independence to Palestine."

"Thank you." Lady Madrigal inclined her head. She turned to her companion. "Tatiana," she said. "Would you fetch the envelope from the top of the piano, please? Give it to Dame Imogen."

Imogen accepted the envelope Tatiana held out to her, saw it had been opened, and looked at the writing on the front. "'Palestine Conference,'" she read aloud. "'Keep for Winston. In case.'"

"Open it," Lady Madrigal commanded. There was a trace of impatience in her voice.

Dame Imogen tilted the envelope. She took the little collection of photographs that slid into her hand and studied them. One by one. She looked at them again. Then she put them back in the envelope. "You know," she said, her eyes on Lady Madrigal's.

"I know."

"Then you know how . . . concerned we are."

"I can imagine. You needn't be."

"Can you tell me why?"

"Because all of the evidence was destroyed. Years ago. By me."

"How can I be sure?"

"What are you going to do? Waterboard me?"

Dame Imogen laughed aloud. "We don't do that."

"You have friends who do."

"Nevertheless."

The two women eyed each other in silence. Lady Madrigal broke it. "Ned—Lawrence—had all of the evidence about what the Prince of Wales was up to. He hid it. After his death I found it. I destroyed it."

Imogen stared into the older woman's gray eyes. "I believe you," she said. "So what happened?"

"Hmm?"

"Lawrence was killed. You destroyed the evidence. But Edward abdicated the throne. Nothing ever came of the plot."

"I never said I didn't do anything with the evidence first." There was a distinct twinkle in Lady Madrigal's eyes.

Imogen nearly choked. "You blackmailed the king?"

Lady Madrigal's answering smile told her everything she needed to know. "What about the other business?" Imogen asked, when she could speak. "The cover story that was more than a cover story? Independence for Palestine."

"There you have me, I'm afraid." Lady Madrigal's expression turned grave. "Until Miss Ryder burst in on me this morning I'd never thought anything of it. The photograph of Ned with Nigel Clarke-Kerr and the Grand Mufti always puzzled me. But I assumed the dear man was just up to his old tricks. Ned loved to throw sand in the eyes of whoever was after him."

"You had second thoughts, though."

"Yes. Miss Ryder—wonderful girl. You or Six ought to recruit her. She convinced me there was something in the Palestine business. She even came up with an interpretation of one of Ned's clues that never occurred to me. It's just possible it may lead her to the proof she's looking for."

"A clue?"

"Yes."

"May I know what it was?"

Lady Madrigal said nothing for so long that Dame Imogen became uncomfortable. Then: "What will you do if Miss Ryder finds something? Proof. The treaty. Whatever Ned had."

Imogen did not reply immediately. Mainly because she did not know the answer. Then she shrugged. "I really don't know," she confessed. "I would think it'd be up to the prime minister."

"If it were any other prime minister than our present one, except for Winnie of course, I'd tell you to take a hike. That girl's got spunk, though. I like her." Lady Madrigal moved the slice of lemon in her martini with her fingertip, then looked up. "They went to Cornwall. Bodmin."

When Imogen got up to leave, begging off another drink, Lady Madrigal rose from her chair. Easily, despite her age. "You know there are others after her, don't you? Besides your people."

"Yes."

"Find her before they do." Lady Madrigal's eyes burned into hers. "She's a good one. Find her and keep her safe."

CHAPTER 52

The spotlit sign drew Ayesha like a beacon. She picked her way down the hillside away from the thicket, the church-yard, and the bog that was now Bryan's grave. As she drew closer she made out the details. In the foreground a pirate. Sinister, eye-patched and with a colorful bird perched on one shoulder. In the background, a sailing ship foundered on rocks beneath a full moon. Two words were emblazoned below the archaic image: JAMAICA INN. She knew something of its infamous history. Once the headquarters of pirates, wreckers, and smugglers. The inn was also reputedly one of the most haunted places in England.

She walked toward the cluster of buildings, aged, stone built, slate roofed. Light showed through the glass panes in a black-painted door. She pushed through it into the tiny entry foyer and stepped inside.

Flickering light. A dying fire. Old, heavy wood. Shiny copper kettles hanging from the beamed ceiling. Christmas tinsel and lights. Rows of gleaming glasses and bottles behind the bar. Smell of strong ale and roast beef. She almost wept with relief. The room swam before her eyes. She staggered, saved herself from falling by grabbing the edge of a table. Almost pulled it over.

"Bob! Call 9-9-9!" A woman's voice. Urgent. Footsteps running toward her.

"No!" Ayesha forced away the darkness. A man and a woman. Fiftyish. Anxious, concerned expressions on their kindly faces. The man had both arms raised, ready to catch her if she fell. "I'm fine," she told them. "Really. I just need to sit down."

"You're sure?" The woman had a light Welsh accent. She bit her lip, worried, obviously still inclined to call for help. "You look as if you need an ambulance."

Carefully, Ayesha let go of the table and straightened. She didn't fall, but she could not hide a wince of pain.

"Come on, dear," the woman urged. "Let's get you sat down." She and the man both helped her into a square-backed wooden chair in front of the fireplace. The man hurried behind the bar and returned carrying a bottle of brandy. He splashed some of the liquor into a glass and handed it to her.

"Here," he said. "Get some of this inside you."

"Can you tell us what happened, dear?" the woman asked. "You look as if you've been in an accident."

Ayesha used both hands to raise the glass to her lips. She drained the brandy and immediately felt the delicious warmth start to work its magic. The fire helped, too. She glanced at a long case clock that stood in a corner. Just after one o'clock. The man and the woman must be the inn's owners. Probably cleaning up before retiring for the night. "I was in an accident," she lied. "A cow was on the road. I tried to miss it. Skidded into a ditch. Car wouldn't start, so I tried to find help. Then I got lost on the moor." She grimaced. "I fell down a few times."

"You poor thing!" the woman exclaimed. "In this weather, too! You might have caught your death of cold." She exchanged a look with the man. "You need to get out of those wet things. Have a hot bath. We've plenty of rooms free at the moment. You can spend the night and in the morning Bob will help you find your car and get things sorted."

"Hot water and a good night's sleep will do wonders for you." Bob added. "I'll give the AA a ring first thing. Would you like something to eat? The kitchen's closed but Honora could fix you a roast beef sandwich."

"Thank you." Her stomach rumbled at the man's words. When had she last eaten? Or slept? The thought of a comfortable bed sounded like heaven. She put down the brandy glass, placed both hands on the sides of her chair, and pushed herself to her feet.

Bob and Honora exchanged worried glances. "Are you sure you don't need a doctor, love?" her hostess asked.

"No. Really. It's just bruises and scratches." She glanced down at her pants. The tear that Tatiana had sewn up had parted under the stress of her journey across the moors. The gash she'd received in the Underground had opened and there was blood on her thigh. Fortunately she'd kept her jacket zipped up. Bob and Honora would certainly have called the police if they'd seen the state of her T-shirt. Or the rope marks on her arms. "I could use a first-aid kit if you have one," she admitted. "I'm pretty good at doctoring myself."

"We've got one in the office," Bob said, heading toward a doorway beside the bar.

"Is there anyone who'll be looking for you, dear?" Honora asked. "Do you need us to call someone?"

"No." Only now did she remember her name and photograph

had been broadcast as someone wanted by Scotland Yard. She doubted that, in her current state, Bob or Honora would recognize her, but if she gave her name the danger of that would greatly increase. "I was on my way back to Plymouth," she said, lying again. "But no one's expecting me." She hesitated. "About payment. I left my purse in the car—"

"Absolutely not." Honora cut her off. "We wouldn't think of it. This is one Christmas when there *is* room at the inn." She chuckled at her own joke, then, with a glance at Bob, who rejoined them with a white tin box in one hand and a key in the other. "What do we call you, dear?"

"Ghayda. Ghayda Ja'bari." Ayesha's sister and her family name.

"Well, Ghayda," Bob said. "Let's get you into a room."

Twenty minutes later she cinched tight the belt of a thick white robe and opened the door of her room.

"Here you go, dear," Honora said, handing her a large tray. It held a covered plate, a bowl of fruit, and a thermos flask. "Is there anything else you need?" She swept a keen glance over her guest, but the robe almost completely enveloped her. None of her wounds were visible.

Ayesha set the tray down on an antique chest of drawers as Honora held something else out to her. A pair of blue jeans. "These are my daughter's. I think you and she are about the same size. Those pants of yours didn't look as if they were fit to be worn."

"I really can't thank you enough." She was touched by the woman's kindness to a stranger. "I'll send them back as soon as I get home."

"Don't bother. Really. Demelza has more jeans than she knows what to do with."

She locked the bedroom door after Honora left and dropped

the jeans on the bed. Then she slipped out of the robe. Naked, she padded across the thick carpet to the luxuriously appointed bathroom, a glory in white tile and gleaming brass fittings.

Much later, she collapsed on the bed. She had soaked her aching, battered body in a steaming hot bath and used up all the complimentary guest lotions provided by her hosts. She had washed and rinsed out her stained T-shirt as best she could and hung it on the shower rail to dry. Then she began the painful business of treating her numerous cuts and gashes. And the burns on her breast. Fortunately Bob's first-aid kit was fully stocked. She made liberal use of the iodine bottle and a burn salve. She bandaged the worst cuts and gashes, then covered each of the burns with Micropore tape. It would do until she could get to a doctor. The pain was considerably eased, and mentally as well as physically she felt like a new woman. Food and sleep would work further wonders.

Once more wrapped in the bathrobe and propped up against the bed pillows, she devoured the roast beef sandwiches, then poured hot tea from the thermos into a cup. A television was mounted on the wall opposite the end of the bed. A flick of a button on the bedside remote control turned it on. She sipped tea and channel-surfed until she found a news broadcast.

Ten minutes later she was fully dressed except for her boots. Demelza's jeans fit her perfectly and she'd dried her T-shirt as best she could using the powerful guest hair dryer. Her remaining cash and plastic cards she'd transferred from one of the zippered pockets in her pants, more than thankful that Nazir hadn't removed them.

She regretted enormously what she was going to do next. There was no alternative, though. Not after what she'd seen on the news. As she watched and listened, stunned at what had happened in

London, Nazir's phone conversation came back to her. A bomb had exploded in Downing Street. Someone had only been injured, not killed. She put two and two together. The bomb was obviously meant for Judah Ben David. Nazir was involved. He'd failed. But he had a backup plan. For tomorrow. Today. *Sagheer.*

Ayesha eased the door of her room shut behind her, crept across the landing in her bare feet, then made her way down the wooden staircase, stopping and listening at each creak of the old wood. The taproom was in darkness, except for a flicker from the fireplace embers. Enough moonlight came through the windows for her to see her way to the office. She was sure that was where she would find the keys to her hosts' car.

CHAPTER 53

Moses Litmann checked the time on his watch. Nearly 7 A.M. He turned back to the *Daily Herald*'s website, open on his laptop browser, and refreshed the screen. "*A broch!*" he muttered. Still nothing. He was frustrated and puzzled. He'd been sure, by the time he showered, shaved, and dressed, there'd be something online under Milton Hoenig's byline. The Christmas Bombing. The meeting of the leaders, today at the Tower of London. These were the big stories. But he'd given Hoenig the scoop on exactly what was going to be announced at the Tower. It should have been all over the Internet by now.

He brought up the BBC page. Scanned the lead stories. Frowned at pictures of soldiers in full combat gear taking up strategic positions around the Tower of London. Nazir had assured him it didn't matter. His backup plan allowed for such things.

The embassy kitchen had sent up a basket of bagels to his room. He couldn't eat anything. A rock sat in the pit of his stomach.

He checked the time once more, then looked at the window. It was still dark. All he could see was his reflection. He gazed into his own eyes. Before the Downing Street assassination attempt, he'd contemplated something. Decided it wasn't necessary. Before dawn, after watching the footage, seeing the huge boost to the Palestinian cause from the sacrifice of the foolish police-man and Sayyed Khalidi's heroics, he'd changed his mind. The cost was worth it. There would be a revulsion of feeling against the Palestinians. The sympathies of the world would be with the Jews once more. The hatred would boil over and, when Judah Ben David was killed, his people would howl for blood. As the new prime minister, he would supply it. One call to Jerusalem had set the wheels in motion. By now everything would be ready. He just needed to give the order.

He found his secure phone. Thumbed a button.

"*Shalom,*" a voice answered.

He replied with two words: "Do it."

CHAPTER 54

D ame Imogen Worsley stood under the shower and let the hot water do its job of waking her up. She'd managed four hours' sleep after getting back to her Knightsbridge apartment. It hadn't been good sleep; she had too much on her mind. The murder of Detective Inspector Holden for one thing. Shot dead, along with the Bodmin postmistress. Neither Ayesha Ryder nor Detective Sergeant Bryan had been found, but she feared the worst. Peta Harrison was another problem. She'd had her picked up. It was only suspicion—yet, but that was too much for someone in her position. Dame Imogen sighed. Harrison's interrogation was another thing on a list that was long and getting longer.

She applied soap to her skin with a bath sponge. She thought about the one good thing to have come out of the night—Lady Madrigal Carey. After visiting the old woman, she'd called on the home secretary. Sir Norman Eldritch had been hugely relieved when she told him the evidence of Edward Windsor's plot with the Nazis had been destroyed long ago.

"This woman sounds incredible," he said. "She was really Lawrence's lover?"

"So it seems."

"And she actually *blackmailed* Edward into abdicating?"

"She as good as said so."

Eldritch hadn't been able to restrain his laughter. "With the abolition of the retirement age, maybe you should think about hiring her."

She rinsed off the soap, smiling. It wasn't all that silly a notion. There was certainly no reason why Lady Madrigal couldn't act as a consultant. None of her old connections were likely to be alive, of course.

Thinking about Lady Madrigal drew her back into their conversation. Lawrence's clue. Something about it niggled her. *The man who taught you to fly.* She thought about that while she applied her makeup. The man who taught Churchill to fly was Jack Trelawney. Ayesha Ryder had figured that out and raced off to Bodmin. Trelawney's old address. It was the obvious thing to do.

Imogen hated the obvious thing. In her experience it was rarely the right thing. She paused in the act of applying her lipstick and gazed at her reflection. Lawrence was fond of the double bluff. A master of guerrilla warfare, he liked to outthink his enemy. *Safe custody.* Her eyes widened in the mirror. Not Bodmin. *Here.* In London.

She dashed to her phone. Told her driver to get to her apartment ASAP. Four minutes later she'd finished her makeup, belted a black Burberry trench coat over a dark suit, and was waiting impatiently for her car to arrive. While she paced, she listened to the BBC and scrolled the unchecked messages on her BlackBerry.

The news had nothing for her. Her messages added little. Speculation was rampant. Reports on the hunt for Jacob Steiner, the man responsible for the Downing Street bombing, were uniformly negative. The Devon and Cornwall police were investigating a report of a possible sighting of Ayesha Ryder at the Jamaica Inn. No sign of DS Bryan, though. Steve Watts needed to talk to her urgently. She knew what that would be: another nail in the coffin of Peta Harrison. She sighed. It was getting light and people were about, heading to work. Her car pulled up.

"Crutched Friars," she instructed her driver as she slid into the backseat.

Before she was appointed to her current position, she was a top field operative. Although she relished her current role and the power that came with it, she often wished she could get out from behind her desk, just for a while. This morning, her heart was racing. It felt good to be doing something. If Ayesha Ryder drew a blank in Bodmin, she might just find her where she was going. If she was still alive.

CHAPTER 55

C rutched Friars. The street near Tower Hill drew its name from an order of monks who settled thereabouts in the thirteenth century. The Walsingham Institute was just a few hundred yards from where Ayesha sat, the lone customer in a shabby café, devoid of a single Christmas ornament, sipping bad coffee. She'd been there, pretending to read the newspaper, since making her way from the London Monument via a stop at a Boots for a bottle of Panadol Ultra to dull the pain of her injuries. She'd also picked up a padded bra, panties, and a new T-shirt, using a public toilet to change. She used her cash card for the purchases. It wasn't as if she was going to hang around the store long enough for anyone to find her.

The London Monument was where the truck driver with whom she'd hitched a ride from Andover, not wanting to risk staying longer with her stolen car, had dropped her. The driver— "Call me Franky"—was heading for Billingsgate. The famous market would have been ideal for her, but it was within the declared security zone for the Tower of London conference. Franky was going to be stuck in traffic for hours, so she said her thanks and abandoned him. He'd tried for her phone number—Franky had guts—but she'd given him one of her rare smiles, and a shake of her head.

She raised her left arm, saw only bandages where her watch should have been, and lowered it again. The watch hadn't been with her clothes; presumably it was back at the old farmhouse on Bodmin Moor. She glanced at the electric clock on the wall over the counter. Just after eight o'clock. She yawned and turned back to the window. It was light, finally, but the bank wouldn't open until nine.

The bank was an old building, unlike many in Crutched Friars, replacements for those destroyed in Hitler's Blitz. The bank, also unlike its more recent neighbors, had style. Understated, as a bank should be, with a porticoed entrance. Late eighteenth century. It wasn't a guess on her part. She knew that Trelawney's Bank had been there since 1774. It was an *old address*.

The knowledge had come to her when Nazir burned her for the fourth or fifth time. Her mind flickering in and out of consciousness, near hallucinating, she'd flashed on an image of the old building she walked past every day on her way to work. Trelawney's Bank. One of England's oldest still operating private banks. One of the few of its kind to have survived the world economic crisis. Somehow her brain made the connection between the bank and the phrase in Lawrence's last clue: *safe custody*. At that point she knew, with no shadow of a doubt, where Lawrence had hidden the Palestine treaty. His clue led in two directions. One, the trail to Bodmin, was a blind. The other, to the bank, was the real one. *Safe custody* could refer to items held *poste restante* at a post office. But the more common use of the phrase related to banks. Banks had strong rooms, where people kept safety-deposit boxes for bonds, deeds, valuables, and documents.

She still didn't know what she'd do when the bank opened. How she'd get access to the box she was sure was there: *identification Ross 352087*. A bank wasn't a country post office. And she had no Scotland Yard credentials to flash. Just let her get into the bank. The rest would take care of itself. She grimaced. The rest. The plot to assassinate Israel's prime minister. Nazir had a backup plan. But that was all she knew. That and a word: *sagheer*. The Arabic word for small, or tiny. She had to tell someone. She'd already decided who. As soon as she'd had a chance to find out what, if anything, was at the bank, she was going to visit Lady Madrigal Carey. It was many years since the old lady had worked for MI6, but Ayesha had no doubt she would know exactly who to call.

A gleaming black Bentley drew up outside the bank. The driver, dark-suited, got out and opened the rear passenger door. A woman alighted. Thick auburn hair. Mid-fifties and beautiful in the way a very few women always are. She was stylishly, almost dramatically, dressed. An air of command, of getting what she wanted. The woman looked at the bank, then swung round to scrutinize Crutched Friars. Her gaze fixed on the café where Ayesha sat. With a glance to check the traffic, she walked straight across the street and pushed through the café door. When she stood in front of her table the woman held out a hand and smiled.

"Hello, Dr. Ryder," she said.

CHAPTER 56

The tiny outpost of Har Yaacov had only just been established, in an area a few miles to the north of Har Homa, in the occupied Palestinian territories. That morning—its last morning—Har Yaacov was a hive of activity. Shouts and calls rang out in numerous languages and accents. Some Hebrew, but English and Russian could be heard, too. A generator thrummed noisily. Somewhere a man chopped wood with an axe. There were no buildings yet on the dry, dusty hilltop. Just trailers and tents. They provided housing for twenty-three families in all. Forty-six adults and thirty-five children.

Some of the settlers were recent immigrants. From the United States and the lands of the former Soviet Union mostly. They were a hardy, tough group. They had to be. Devoutly religious, they believed, in the face of the world and their Palestinian neighbors, that the land was theirs. God-given and Jewish. That morning all of the adults, some of the children, too, were hard at work. Clearing the land. Digging latrines. Laying out foundations and fields. Looking for places to dig for water. A group of children attended classes in an open-sided tent. High in the cool, cloudless sky something flashed, just for an instant. No one in the outpost saw it.

The settlers had sentries posted. They were expecting trouble. From the Palestinians, who said this was *their* land. But trouble usually came at night. Not in broad daylight. And if any trouble did materialize they could call in the IDF. The outpost might be illegal, but they were Israelis and their country possessed the world's fourth-largest military.

The two sentries died first. They had taken up vantage points where they could watch the valley below, with plenty of time to give warning. They hadn't reckoned on sniper rifles with thousand-yard range, though. Or snipers with the ability to hit a target over that kind of distance. They died where they sat, without making a sound. The crack of the shots that killed them was lost in the noise of the outpost.

Seven minutes later the shooting started in earnest.

Two covered trucks, old, battered, green painted, rumbled into the heart of Har Yaacov and stopped. Men piled out of the back. Heavily armed men wearing green military-type fatigues and black-and-white checkered kaffiyehs.

"*Allahu Akbar!*" the men cried as they spread out and opened up with their weapons on the defenseless colonists. Except for one man, who strode back and forth, filming with a handheld video camera. It was the reason they'd decided to go in in daylight. It would have so much more impact when the video was uploaded to the Internet.

The man with the video camera seemed impervious to the screams that filled the air. He filmed as a grenade was thrown into the open-sided tent, killing fourteen children and their teacher, who had taken shelter beneath their makeshift desks. Those who weren't killed outright were dispatched with a bullet to the head. The video camera caught it all. The sobbing, unheeded cries for mercy. The brutality of death.

Men were shot protecting their wives. Then their wives were shot. Quite a few of them were pregnant. Some tried to hide inside their trailers and tents. Grenades took care of them. One man, the man who'd been chopping wood, ran screaming into the outpost, waving his axe. They let him get close so the camera could capture the moment bullets riddled his chest.

It took perhaps twenty minutes. From the time the sentries were taken out, until the last child was shot through the head. When there was no one left to kill, the men climbed back into their trucks. The man with the video camera took some last footage of the silent colony of Har Yaacov. Then he joined his companions and the trucks drove away.

CHAPTER 57

"Imogen Worsley," she said. "I'm with the Security Service. We've been looking for you."

Ayesha tensed, then glanced through the window. The woman's Bentley was still there. The driver hadn't moved.

"Please." Dame Imogen had caught the look. "Don't run. I . . . we . . . mean you no harm. I know what you've been doing, and I want to help. I know why you're here. Trelawney's Bank."

Ayesha jerked back in her chair, almost tipping it. She grabbed the table to steady herself, her sleeves riding up to reveal the bandages that only partially concealed the deep lacerations on her wrists and arms.

"You've been hurt." Dame Imogen pulled out a chair and sat down opposite her. She looked from her arms to her face. "Badly."

Ayesha looked into the blue eyes of the auburn-haired woman. Somehow she knew about Trelawney's. How? Imogen Worsley had guessed right about her intentions. She had been about to run. Still might. As soon as she thought it, however, she knew she wouldn't. There was something about the woman, some quality Ayesha trusted instinctively. "I'm okay," she replied, deciding to wait.

"How did you know?" Ayesha asked. "About Trelawney's?"

"I talked with Lady Madrigal Carey. She showed me Lawrence's clue. Later I remembered the bank and made the connection." Dame Imogen glanced toward the counter, where the waitress was busy scouring something, then, with lowered voice, asked, "Who shot Detective Inspector Holden?"

"Bryan."

"Ah. Do you know where Bryan is now?"

"He's dead."

Dame Imogen opened her mouth to speak, but Ayesha cut her off. "Bryan was working with someone. A man called Nazir. Nazir and Bryan tortured Evelyn." She drew breath, felt the hurt. "They killed him. Nazir wants Lawrence's treaty."

"Go on," Dame Imogen said.

"I . . . encountered him—Nazir—many years ago. When I was . . . when I was . . ."

"I know about your past. What you did. It doesn't concern us."

Ayesha thought about that, filed the information for future consideration. "When I . . . knew him, Nazir was with the Israeli army."

"He isn't now. Hasn't been for a long time. We believe he works with certain people who concern us. You've heard of *Shamir*?"

"Of course. That explains it. They must have learned what Evelyn was looking into."

"And what was that?" Dame Imogen prompted.

"Lawrence's treaty. It's important enough to kill for." Her eyes widened. "It was *them* who shot the man at St. Paul's?"

RYDER

"We believe so. It was our people who came to pick you up. They'd lost you in the Underground."

"Listen to me." Ayesha leaned forward in her seat. "They intend to kill Judah Ben David. They were behind the bombing yesterday. They're going to try again. Today."

"How do you know?" Dame Imogen's mask dropped slightly. One manicured eyebrow twitched upward.

Quickly she recounted what she'd heard of Nazir's phone call.

"You've no idea who he was speaking to?"

"None."

"*Sagheer*. What could that mean?"

Ayesha shrugged. "It means tiny. In Arabic."

"Anything else?"

"That's all I heard."

The head of MI5 pushed her chair back. "I have to make some calls, get my people onto this. Please, wait here."

Dame Imogen left the café and strode to her car, speaking rapidly into her cellphone. Ayesha watched her through the window, then looked toward the back of the café. There'd be another exit through the kitchen. She could disappear in less than a minute. But where would she go? She turned back to the window. Dame Imogen paced next to her car, gesticulating with one hand as she spoke into her phone. Ayesha admired the calm manner with which the woman handled herself under stress, then she switched her gaze to the bank. A man in a suit walked up the steps and pushed through the front door. She could have howled with frustration. To be so close. Dame Imogen was going to investigate once she'd issued orders to her subordinates. It was why she'd come to Crutched Friars. Ayesha glanced at the clock on the wall. The door opened and Dame Imogen reentered the café.

"We have an appointment," Dame Imogen told her, "at the bank. If you'd care to accompany me, that is?"

One of Dame Imogen's calls had been to Joseph Trelawney, descendant of the bank's founder and the current chairman of the board. He'd grumbled, but just for show. Trelawney was angling for a knighthood, so there was never any doubt he would cooperate. The fact MI5 wanted to look at a safety-deposit box, which, if it existed, belonged to someone who'd been dead for more than three-quarters of a century, no doubt played a part in his decision.

While the bank manager, a fair-haired, conservatively dressed type, alerted by Joseph Trelawney to the reason for their visit, tapped keys on a computer, Ayesha let her gaze sweep over the largest Christmas tree she'd ever seen. She tilted her head back to look at the ceiling high overhead. Plaster columns, fluted and gilded, rose at least thirty feet to support it. A massive chandelier hung from its center. She lowered her gaze. Dark wood and brass fittings had been burnished till they shone. The whole chamber reeked of age, furniture polish, and old wealth. Except for the computers it must have looked the same when Lawrence had visited—if he had.

"Ross 352087," the manager said. "We do have a box with that description."

She let out the breath she'd been holding.

"Hmm." The manager read the computer screen. "It was last opened in 1936." He frowned. "That's odd. It doesn't say who by. If you'd care to come with me." He led the way to a broad marble staircase.

"You're sure it'll still be there?" Dame Imogen asked as they clattered down the steps.

"The computer says so. And the computer never lies." The manager laughed softly. "Well, hardly ever." On the lower level, he strode ahead along a short passageway that ended at a solid metal door. He used two different keys in two different locks, spun a combination dial several times, then turned a massive brass lever. The door swung open.

The vault was comfortably furnished. Two chairs, upholstered in dark leather, sat at a heavy antique table. A massive leather-bound register lay on the end of the table nearest to them. The manager opened it and paged through it. "Yes, here it is." He closed the register and walked around the table to the far side of the vault.

Keys rattled. The manager opened one of hundreds of small doors set into the vault walls, metal slid on metal, and he withdrew a flat gunmetal box. He carried this over and placed it on the table. "I'll leave you to it," he told the two women. "When you've finished, please come back upstairs and let me or one of the staff know."

Ayesha stared down at the box, heart hammering. She wanted to open it. Then again, she didn't. If it stayed closed there was still hope.

"The honor is yours," Dame Imogen said, breaking the spell.

Ayesha nodded her thanks, then rested her hands on the box and closed her eyes. When she opened them again she lifted the lid.

Dame Imogen sighed heavily. Ayesha turned away so the other would not see her disappointment.

The box was empty.

CHAPTER 58

Judah Ben David rinsed his razor, washed his face and patted it dry with a hand towel. He dabbed a little cologne on his skin, then dressed in crisply pressed pants and shirt. He'd managed only a few hours' sleep. His body ached and it hurt whenever he turned his neck, but the shower and shave worked wonders. The horror of the day before—Rachel Singer's death particularly—was still with him. Then there'd been the call from Rex Parker, owner of the *Daily Herald*, not long after midnight. Someone had leaked to one of Rex's journalists the whole story of what he and Sayyed Khalidi were planning. If not for their forty-year friendship and the fact Rex owed him his life, it would have been all over the front pages tomorrow. Rex refused to give him the source of the leak, though, and that cost him another hour's sleep, until the sleeping pills kicked in. He'd woken with the knowledge that one of his closest colleagues was a traitor. Devastating as that knowledge was, the thought of what he was going to do this day, the changes it might bring, filled him with a sense of keen anticipation that helped to dull his unease.

He walked back into his hospital room—he and Sayyed Khalidi had been kept overnight at St. Thomas's, ostensibly for observation, in reality to help the British Security Services keep them safe—and glanced at the stack of papers next to his laptop computer. He looked at the top paper, a Syrian peace initiative. That was important. He flipped through some of the other papers, sighed heavily. No matter what happened, the paperwork would find him. Even being hospitalized was no barrier.

He was looking around for his shoes when someone knocked on the door. It opened, letting in a burst of noise from the anteroom beyond, and Moses Litmann entered.

The foreign minister's cadaverous features were grimmer than usual. "Prime Minister," he said, shutting the door behind him. "Judah. I have bad news. Very bad news. The worst."

"Tell me." He forgot about his shoes. Litmann wasn't one to exaggerate.

"The outpost at Har Yaacov. The new one—near Har Homa."

"I ordered that shut down, dismantled."

"You did. It hadn't been done yet." Litmann swallowed audibly. "There's no need now. The settlers are all dead. Murdered."

"What are you saying, man?" Surely he'd misunderstood.

Litmann remained silent, allowing his words to sink in.

"Explain." Ben David's voice was soft, but with a cutting diamond-hard quality.

Litmann gestured to Ben David's laptop. "May I?" he asked.

He jerked a nod.

Litmann lifted the laptop and placed it on top of the stack of official papers, then he opened a Web browser and brought up YouTube. He typed a few keywords, enlarged the image to full screen size, and turned up the volume.

Ben David leaned forward. The video image was small on the screen and slightly grainy, but it had been made by a steady hand.

He watched as the camera zoomed in on the sprawled corpses of the sentries. One of the men still had his rifle clasped across his chest. He'd never got a chance to use it. When the first women and children were shot, Ben David moaned aloud with the pain of a mortally wounded animal. "This isn't happening," he rasped. "It can't be." He watched in agony while the video played on. When it ended, the screen frozen on an image of children's bodies, he gazed at it for a long time. When he straightened up, he wiped the tears from his eyes and turned to his foreign minister. "Who?" he demanded gruffly.

"You saw their kaffiyehs." Litmann spoke solemnly, regretfully. "You heard them shouting. *Allahu Akbar*." He nodded at the laptop. "They call themselves 'Free Palestine.'" He shrugged. "What does it matter *what* they call themselves? They're all the same. Murdering scum."

In vain Ben David struggled to comprehend what he'd seen. His stomach heaved and he ran into the bathroom, leaned over the basin, and vomited. When he had nothing else to throw up, he stayed there, clinging to the cool white enamel.

Litmann was still waiting for him when he returned. Ben David glanced at his laptop. It was closed. Thank God. He couldn't bear to see those images again. He heard voices on the other side of the door to his room. Voices raised in anger.

"Murderer!" a woman screeched. *"Ben Zonah!"* Sounds of a struggle, then something crashed against the door and it burst inward. Sayyed Khalidi stood in the doorway. The Palestinian leader, dressed in his hospital robe, was disheveled. A cut on his cheek bled profusely. Men, uniformed security, gripped both of his arms. Other men and women crowded the anteroom behind him. Some had been crying. All of them were staring at the Palestinian with murder in their eyes.

"Judah!" Sayyed Khalidi cried. "This was *not us. Not* our people. You *must* believe me!"

The Israeli stared at his friend. His hands twitched. He took two steps toward Khalidi, his arms raised as if reaching for his friend's neck.

The Palestinian leader did not move. The blood ran down his cheek unheeded. Blood, Ben David saw, mixed with tears. Those tears, and the simple pleading in the other man's soft brown eyes, broke through the hate ripping through him. With a despairing sigh, he let his hands fall to his sides and bowed his head. He squeezed his eyes shut, but all he could see were the dead of Har Yaacov. He opened them again and looked at Khalidi. His old friend did not flinch, did not turn away. Ben David looked into his eyes and saw a reflection of what he knew would be in his own. Horror. Horror and immense sorrow. "Let him go," he ordered. The guards hesitated, then obeyed.

He stepped forward and seized Khalidi's arms himself, held them in a firm grip. Not taking his eyes off the Palestinian's face, he spoke to the grief-stricken members of his staff and security details who had crowded into the anteroom: "If my friend says that this . . . this *thing* was not committed by his people, then I believe him." He swung on Moses Litmann, glaring. "So now we find out who *did* do it."

CHAPTER 59

Ayesha's soul felt wrenched from its moorings and she had no idea what she was going to do next. She watched, disinterested, as Dame Imogen Worsley reached into the empty safety deposit box. When the head of MI5 withdrew her hand something glittered in her palm.

Ayesha stared down at a tiny gold earring. She picked it up. When she looked at Dame Imogen her face was a question mark. "It's a double clef. Lady Madrigal wears jewelry like this."

"Yes. It's hers." The auburn-haired woman did not seem surprised.

"But how?"

"The Palestine Conference was a cover." Dame Imogen spoke slowly; Ayesha could tell her words were chosen with great care. "I'm afraid I can't tell you what was really going on. It's why we were interested—the Security Services. Why we needed to find you. We thought you might be on the trail of this secret."

Something clicked in Ayesha's head. "The photographs. Edward, Prince of Wales, with the Nazis."

"Yes."

Ayesha frowned. "Surely that's old news?"

"I'm afraid I can't comment."

"I see." Ayesha put the earring down on the table. "You said it's why you needed to find me. Past tense."

"Perceptive of you." Dame Imogen picked up the earring. "How much do you know about Lady Madrigal?"

"What I read on the Internet. Her wartime service. SOE. Captured and tortured by the Nazis. She admitted she was a spy, that she was Lawrence's lover as well as his liaison with the MI6."

"Then you know about Lawrence?"

"Yes. I'd guessed as much before I met Lady Madrigal. She confirmed it."

"Bugger." Dame Imogen sighed. "Have you ever signed the Official Secrets Act?"

"No. And I'm not going to, either."

The head of MI5 scowled. She tapped the earring on the tabletop.

Ayesha waited.

"Lady Madrigal figured out years ago what Lawrence's clue meant. That it was a reference to a safety-deposit box here at Trelawney's. It contained evidence Lawrence had gathered, damning evidence. Lady Madrigal destroyed that evidence. Once she told me that, our search for you became less urgent." Dame Imogen cleared her throat. "Upstairs, when the manager said the box had been opened in 1936—*after* Lawrence's death—I guessed, but I didn't *know*"—she looked at the earring—"until now, that this was where the papers had been hidden."

Ayesha struggled to comprehend what Dame Imogen had said. What she had not said. She flashed on an image, seized it as a drowning person will a lifeline. "The other photo! The one of Lawrence with the Grand Mufti and the man from the League of Nations. At Clouds Hill. That can't have had anything to do with the Nazis. At least—"

"No, you're right. It was taken years before the Grand Mufti got involved with Hitler's gang."

"Then what?"

"It's why I came here this morning. And why Lady Madrigal encouraged you to go to Bodmin."

"Why?" She was lost.

"Because the cover story wasn't just a cover story. . . ."

"It's true, then," Ayesha said, some minutes later, when Dame Imogen had finished her explanation. "It did happen." She felt no triumph in the knowledge. Regret, that she felt. Regret that Evelyn was not here to share this with her. A lump formed in her throat.

"Yes. It's something I've only learned in the past twenty-four hours. The whole thing was suppressed. You convinced Lady Madrigal of the possibility. Then you came up with the other interpretation of Lawrence's clue, something she'd never thought of. Lady Madrigal thought it possible Lawrence secreted papers in two places. One collection here, relating to the prince—"

"And the Palestine treaty in Bodmin," Ayesha completed.

"I gather there was nothing there?"

"No. There was. A parcel sent *poste restante*. But it contained only old newspapers."

"That's when Bryan dropped his cover, I suppose?"

She nodded.

"And they took you."

"Yes. It's still out there somewhere."

"What?"

"The Palestine treaty."

Dame Imogen looked doubtful.

"I'm sure of it. What now? Can I go?"

Dame Imogen pursed her lips. "Not for a day or two. *Shamir* is still looking for you. They believe the Palestine treaty exists. And as long as they think you might still lead them to it, they'll come after you. I'm going to put you in a safe house. I want a doctor to look you over, too. Once the Tower of London meeting is finished we can debrief you fully."

"Do I have a choice?"

"Only if you want to keep on the run. With both us and *Shamir* looking for you."

"Let's go, then."

Moses Litmann hurried to his room at the Israeli embassy. Judah Ben David believed Khalidi. Litmann had hoped the massacre at Har Yaacov would push his prime minister over the edge, but he'd drawn back. Of course the man really had no choice. Not if all his plans were not to collapse and die. Not that it mattered. The world had seen the video and the world believed that Palestinian terrorists had murdered eighty-one virtually defenseless men, women, and children in cold blood. Whatever Ben David and Khalidi tried to do now, it would be drowned in the cries for revenge that were already rising on all sides. Personally, he felt nothing for the murdered settlers. He had to pretend, of course, but the settlers of Har Yaacov were casualties of war. They had died for a great cause.

He took out his phone and entered a number. "Hoenig?" he said, when the journalist answered. "What's happened? Why is your story not published?" He listened, frowning, then, "I see. What's the name of your publisher?" His brow cleared. "Rex Parker? That explains it. Judah Ben David got to him. They're old friends. . . . No, no. Leave it with me. I'll get back to you. . . . A quote? . . . Hmm. Let's see. Okay. How's this: *The massacre at Har Yaacov will go down in history as an atrocity of such evil that the Jewish people rose up and threw the Palestinians from their land forever.* . . . No, that's okay. Just wait till the end of the day before you use it."

He ended the call. His gaze was caught by a spider that chose that moment to descend from its web in the corner of the room. He watched it, until it vanished in the shadows. Then he shrugged. The story about what Ben David and Khalidi were going to announce would not be published in the *Daily Herald*. Even if the two leaders persisted in their madness, after Har Yaacov it hardly mattered. He raised his phone again. Entered another number. Almost immediately he jabbed the button to end the call, his brow clammy with sweat. He checked the call screen. He'd called the right number. But it hadn't been Peta Harrison who'd answered.

He dropped the phone and crossed to the writing desk. He withdrew the metal box, unlocked it, and lifted out the Jericho. He stood there, holding it, finding comfort in the pistol's loaded weight. Time was running out. He would succeed. If God willed it.

CHAPTER 60

The analyst looked up at the large man in the tight-fitting suit. "Yes, Mr. Danforth," he said. "We've had a couple of the new unmanned stealth drones over the occupied Palestinian territories for the past month. Lovely things, only a ten-foot wing-span, eighty-mile range, and flight time of over ten hours. The new-generation stealth technology makes them almost impossible to detect—with anything the Israelis have, anyway."

"Makes it easy, seeing as how we sell them most everything they've got." John Danforth, CIA's London station head, chuckled. "Still, it was taking a risk putting them up over their airspace. If they catch us spying on them there'll be hell to pay."

"Langley cleared it with the president," the analyst replied. "The president thought the risk was worth it. In case things really go south after the London conference. We'll be in a position to monitor events on the ground, see what happens."

Danforth looked down at the younger man, a career officer and one of the top analysts in his field. The analyst didn't know it, but the resources at his disposal were possibly all that stood in the way of another Middle East bloodbath. Danforth knew it. The secretary of state knew it, too, although she was skeptical.

Diana Longshore had swept into his office on an upper floor of the U.S. embassy in Grosvenor Square ten minutes earlier. About to head down to CIA's subbasement operations center, Danforth was not surprised at the visit. "Diana," he drawled. "You're looking particularly lovely this morning."

"No bullshit, John," snapped the secretary, shutting his door behind her. "I've been on the phone with Judah Ben David. The Har Yaacov massacre. He doesn't believe it was the Palestinians. Khalidi denies it, too." She snorted. "He would, of course."

"Actually our sources, such as they are, tend to agree." He leaned his ample backside against his desk and contemplated his nation's top diplomat. "No one knows anything about this group that's claimed responsibility. 'Free Palestine.'"

"Come on, John. Free Palestine is just another splinter group. Even if Khalidi didn't know about it, it's obvious it was the Palestinians."

"I'm not saying you're wrong, Diana. At the moment all we have is circumstantial, though."

The secretary chewed her lip. "If it wasn't the Palestinians, then who do you think it was?"

"If I had to guess—and you know how much I hate doing that—I'd put my money on *Shamir*."

"You can't really think they'd kill their own people?" The secretary of state sounded shocked.

"You haven't forgotten Rabin, have you? A Jewish law student shot and killed his own prime minister to keep him from handing land to the Palestinians. Granted, this is on a much bigger scale. But I'm not going to rule anything out until I know more. Can you think of a better way to kill any talk of rapprochement between Jews and Palestinians?"

"I hear what you say." The secretary paced his office. "But what evidence is there?"

He shrugged. "We're shaking the bushes. I was just about to head downstairs to see what else we can do."

The secretary of state left and he took the elevator to the sub-basement. "Listen, son," he said to the analyst. "You've got the coordinates for this Har Yaacov place?"

"Yes, sir. I think there's a good chance one of our drones was in the area when it all went down."

"I hope you're right. It's about time we had a stroke of luck." He sent up a silent prayer. "Come on then, let's see if we've got anything."

The analyst bent over his computer. Danforth leaned over the man's shoulder, peering intently at the screen.

CHAPTER 61

Ayesha looked through the window of Dame Imogen's Bentley at Russell Square. A few flakes of snow were falling. Perhaps there'd be a white Christmas after all. Not that she cared. She was sunk in gloom after the visit to the bank and the shock of the empty box. Still, a glimmer of hope remained—from the knowledge, confirmed by Dame Imogen, that Lawrence's Palestine treaty was real.

Something niggled at the back of her mind. Something she'd overlooked. As she racked her brains to remember what it was, the car turned into a side street. One more turning, then the driver slowed. He drew the car into the curb in front of a four-story brick terrace. The ground floor housed a used bookshop, not yet open.

Dame Imogen alighted and waited for her on the pavement. "This way," she said, and walked up to a casually dressed man who stood in the bookshop doorway. He stepped back for them to enter.

Ayesha breathed in the distinctive musty scents of old books. The man led them into the further recesses of the shop. He ushered them through a door behind the counter, then into a dingy hall crowded with more books piled on the floor along the walls. Another doorway at the far end of the hall opened into a cozy living room, cheap but comfortably furnished with a sofa and two armchairs, a bookcase filled with popular novels and magazines and a 1990s vintage television.

"Kitchen, bedroom, bathroom," the man said, gesturing at the other doors. "All mod cons. I'm Bruce. I'll be looking after you while you're here. Anything you want, just ask."

"Bruce will get a doctor to have a look at you. And anything you need. But no calls. And you can't leave here. Not for a couple of days at any rate." Dame Imogen touched Ayesha's shoulder. "Thank you for what you've done. You've been through hell. But your information just might save lives." She hesitated, searching her face, then, with a nod to Bruce, she swung on her heel and left.

Ayesha turned to her guardian. Or *jailer*, she thought grimly. "Which one's the bathroom?" she asked.

Ayesha closed and locked the bathroom door behind her, used the toilet, then washed her hands in the basin, letting the warm water run over them. It felt good. Safe. She glanced at the tub. She could run a hot bath, soak in it. Get her wounds properly tended by a doctor. Eat something. Turn on the television and catch up with the news. Read a good book—the shop looked like just the sort of place she could spend hours browsing in.

It was no good. She couldn't sit still and do nothing. Lawrence's treaty was still out there somewhere. She was convinced of it. A thought hit her. Her eyes widened. The second piece of paper! How had she forgotten it? The madrigalism, or whatever it was, in Lawrence's envelope. It must be another clue. But to what? She squeezed her eyes shut and tried to picture it: the neatly ruled lines, the musical notation.

Minutes passed before she accepted that she could not remember how the notes were arranged. She crossed to the one small window and peered out. There wasn't much to see. A tiny yard with a corrugated iron fence. A gate that gave on to an access lane. The yard itself was empty—just weeds and old garbage bins. She tried the window. It wouldn't open. Two screws secured it to the frame. She went back into the living room. Bruce had turned on a radio, was listening to the news. There was no sign of Dame Imogen.

"Make yourself comfortable," he told her. "I'll be in the shop. Sing out if you want anything."

She went into the kitchen. Methodically, she searched the drawers and cupboards. There wasn't much. She selected two knives and a pair of scissors. She took them to the bathroom, locked the door, and turned on the taps in the bathtub. The screws that secured the window were stiff, and neither the knives nor the scissors was ideal for the task. Nevertheless, she had the window open in seconds. Wriggling through the small opening, she dropped into the yard. Two minutes later she was jogging across Russell Square Gardens in the direction of Mayfair.

CHAPTER 62

For the third time Bryan's phone rang, unanswered. With a snarl of rage, Nazir hurled his phone across the room and slammed his fist into the mantel over the fireplace. The old wood cracked under the impact. "Fuck!" he yelled. He kicked the wall, then stormed across the room. He flung the kitchen door open, ready to vent his anger. No one was there.

He clenched and unclenched his fists. He took a ragged breath. Kaleb Bryan was never going to answer. *Ayesha Ryder.* Somehow the woman had bested him. Like she'd done twenty years before. He didn't have to close his eyes to picture the scene. It was there before him, always.

He'd drawn out the torture. Relished every second of it. Used her body. The girl had been helpless, defeated—until she wasn't. Until she erupted from the table with stunning violence. Sweat broke out on his brow and his hands shook at the memory of what she'd done to him. How she used the jagged glass to hack away his manhood. For years he'd fantasized about finding her and taking his revenge. Then, from nowhere, she'd reappeared. He hadn't recognized her at first. Then he'd seen the scars on her neck and breast, his own handiwork. Even then he couldn't believe his luck. The bitch was still alive.

He'd anticipated, almost with ecstasy, what he would do to her. He hadn't even minded the interruption, the need to return to London. It had merely prolonged the pleasure, given him more opportunity to exercise his imagination. He'd fantasized about how long he would draw out the torture this time, making it last for days, until she begged him to let her die. Now, after he had finally found her, she had escaped. Again.

His phone was ringing. It took a moment for him to find where it had fallen.

"Yes?" he said. A familiar voice spoke furiously in his ear. While he listened, he walked back and forth across the room. It took all his willpower not to snap into the phone, tell Moses Litmann to pull himself together.

"Yes," he answered calmly. "Yes. You are right to be worried. Do not call that number again. And get rid of that phone. Use one of the others I gave you. I don't think it can be traced. But it is better not to take chances. . . . Everything is under control. I will be meeting Sagheer shortly to give him his final instructions. This time Judah Ben David will die. . . . Yes. The Ryder woman." Again he felt the thirst for revenge rising inside him, forced it down. "Something has happened. She may have gotten away."

Nazir held the phone away from his ear and let the man rant for a full minute before he interrupted. "She will turn up. If she is still alive, she will turn up. When she does, I will find her. . . . Count on it."

When he ended the call Nazir stared into space. All he could see was the room below the old fort outside Beersheba. A naked, broken woman. And a howling emptiness.

RYDER

CHAPTER 63

"So there *was* something." Lady Madrigal Carey contemplated Ayesha across the rim of her martini glass.

"Yes, but like I said, it was a false trail. Just a parcel of old newspapers." Ayesha had told Lady Madrigal the whole tale. She left out the details of what Nazir had done to her, but the old lady had watched her shrewdly as she spoke. She didn't miss much, or anything.

"I'm sorry. I hope you don't think I sent you on a wild goose chase."

"Of course not. Dame Imogen said you thought Lawrence might have hidden papers in two locations."

"That's right. You convinced me there might be something in this business of Lawrence's treaty. I knew the box at Trelawney's Bank didn't hold anything relevant. The Bodmin Post Office seemed a plausible alternative. If I'd dreamed—"

"Please." Ayesha cut her off. "I'm fine. I'm only interested in finding the treaty." *And Nazir*, she thought. Evelyn's murder would be avenged. "You really think a copy of the treaty still exists?"

"I'm sure of it. At least, I can't stop looking until I know for sure it doesn't. Could I have another look at the second piece of paper that was in Lawrence's envelope? The one with the musical notes on it?"

"Of course." Lady Madrigal picked up the envelope from the table next to her armchair and held it out.

Ayesha opened it and drew out the two sheets of paper. She replaced the one with the Trelawney's clue and held up the second. She pondered the lines of music. "Would you mind if I played them?"

"Help yourself."

As she opened the lid and propped the sheet of paper on the music stand of the baby grand piano, her glance was caught by the framed photograph of Lady Madrigal sitting with Lawrence on his motorcycle. He looked so obviously in the prime of life. Happy. Carefree. *Those eyes.* Even in the black-and-white photograph they seemed to reach out to her soul. "What was he like?" she asked impulsively.

"He was a god," Lady Madrigal replied evenly. "And the nicest man I ever knew."

Ayesha studied the piece of paper propped in front of her, flexed her fingers, and played the notes. As she had done with the clue from Lawrence's dagger, she played them several times, straining to discern any meaning. It was no good. Defeated, she stopped.

"I'm sorry." Lady Madrigal shook her head.

"Clapping!" Tatiana said suddenly. Lady Madrigal's companion had entered the room while Ayesha was playing. "It sounds like clapping. Applause."

Ayesha played the notes again. Then again. "You're right. It *could* be clapping. Repeated clapping." Her heart jackhammered.

"Significance?" Lady Madrigal asked. "What is the significance of repeated applause?"

"An encore?" Tatiana suggested.

"Encore?" Ayesha echoed. "*Encore* means again." She jumped up, knocking the piano stool backward onto the carpet. "*Again.* Play it again. Could there be a second box at Trelawney's Bank? A box containing Lawrence's treaty?"

"A second box!" Lady Madrigal exclaimed. "Of course! I do believe you've got it."

"The first box was under the name of Ross, and his service number. If there is a second box, Lawrence didn't leave us a clue to the name."

"Oh yes he did." Lady Madrigal laughed. "Encore. Again. A second act. Or a second enlistment. Under a second name: Shaw."

The red-haired man yawned, shifted uncomfortably in his chair, and adjusted his crotch while he kept his eyes on Lady Madrigal Carey's apartment. He had been there, in the van, for hours, just as Nazir had ordered. He had watched as Ayesha Ryder entered the building, then he had called his boss. Now he waited to observe her departure, glancing at his watch from time to time. His relief was overdue and his bladder was full. He was about to use the bottle he'd brought for the purpose when he grabbed up his phone, forgetting his need to pee. Ryder was hurrying along the sidewalk.

Farther along the street another man watched Lady Madrigal's building. This man, who wore a light-colored trench coat, sat in the window of an upmarket café and drank very expensive coffee while he tapped on the keyboard of his Mac, working on the novel he was determined to finish. He too had observed the arrival of Ayesha Ryder. And he too had reported that fact to his head-quarters. Now, as he pondered a particularly difficult paragraph and debated whether to kill a minor character, he saw Ryder leave Lady Madrigal's building. Unlike the red-haired man, he did not reach for his phone. The proprietary and highly secret instant messaging software installed on his Mac served the same purpose.

CHAPTER 64

IA's London station chief squinted at the screen in front of the analyst. Danforth was just able to discern the tiny figure of a man as it collapsed to the ground. "That's it!" he exclaimed. "Can you magnify it?"

"Yes sir." The analyst toggled a joystick and the image zoomed in, greatly magnified.

Danforth could see everything. Once more he watched the same events he had seen on the Internet video play out, this time from a bird's-eye view. Or a drone's view. The difference was that, where the Internet video stopped when the trucks departed from Har Yaacov after the settlers were massacred, the cameras in the drone had kept on filming.

"Okay," he said grimly, "let's see where these fuckers went."

The analyst entered commands into the computer. A minute ticked by. Two. Then Danforth grunted with satisfaction. The image zoomed in once more and he could see the trucks moving along a road.

The CIA station chief never took his eyes off the screen. He was terribly afraid the trucks would drive out of range of the drone. They didn't, though. They turned off the road and headed down a dirt track, stopping behind a cluster of what appeared to be farm buildings. He watched as men emerged from the trucks. "Can you zoom in more?" he breathed.

The analyst nodded.

This time when the image enlarged Danforth was looking at the men—or not quite. The angle meant that they appeared foreshortened and he couldn't see their faces. He could see that none of them wore Arab headdress. "What's that?" He pointed at one side of the screen.

The analyst moved the viewpoint slightly. Two men were opening the doors of a building—a barn. A minute went by, then a bright yellow bus—a school bus, it looked like—was driven out of the barn. As the men on the ground boarded the bus, and others milled about while waiting to board, one stretched his arms wide, leaned back, and looked directly into the sky.

"Yes! You got that?"

"Yessir! I'll run it through the databases as soon as we've finished here."

The CIA station head continued to watch as the bus left the farm, turned onto the track, then back onto the road. It headed west—for Jerusalem. The analyst sped up the video, then slowed it again as the bus stopped. At the Az Zayyem crossing point from the occupied territories into Jerusalem.

"This will tell us something," he muttered.

Both men watched intently as, with barely a pause, the bus moved through the crossing point. The analyst looked up at Danforth. They exchanged grimaces. Both knew that any busload of Palestinian men seeking to cross into Israel would be subject to a lengthy scrutiny by the guards, then probably turned away. They continued to watch as the bus moved into Jerusalem, its distinctive color enabling them to pick it out easily from the traffic swirling around it. That did not assist them for long, however. The vehicle stopped at a bus station and the occupants quickly alighted. Danforth hoped that one or more would look up, but none did. The men went their different ways, almost immediately indistinguishable from the pedestrians around them.

"Okay, son," he said to the analyst. "We've got one chance. Let's make it count."

CHAPTER 65

"Miss Ryder." The manager of Trelawney's Bank gestured to the visitor's chair in front of the ornate antique desk. "Please, sit down." He waited until she had accepted his invitation, then sat. "Did you want to have another look at that box?"

Ayesha heaved an inward sigh of relief. *Yes.* After leaving Lady Madrigal's apartment, she'd walked the short distance to the Millennium Mayfair Hotel, then took a cab back to Crutched Friars. It was now business hours and the bank was open to the public, although there'd been only one customer in sight when she entered the lobby, her heels echoing on the marble floor, bracing herself to bluff for all she was worth. A uniformed lobby guard sent her name up to the manager. He appeared almost immediately, all smiles, and invited her to sit down at the desk—the bank's idea of a workstation. Would he ask to see identification? On their earlier visit Dame Imogen had introduced her as a colleague from MI5— to do otherwise would have been to create unnecessary difficulties. Ayesha's current strategy depended on the manager not being overly bureaucratic. She had one other weapon.

"Not that box," she replied. "Another one. Same time period, though." As she spoke, she crossed one leg slowly over the other. The manager's eyes followed the silken movement. When he looked up, she looked into his eyes and smiled.

"W-what details do you have?"

She smiled again and placed a piece of paper on the desk in front of the manager.

He took the paper, turned to the computer, and entered the information. The tips of his ears were bright pink. She held her breath while he read whatever information had appeared on his screen. He frowned, and her hopes dived.

"Yes," he said, "we have a box under that name: Shaw 7875698. It was opened on May twelfth, 1935. According to our records it has not been opened since."

The second box, the *encore*, really existed! And no one else had looked at it since it was opened in May 1935. Ayesha's heart beat wildly; she had to work to hide her excitement as she accompanied the manager down to the lower level. "It's incredible," she remarked as he unlocked the door to the vault, forcing herself to make conversation, "that you've kept these boxes for so long."

"Bank policy," the manager replied, stepping back to allow her to enter. "If a box hasn't been opened in a hundred years we start to try to trace the owner. If none can be found we open the box and see what's inside. If the contents are valuable we auction them. The proceeds go to charity."

The manager followed the same procedure as on her previous visit. When he had placed a second gunmetal box on the table he turned to her with a shy smile. "If there's anything else I can do," he said, "please let me know."

Impatient for him to be gone, she controlled herself enough

to thank him. *Don't let him ask me out*, she thought. She could see the question trembling on his lips, but this man didn't have Franky the Trucker's nerve. With a final smile, cheeks pink, he left her.

She stared at the box for several rapid heartbeats. Then she reached out and lifted the lid.

Inside the box was a plain brown envelope. The flap wasn't sealed. She tilted the envelope and allowed the contents to slide out onto the table. A heap of documents lay in front of her, yellowed slightly with age. She slid the top document toward her. It was a small collection of pages held together by a staple in the top left-hand corner. A tiny circle of brown rust had bled from the staple onto the cover sheet, which was blank except for six words: PALESTINE, TREATY OF FEDERATION AND ADMINISTRATION.

The hairs standing up on the back of her neck, the palms of her hands suddenly damp, she turned the pages. There weren't many; treaties to create states are not long documents. *It is hereby agreed between the League of Nations and His Majesty's Government . . .* The articles were concise, beautifully composed. Lawrence's prose rendered them so. It wasn't just the words, though. It was the ideas. Well before she reached the end, tears streamed down her cheeks. Her vision was blurred and she could hardly see to read the words. *If only.* The phrase ran through her mind, over and over.

Laying the precious treaty down, she wiped her eyes and face with the back of her hand. *If only.* If only Lawrence hadn't been murdered. If only Evelyn had lived to see this document. To read these words. She knew if she didn't stop thinking about it, she would break down and start to sob, something she hadn't done since she was a child. Instead she forced herself to concentrate, looked through the other documents. Typewritten, all of them, on the same typewriter. Lawrence's probably. The same superb

RYDER

prose, but unlike the treaty these pages revealed nothing of importance—a draft constitution that backed up the words of the treaty.
Administrative proposals. Handover procedures from the Mandate
authority to the new Government of Palestine. A suggested election timetable. Lists of British laws that could be adopted without
amendment. Proposals for new laws. Maps too, hand-drawn works
of art showing the borders and divisions of the new federation. In
all of them she recognized Lawrence's hand. He was a natural
mapmaker.

She forced down the emotion that threatened to break her and
lifted the last document, a single sheet of paper. She gazed at the
heavily underlined words at the top of the page: *Exodus 25:10.*
With an effort that was almost physical, she lowered her eyes to
the text and read:

*In December 1917, shortly after Allenby captured Jerusalem, I
was taken by a trusted friend to Bethlehem. There, in a secret chamber below the Church of the Nativity, I was shown the Ark of the
Covenant. I have no doubt that it was indeed the Ark and not a for-
gery. The object matched the dimensions given in Exodus, and was
clearly of great age. It is guarded by the same family that has kept
it safe for generations. They sought my advice on whether, with the
Ottoman Empire in ruins, the time had come for them to reveal their
great secret. I told them they must wait until Palestine is truly free.*

The page was signed *T.E.S., May 1935.*

Her mind struggling to grapple with the implications of what
she had discovered, she returned the papers to the envelope, put
the lid back on the box, and walked back up the stairs to the bank-
ing chamber. Her heart was racing. The envelope gripped tight
in one hand, she told the manager she was leaving, then, dazed,
pushed through the bank doors into Crutched Friars.

What to do, she wondered. The Palestinians, the delegation to the London conference, Sayyed Khalidi. That's who the papers should go to. But how? There was no way she'd get past the heavy security arrayed about the Tower of London. Imogen Worsley? No. Perhaps Lady Madrigal could help.

She had made up her mind to return to Upper Brook Street when she felt rather than heard a movement behind her. She started to turn. Too late. She was seized from behind, her arms pinioned to her sides.

The envelope dropped from her hand and she lashed back with her right leg, viciously raking her attacker's shin with the heel of her boot. At the same time she threw her head back, felt it connect with something hard that gave with a crunching sound. Her attacker grunted and released her. She shifted her weight, raised her right shoulder, then something cold and metal was jammed into the back of her neck. She froze.

"We don't have to take you alive, bitch." The harsh male voice grated in her ear.

A car, a dark blue Ford Galaxy, drew up, the rear door swung open. "In," the man behind her growled. The pressure against her neck increased.

Crutched Friars was deserted. If anyone had seen her brief struggle, they hadn't stayed to do anything about it. The gun moved from the back of her neck and ground into the small of her back. "*Move!*"

She stepped forward. The gun never shifted from her back, although she was aware of the man who held it bending to scoop up the fallen envelope. All of her senses were alert, waiting for the instant when the man let his guard down. But he did not, and she was forced into the back of the Ford. Another man sat there. He too held a gun. When she lowered herself onto the cushions he jammed its barrel into her rib cage. A powerful odor assaulted her nostrils: stale cigarettes and burritos. The man who'd jumped her climbed into the front passenger seat. He pressed a blood-soaked handkerchief to his nose. The sight gave her small satisfaction. These men weren't MI5. She had no doubt who they did work for, though. No doubt at all. *Shamir. Nazir.* She ground her teeth in despair. So close. She was so close. It couldn't be the end.

CHAPTER 66

"This is him? The same man? You're sure?"

"Yes, sir. It's a one hundred percent match for the image captured by the drone."

"Who is he?" Danforth studied the photograph, a head-and-shoulders picture of a man in military uniform.

The analyst held out a slim folder. Danforth took it and opened it. "Moishe Bortnick. *Samal.*" He looked up, his forehead creased in a deep frown. "What's a *Samal*?"

"Hebrew word for a sergeant. IDF rank."

"Sergeant." Danforth nodded. "In the Golani Brigade." He gave a low whistle. "Dishonorable discharge, 2009, after Operation Cast Lead in the Gaza Strip. What'd he do?"

"It's all in the file. Bortnick was accused of using Palestinian civilians—children—as human shields. He was court-martialed, found guilty, and dishonorably discharged."

"Sounds like our guy. Any chance an Israeli Arab might have served in the Golani Brigade?"

The analyst shot his superior an incredulous look. The Golani

Brigade, formed during the 1948 Arab-Israeli War, was one of the most highly decorated formations in the IDF. "None at all. I also doubt there's any Israeli Arab with the name Moishe Bortnick."

"Known associates?"

"Those in the database are all ex-military. Some of the others also show dishonorable discharges." The analyst allowed himself a tiny smile of triumph. "One of them, name of Dershowitz, ex-paratrooper, is in Israel's Gilboa prison for the murder of the mayor of a Palestinian village two years ago. He's admitted to being a member of *Shamir*."

"Well done, son." He clapped the analyst on the shoulder so hard that the younger man winced. "This ought to give our beloved secretary of state something to think about." He grabbed up the nearest phone. He hoped there was still time.

CHAPTER 67

Ayesha's nose wrinkled as she was pushed along the dark hallway of the old house. Whitechapel, she knew that much. Safe house probably. The smell was the same as the car, only more so. Stale takeout and male bodies living in close quarters. She came to an open doorway on her left, hesitated. A violent shove sent her through it.

"Where is Bryan?" Nazir snarled.

She was going to die. This time there wouldn't be any escape. Apart from Nazir she counted five other men in the room. Broken-nose. The two who'd been in the car. A heavyset man she recognized from Bodmin. And a red-haired stranger. A door opened on the other side of the room. She glimpsed another man silhouetted in the doorway. The newcomer was tall, at least six foot five or six. She might have taken two of them, even three—the red-haired man looked as if he'd be useless in a fight. Not seven, though, and there might be more.

"Bryan?" She faced Nazir. "He drowned. I killed him. He got

to keep his balls, though." She smiled. "I only do that to *really* sick fucks. Like you."

Nazir landed a haymaker in the pit of her stomach. The muscles there were well developed from years of workouts. Even so, her knees buckled. Through a red mist she saw the next blow coming. She tried to raise her arms, couldn't. The blow slammed into the point of her jaw. Her head snapped back and she hit the floor.

She lay there, her eyes closed, feigning unconsciousness. She nearly was. Only the pounding in her skull told her she had not passed out. Heavy breathing rasped close to her face confirmed it. Nazir was going to make sure. She knew it was coming, but when the brutal kick smashed into her side it took everything she had left not to give any sign. Through the darkness and pain she heard Nazir move away.

"Sagheer," he said. "You are ready?"

Sagheer. She pushed aside the pain and concentrated on what was being said.

"I am."

"Good. The rest of you, pack our gear. We need to get out of here. Sagheer, come with me. I have a plan of the Tower. I want to be sure . . ."

Nazir's voice faded. Ayesha's heart sank. He and Sagheer had moved out of earshot. While footsteps moved back and forth around her, most of them leaving the room and tramping up a nearby staircase, she fought to focus her thoughts. The tall man in the doorway. His name—*Sagheer*. Arabic for small, or tiny. It was a joke name. He—Sagheer—was the backup plan. Sagheer was going to assassinate Judah Ben David.

Heavy objects were moved around on the floor overhead. A

door opened and two pairs of footsteps crossed the room. One pair came back. Nazir spoke. "Sagheer is on his way. . . . We have Ryder. . . . Yes, of course . . . I don't need to. She had the papers you were looking for.

"I have them here," Nazir continued. "Hold." Silence except for thumping sounds overhead, a rustle of paper, then, "A treaty. For a Federated Palestine." Nazir snorted. "Other legal papers. Maps. Something handwritten. Wait." Another silence, while, Ayesha guessed, Nazir tried to read Lawrence's writing, then, "The Ark . . . According to this writing it is hidden in a cave below the Church of the Nativity in Bethlehem. . . . I do not know. It is signed T.E.S. . . . You will have the papers before the day is out. . . . Ryder is dead."

She opened her eyes. Nazir stood over her. The man with the broken nose stood there, too, grinning with anticipation. The pistol Nazir held was pointed at her stomach.

"One shot," he said. "It will take you a very long time to die. I shall enjoy watching."

She stared into his eyes, refusing to give him the slightest sign of fear.

The shot, when it came, was deafening.

CHAPTER 68

The shot took Broken-nose between the eyes, bursting his head apart like a ripe melon and showering Ayesha with blood, brains, and fragments of bone. Nazir twisted, firing wildly at the door to the hall. Someone cried out. Nazir squeezed the trigger again, as, adrenaline surging through her body, she scissored her legs and jerked him sideways. He fell heavily, his gun flying from his hand.

Nazir was on his knees in an instant, cursing and scrabbling desperately for his weapon, but she lurched to her feet and kicked it beneath the sofa. Nazir swung round on her with an animal-like roar of rage. He lunged, his hands reaching for her throat. Another shot rang out. Nazir staggered, fell across the sofa, then rolled across the floor and through the open doorway on the far side of the room. It slammed shut behind him.

She threw herself after Nazir. She was dimly aware of more shots from the hall and the upper floor. Screams, too. The acrid smell of tear gas filled her nostrils. Her eyes stung and she felt sick. Someone yelled at her to stop, but she ignored the command.

Her entire focus stayed on the door through which Nazir had fled. She tripped over a coffee table. Lawrence's envelope lay on it. She snatched it up and thrust it into the top of her jeans beneath her jacket and ran to the door. She turned the handle, pushed against it. The door gave slightly; something was jammed against the other side. She heard more gunshots. Shouted commands. Her eyes watered from the tear gas.

Ignoring her injuries, she hurled herself against the door, ramming it with her shoulder. It slammed backward and she tumbled into the kitchen, sprawling painfully over the wooden chair that had been used to jam the door.

Nazir was on the other side of the room, pounding at the lock of another door with a screwdriver and a kitchen mallet. As she scrambled to her feet, he swung round to face her. A kettle steamed shrilly on a hot plate.

She slammed the door shut behind her and jammed the chair back under the handle. It hurt every time she took a breath—one rib, at least, was cracked or broken, and she had no weapon. She was beyond caring. With a scream of pent-up rage and fury for Evelyn, and for all that he and she had suffered at Nazir's hands, she launched herself across the kitchen.

Snarling, Nazir stabbed at her with the screwdriver. The blade penetrated the sleeve of her leather jacket, biting deep into the flesh of her forearm. She barely felt it. With her left hand she swept the kettle off the stove and swung it with all her strength against Nazir's skull. He screamed as the hot metal struck his flesh, as scalding water splashing over his face and neck. Staggering backward against the stove, he dropped the mallet and screwdriver.

She pounced. She seized Nazir by the hair and rammed his head down onto the hot plate. She held it there while he screamed a high-pitched primeval wail of purest agony. She did not let up. She forced his face against the red-hot coil, until the flesh charred and his hair caught fire and melted away. When, finally, she let him go, Nazir dropped to the floor, sobbing piteously. The side of his face that had been pressed against the hot plate bore its coiled imprint, burned deep into what was left of his flesh. His ear was no more than a carbonized stub.

She stared down at Nazir. There was no pity in her heart, only an ice-cold satisfaction. It was not finished, though. She crouched down, picked up the screwdriver and kitchen mallet. Held them up in front of Nazir's face. She kept them there until his rolling eyes focused, until she was sure he understood what was going to happen. "For Evelyn," she said. Then she hammered the screwdriver upward with the mallet, beneath his rib cage and into his heart.

Nazir's body jerked once, twice. His mouth open in a silent howl, his twitching, terrified eyes locked on hers. Then he ceased to move.

She straightened, turning as the door behind her burst open. A man wearing body armor and a gas mask covered her with a submachine gun.

As she raised her arms, another person stepped into the kitchen. She walked across the room, stood motionless over Nazir's corpse.

"Hello again, Dr. Ryder," Dame Imogen Worsley said, raising her gas mask.

CHAPTER 69

Israel's prime minister was ringed by heavily armed police officers as, bound for the peace conference at the Tower of London,
Judah Ben David motored across the Thames in a police launch.
When he boarded the launch on the Southwark side of the great
river, his escort tried to get him to remain below, in the aft cabin.
The cabin was stifling, though, and Ben David needed air, to clear
his head and think. He'd been in a state of shock since watching
the video of the massacre at Har Yaacov. Numb. He'd shut everyone out of his room except for Sayyed Khalidi.

The two politicians had tried to discuss what to do, how to
respond. All they came up with was the need to maintain a united
front. They knew the massacre probably spelled the end of all of
their hopes and dreams. Neither man lacked for courage, however,
or stubbornness. They were determined to go forward. Another
chance might not come again for a generation. If ever.

His vessel was in the center of a flotilla of other launches.
Tower Bridge, up to their right, was closed. Soldiers in full combat
gear patrolled it. Snipers had taken up positions atop the bridge's

iconic towers. Others observed them from vantage points along the embankment and from the battlements of the Tower itself.

Ben David's method of entry to the Tower was a closely guarded secret that was only now becoming apparent. For weeks in the lead-up to the London conference, the view of the Thames embankment adjacent to St. Thomas's Tower had been blocked by a specially constructed cofferdam. That cofferdam had only come down in the past few hours to the astonishment of all who now saw what it had concealed.

In the thirteenth century, Edward I directed construction of a water gate to provide direct access to the Tower from the river. For hundreds of years it was the means by which alleged traitors, many of them famous—like Anne Boleyn, and the young Princess Elizabeth—were delivered into captivity in the Tower. The name, Traitors' Gate, had stuck. Although the great wooden gate was still there, access to the river had been bricked up in the nineteenth century. Now, once again, it was open. Everyone—the press, potential assassins—would expect the two leaders to arrive through the main entrance. It was hoped that everyone would be taken by surprise.

"Sir?"

Ben David turned. The Israeli stared at his temporary aide, a young man whose name he hadn't troubled to try to remember. "What is it?"

"Sir, it's the American secretary of state." The aide held out a cellphone. "She insists it's urgent."

He accepted the phone and held it to his ear. "Madam Secretary?" He heard Longshore's voice, staticky and too faint to compete with the noise around him. "Wait," he interrupted. He walked down the short flight of steps, bending his head as he entered the steering cabin. The pilot, a grizzled veteran of the Thames Division, was smoking a pipe. If he was surprised at the sudden visit by Israel's prime minister he did not show it. He merely nodded and kept his attention focused ahead on the now open water gate.

Ben David peered over the pilot's shoulder, through the window. On the steps beyond the gate, surrounded by a blue-uniformed phalanx, he could make out the figure of Susannah Armstrong. The British prime minister was somberly clad in black and gray. A mark of respect to the victims of Har Yaacov and Downing Street. "Madam Secretary," he said, turning away from the view. "Do you have news?"

As he listened to the familiar voice, his hand tightened on the phone. "You're sure? There's no doubt?" Tears came to his eyes. The news was awful. The worst. But it would save his plan. His and Sayyed Khalidi's. And, just perhaps, the future of their two peoples.

CHAPTER 70

"Sagheer is a man," Ayesha blurted, relieved but not surprised to see the head of MI5.

Dame Imogen Worsley, her mouth open to remark upon the blood that was liberally spattered over the younger woman's face and body, froze. "Tell me!" she commanded.

The room tilted. Ayesha staggered.

Dame Imogen dived for the sink. She snatched up a glass and filled it with water. "Here," she said, thrusting the glass into Ayesha's hands. Both women ignored the body sprawled at their feet.

Ayesha swallowed the water in one long gulp. It helped. She splashed cold water over her face. Better. She accepted a handkerchief from Dame Imogen and dabbed the water from her face. When she looked down at the handkerchief it was pink with blood. "Not mine," she said. Then she looked at the sleeve of her jacket. "That's mine." She closed her eyes. Concentrated. When she opened them again, she looked unblinkingly at Dame Imogen. "He's very tall. Six five or more."

"Tiny," the MI5 head said, understanding instantly.

"Dark hair, short cut." Ayesha closed her eyes once more. Remembered the silhouette in the doorway. "He wore a suit. A dark suit. He's going to the Tower."

"Very," repeated Dame Imogen. "Over six foot five. Short dark hair. Dark suit. There's no one like that here." She glanced at Nazir's corpse on the floor. "Alive or dead. Anything else? Where at the Tower?"

"No idea. But I'd recognize him." She was sure of it.

Dame Imogen issued orders into her phone at rapid fire. "You can walk?" she asked Ayesha. "Not going to bleed out?"

"I'm fine."

Dame Imogen's eyes narrowed. "Come on," she said, jerking her head toward the door. "I hear there's no entry charge at the Tower today."

From somewhere deep within herself Ayesha summoned up the hint of a smile.

CHAPTER 71

Ayesha ran side by side with Dame Imogen, their feet pounding on the cobbled walkways of the Tower of London. Both women wore heels, but both had years of experience negotiating the ancient streets of England and Europe. They moved faster than the two armed policemen who ran beside them, weighed down by their weapons and body armor.

Dame Imogen had commandeered a police car to get the short distance from Nazir's safe house to the Tower of London. All of the streets around the Tower were sealed off, and the security zone extended some distance beyond that. Dame Imogen's face, and her credentials, got them through the barriers, but it took precious time. She reached Judah Ben David on her cellphone on the way, pleaded with him to turn back. Israel's prime minister refused.

Before leaving the safe house, Dame Imogen relayed Ayesha's information to her people and those coordinating security at the Tower. A huge manhunt was now under way for a tall man with short dark hair in a dark suit. It was an impossible task. There were hundreds of people at the Tower. Diplomats and members of the delegations. Susannah Armstrong's people. Tower personnel. The press. Even the famous Beefeaters, the Yeoman Warders in their distinctive Tudor dress. The only real hope was that Ayesha would recognize Sagheer.

"This way," Dame Imogen gasped as they passed the Bell Tower.

Ayesha, one hand clasped tight to her side, glanced upward. Snipers on top of the battlements. Sagheer could be one of those. He wore a suit. So not a sniper. Lots of suits ahead—the dignitaries and hangers-on gathered at the top of the steps above Traitors' Gate. They drew back, applauding. She recognized Israel's prime minister. Judah Ben David looked drawn and haggard as he shook hands with Susannah Armstrong. The British leader threw protocol to the winds and hugged him. Sayyed Khalidi limped forward, cane in one hand, the other outstretched to greet his friend. Ayesha ran on.

She neared the group of dignitaries, her breath coming in short gasps of pain. The security personnel and armed bodyguards at Traitors' Gate had been warned to expect her, but the tension that radiated from them at the sight of her grim and bloodied appearance was palpable. Ayesha was aware of their reactions, of the raising of weapons, and of Dame Imogen taking command, explaining, soothing nerves, but it meant nothing to her. She pushed through the fringes of the group gathered around the top of the water-gate steps, peering, trying to see faces, silhouettes. One man, gray-suited and gray-faced, standing next to the American secretary of state, swung round to see what was going on. He looked straight at her, his eyes widening in sudden shock. Moses Litmann, Israel's foreign minister.

She ignored the Israeli and elbowed her way between the

distinguished men and women toward the little tableau being enacted above Traitors' Gate. Judah Ben David was shaking Sayyed Khalidi's hand, holding the pose for the cameras, showing that their friendship was still strong despite the bloody horror of the Har Yaacov massacre. Not concerned with the significance of handshakes, her gaze traveled over the Palestinian's shoulder. "Sagheer!" she gasped.

"Where?" Dame Imogen was right behind her.

She didn't answer. Sagheer was Sayyed Khalidi's bodyguard. That was how he'd gained access to the Tower. The assassin stood only three feet from Judah Ben David. She'd seen Sagheer's hand disappear inside his suit coat. Seen the telltale bulge beneath the armpit that said he was armed.

With incredible clarity, now the moment had arrived, she calculated distances, obstacles. Knew she would not have time to reach Sagheer. The American secretary of state, decorous in dark green, stood in her way. With a violent shove Ayesha sent her sprawling to the ground. She dashed forward, weaving through the crowd with the skill of a soccer forward. She was oblivious to the cries of outrage, the shouts of alarm, the barked commands. Her attention stayed riveted on Sagheer. His hand was out of his coat. His gun glinted in the watery sunlight as he raised it. His finger tightened on the trigger. With gritted teeth Ayesha threw herself at Judah Ben David. As she crashed into him, a blinding flash of light exploded inside her head.

CHAPTER 72

Ayesha was blind. She couldn't see. She felt a burst of panic, put up a hand, and wiped it across her face. Her vision cleared. Her hand was covered in blood. She had trouble focusing. Her hearing was affected, too. It came and went in bursts, as if a child were gleefully switching the sound on and off. Then it came back on, turned up full volume. Booted feet slammed past her head. Women screamed. Men shouted, cursed. She lowered her hand. A man lay on the ground inches away. His face was turned toward her. Between his eyes was an ugly black hole. It seemed to have bled very little. Sagheer.

She raised her head slightly, wincing as lightning rocketed through her skull. Judah Ben David was there, unhurt. Others, too: Khalidi, Secretary of State Longshore. Moses Litmann. They—and she—were surrounded by an anxious cordon of armed police officers, staring outward, ready to protect the leaders against any fresh attack. None of them were looking at her. Movement to her right caught her eye. Moses Litmann. He reached inside his coat. She frowned. Why would he have a gun? Then she remembered.

The foreign minister had recognized her. Had been shocked to see her. Like he was seeing a ghost. Because he thought she was dead. Because he was *Shamir*.

Litmann, his face a mask of grim determination, raised a Jericho semiautomatic and pointed it at Judah Ben David. "Death to all traitors!" he shouted as he squeezed the trigger.

Ayesha's head, face, and the upper part of her body were spattered with blood. She'd no doubt everyone thought she was dead. Until she exploded from the ground with a low growl, like some revenant rising from the grave. She swiveled on her left heel and swung her right leg upward, slamming her booted toe into Litmann's crotch, levering him backward off his feet at the very instant he fired. The barrel of his gun jerked up and the bullet ricocheted harmlessly off the wall of St. Thomas's Tower. The back of the Israeli's skull hit the cobblestones with a dull thud and he lay still.

Judah Ben David stared from the gun to the motionless body of his foreign minister, then, finally, he turned to look at her. She held his gaze until a great roaring filled her ears and he vanished from view.

CHAPTER 73

Ayesha peered up at the heavy pale stone arches that lowered over her. Daylight filtered through window slits. "Where?" she croaked. She moved her head. It was a mistake. A heavy-metal band climaxed its act inside her brain.

A dark-skinned face looked down at her, showing brilliant white teeth. He wore the navy blue uniform of the London Ambulance Service. "You're in St. John's Chapel," the paramedic answered. "Inside the White Tower."

She nodded. The pain imploded and she wished she hadn't. The White Tower was the original keep. A fortress within a fortress. The most secure part of the Tower of London. She struggled upright. She was lying on a wooden pew, her head cushioned on a hassock. A blanket had been draped over her. It slid off and she realized her jacket had been removed. Her right arm, where Nazir had stabbed her, was swathed in a heavy bandage. New dressings, too, on her wrists. She pulled the blanket up and peered into the gloom of the Norman chapel. People crowded the small space, many of them in uniform and carrying arms. She ignored the stares directed at her, kept searching until she spotted Israel's prime minister. He stood by the altar in animated conversation with Sayyed Khalidi.

"Would you look at me for a moment?" The paramedic held up a penlight. "I need to check your eyes."

She held still impatiently while the paramedic shone his light into each of her eyes. He switched it off with a grunt that might have meant anything. "What is your name?"

"Ayesha Ryder."

"Where do you work?"

"The Walsingham Institute."

"What day is it?"

"Wednesday."

"Where are you now?"

"St. John's Chapel, in the White Tower."

"Okay. I don't think there's concussion. But we need to get you to a hospital. You've been through the mill, quite apart from getting shot."

She glanced down. She still wore her T-shirt, but the paramedic must have seen her burns. She wondered if anyone else had. Lifting her hand to her head, she felt thick bandages. "Where was I shot?"

"Bullet glanced off your skull behind the top of your right ear. You're a very lucky lady. There's a nasty flesh wound. You've lost a lot of blood, and I'm sure you've got a hell of a headache, but you should be okay. We'll run some tests to make sure." The paramedic bent and picked up something that lay on the next pew. "I found this." He held an envelope out to her.

"Miss Ryder?" Judah Ben David said.

"You're okay." She saw Sayyed Khalidi behind the Israeli, smiling at her.

"I am." Ben David smiled, too. "Thanks to you." He bowed formally. "Thank you for saving my life, Ayesha Ryder. Twice."

"Litmann?"

"He's alive. Under arrest." Ben David pursed his lips. "We think he's behind *Shamir*." "Then he's responsible for Evelyn's death."

"Evelyn's and many others."

She held the Israeli's eyes, then looked past him at Sayyed Khalidi. "Mr. President. There are some papers in this envelope. I'd like you to have them."

The Palestinian accepted the envelope. He lifted the flap and let the documents drop into his hand. When he read the title on the first, his jaw dropped. He sank onto the pew next to her. "These are Lawrence's papers?" His words drew a swift intake of breath from Judah Ben David.

"Yes."

Ben David sat down next to his friend, then, their heads close together, the two leaders pored over the documents.

"Incredible!" Ben David exclaimed.

"I agree. Truly, it *is* incredible."

Khalidi unfolded the hand-drawn maps. He spread them on the pew. When he looked up, tears shone in his eyes. "Judah, this is . . . it's . . ."

"Wonderful," the Israeli finished.

"There's one more thing you need to see." Ayesha gestured to the single sheet of paper that jutted out. "It's Lawrence's handwriting."

This time Ben David was the first to look up. Now he, too, had tears in his eyes. "Thank you," he croaked. "With all my heart and soul, thank you." He broke off, overcome. "Dame Imogen," he said, rising, Lawrence's handwritten note clutched tight. "Can you tell us what's happening?"

Ayesha looked at the head of MI5. Their eyes met. She saw the strain in the older woman's expression. Her hair was a mare's nest and a cut on her cheek had left a trail of blood that dripped onto her collar. Dame Imogen nodded to Ayesha, then turned to Ben David. "Mr. Prime Minister. Mr. President." She looked to her right as two more people joined them—Susannah Armstrong and a man Ayesha recognized as the home secretary, Sir Norman Eldritch.

"Situation?" the British prime minister asked.

"The Tower has been secured," Dame Imogen replied. "It's locked down. I'd like to process everyone out as soon as possible. Evacuate them from the Tower and do a clean sweep."

"I agree," the home secretary said. He touched Dame Imogen on the shoulder, seemed concerned about her.

Ayesha noticed this while her heart despaired.

"No!" Sayyed Khalidi exclaimed. The Palestinian jumped to his feet; his cane clattered to the floor. "We have to go on with the press conference. Judah, surely you agree?"

Ayesha felt a surge of hope. The Israeli prime minister looked down at her, held her eyes for a moment, then turned to Susannah Armstrong. "I beg of you," he said. "Let us do what we came here to do. This is our time. Here and now. If we walk away today we may never get another chance."

The British prime minister sat down on the pew and took both of Ayesha's hands in her own. "Dr. Ryder. You more than anyone have a right to say what we should do. What do you think?"

Ayesha smiled through the tears that pricked at her eyes. "We go on," she answered. Emotion welled up inside her, threatened to overwhelm her.

Susannah Armstrong looked up at Dame Imogen. "We've beaten off two assassination attempts. Thanks to Ayesha Ryder. If there's a third—well, tell me where there's a safer place than the Tower of London?"

CHAPTER 74

Together Judah Ben David and Sayyed Khalidi walked down the steps from the White Tower. The Israeli and the Palestinian took their places atop a specially built platform on Tower Green. The podium was bristling with microphones. The invited dignitaries and representatives of the world's media sat in rows in front of the platform and seethed with nervous anticipation. The few flakes of snow that fell from the lowering clouds were ignored.

Like schoolchildren, Ayesha thought. Bundled in a blanket, she sat away from the crowd, near the little paved area where two English queens, both wives of Henry VIII, had lost their lives to the axe. After deciding the press conference should go on, Susannah Armstrong consulted with the paramedic. He agreed that, as long as she was kept still and comfortable, it would be all right for Ayesha to attend. He had an ambulance standing by, though, and insisted she be taken straight to the hospital as soon as the press conference was over.

Some of the excitement among the waiting spectators sprang

from natural human exhilaration at having survived the deadly violence recently unleashed within the Tower. People who had never experienced fear for their own lives had seen guns pointed at them. Many of them still nervously eyed the armed police and soldiers who looked down on the Green from every possible vantage point along the ancient battlements. Another reason for the excitement, to Ayesha's embarrassment, was her own newfound celebrity. Foiling the assassination attempts on Judah Ben David had been captured on camera. The footage had already been uploaded to the Internet and was being viewed around the world. By those in the crowd, too, who had mobile devices.

Adding to the electric current of excitement was the news, spreading rapidly, that the Har Yaacov massacre was not the work of Palestinian terrorists, but Jewish ones—*Shamir*. Judah Ben David had authorized the release of this information along with the facts that Moses Litmann was the suspected mastermind behind the underground group and that *Shamir* was also behind the Christmas Bombing and his own attempted assassination.

"Ladies and gentlemen." The voice of Israel's prime minister boomed through the loudspeaker system. He waited until the chatter subsided. "Yesterday a British policeman, a Palestinian by birth, saved my life in Downing Street and in the process lost his own. Today a young woman, also a British citizen of Palestinian birth, has twice saved my life. I have already thanked her, but I now do so again, before the world." He looked across the heads of the assembled VIPs and press at Ayesha. As did everyone present. Cameras clicked. "Ayesha Ryder," Ben David said, "thank you."

Wishing the ground would open up and swallow her, she did her best not to scowl. She could do nothing about the flush that warmed her cheeks, though, as the crowd shot to their feet roaring their approval. Snowflakes fell more thickly, for which she was grateful.

Ben David waited for the applause to die down, for people to resume their seats. Then he turned to the man at his side. "Sayyed Khalidi, thank you also, for your part in saving my life yesterday." The Palestinian leader smiled, nodded. Again there was applause and again Ben David had to wait. "The news you are all now hearing, about Har Yaacov, is true. It is true, and shocking. That Jew would kill Jew for political gain is beyond words. These murders were committed from fear. They were committed to stop what Sayyed Khalidi and I have come here today to announce. Those responsible for this evil—*Shamir*—have failed." Ben David looked out over the crowd. Then, in solemn, measured tones, continued: "Sayyed and I have to thank Miss Ryder for something else. She brought us some papers. Extremely important papers." He had the crowd hanging on his every word. Even Ayesha held her breath.

"Over three-quarters of a century ago, British prime minister Ramsay MacDonald came to an extremely important decision. He decided it was not practical for two peoples to exist separately in what was then Palestine. At his request a very famous, wonderful man, T. E. Lawrence—whom we all know as Lawrence of Arabia—drafted a treaty to create a new state. An independent state of Palestine. A state where Jews and Arabs would have equal rights, and equal say, in the running of that state."

Ben David stopped. The rising tide of voices on the Green left him no choice. He held up his hands, pleaded for calm. When, finally, it came: "That treaty—Lawrence's treaty—never came to fruition. It was suppressed, out of fear and greed." The crowd gasped. "If Lawrence's plan had gone forward, there would now have been an independent state of Palestine for over seventy-five years. Jews and Arabs would be living side by side, governing one country together, making use of all of its resources for the common good. Living at peace with its neighbors." Ben David let that sink in.

"As we all know, to our sorrow, that did not happen." Israel's prime minister surveyed the men and women in front of him, most of whom were staring at him, openmouthed and bewitched. Then, in ringing tones: "My government and I have agreed with the government of Palestine to do now what should have happened all those years ago: We will merge our two states and create *one new state!*"

For a second there was utter silence, as if the whole crowd had drawn breath at once. Then, magnified by the walls of the ancient buildings, a thunderous sound erupted. Everybody was on their feet, some shouting, gesturing angrily. More, many more, were smiling and weeping and applauding wildly. Some stood on their chairs. Others, complete strangers, hugged each other. It took nearly fifteen minutes before Ben David could make himself heard again. This time, when the Israeli prime minister spoke, his voice was raw with emotion. "*Palestine* and *Israel* are powerful words." He turned to Sayyed Khalidi. The two men smiled at each other, then Ben David faced the people in front of him once more. "So we have agreed on a new name for our new state. A name that is at once old and new. One that reflects the heritage of all our peoples—Jews, Muslims, and Christians." He paused, and this time the effect was brilliantly calculated. "The Holy Land."

The cheering that greeted this new announcement, mingled with delirious applause, completely drowned any sound of dissent. Susannah Armstrong, tears running freely down her cheeks, ran forward onto the podium and embraced both men. Diana

Longshore looked confused, as if she wasn't sure how to respond to the announcement. The American secretary of state had a large bandage on her right knee. Ayesha remembered pushing her to the ground. Then, with tears misting her eyes, she tried to raise her hands to clap. The effort was too much. An overwhelming weariness descended upon her. The last thing she saw was the two leaders, Palestinian and Israeli, holding up a large cloth between them, spreading it so everyone could see it. The cloth was white. In its center was the blue Star of David. Within the central panel of the star was a large red Greek cross, surrounded by four smaller crosses. Partially encompassing the emblems of both Judaism and Christianity was a green crescent moon, symbol of Islam. The flag of the Holy Land.

CHAPTER 75

Ayesha sat in the library of her St. John's Wood apartment. Once Evelyn Montagu's apartment, it and everything in it were now hers. Evelyn had left it all to her in his will and she'd moved in the previous week, not without some heartache over the sale of her aunt Harriet's apartment. The sale had made her a wealthy woman, though, and she was certain Harriet would have approved. Harriet too would have supported her decision to keep her job with the Walsingham Institute. The money, more than anything, meant real freedom. Ayesha could travel, although she had no plans to do so. Three months had passed, but she was still recognized wherever she went. The film of her heroics at the Tower of London was the most downloaded on YouTube. Images of her throwing herself between the assassin's bullet and Judah Ben David, or covered in blood, kicking Moses Litmann in the crotch, still appeared on magazine covers. She was forced to go everywhere wearing dark glasses and a headscarf. In three days' time, at Buckingham Palace, the queen was going to honor her with the George Cross. At the thought of the publicity that would stir up, Ayesha shuddered.

"You can't turn it down," Lady Madrigal Carey had said when Ayesha begged her to use her influence to help her get out of it.

"Lawrence did. He turned down all his honors."

"Yes, and it was stupid of Ned. He needlessly offended people who only wanted to thank him for what he'd done." Lady Madrigal surveyed her critically. "Now, what are you going to wear?"

Ayesha smiled grimly at the memory. Lady Madrigal had taken her shopping, to some very exclusive couturiers. It had not been a success, although Dame Imogen Worsley had joined forces with the old woman. The head of MI5 had an ulterior motive—to persuade Ayesha to sign the Official Secrets Act. Whatever Lawrence had uncovered about Edward, Prince of Wales, and the Nazis, it was obviously of huge concern to the British government. Ayesha couldn't care less. Dame Imogen appeared finally to have conceded defeat. As had Lady Madrigal on the matter of what Ayesha would wear to the investiture.

Rising easily from the desk—her injuries had healed, although she was still having plastic surgery for the ugly scars on her breasts—she went into the kitchen. She filled the kettle with water, turned it on, leaned against the sink, and contemplated the poster on the wall.

At first she didn't think she could live in Evelyn's apartment, had decided in fact that she would have to sell it. When she visited, however, she found she wanted to be there. The books and mementos had been restored to their places, and Evelyn's spirit, if there was such a thing, was at peace here.

While she waited for the kettle to boil, she glanced at the

newspaper. Things were still dangerously unsettled in the Holy Land. There had been riots, deaths. There would be more. No one doubted it. But most—Jews, Arabs, Christians—were willing to give the new country a chance. She sighed. If only they'd found the Ark of the Covenant. Sayyed Khalidi's people had visited the Church of the Nativity in Bethlehem. With the aid of archaeologists they'd found the secret chamber. But it was empty. The Ark had been there. It was depicted in a mural on a wall of the chamber. But where it had gone, nobody knew or was saying.

The phone rang and she started out of her reverie. She lifted the handset. "Hello?"

"Ayesha?" a familiar voice said. "How are you?"

"Sayyed! I'm fine, thank you. How nice to hear from you."

"I'm calling with some news." Sayyed Khalidi, co-president of the Holy Land, sounded excited. "You know we've had an archaeological team working on the Church of the Nativity?"

"They've found something?" Ayesha's heart soared.

"It's hard to say. They found an inscription. Some words." Khalidi hesitated. "We've no idea what they mean," he continued. "But they're in English. And Ayesha, the words are preceded by a series of musical notes—"

"Lawrence!"

"Yes, that's what I thought as soon as I heard. After what you told us about his madrigalisms."

"What are the words?"

"'Walsingham. Psalm 115:6.' Have you any idea what that means?"

"None. What does the Psalm say?"

"'They have ears, but cannot hear, noses, but cannot smell.'"

Ayesha stared at the old poster on the wall, not seeing it, thoughts swirling. "I don't know what it means, Sayyed."

The Palestinian chuckled. "But you're going to find out?"

"Oh yes," she murmured, her gaze still on the framed poster of *She. Evelyn.* "Oh yes. I'm going to find out."

ACKNOWLEDGMENTS

The writing and publication of *Ryder* would not have been possible without the support of many people, to whom I owe huge thanks. First and foremost, my wife, Pamela, whose love and belief in me kept me going through the darkest hours—and who refused to tell me something was good when it wasn't (the best kind of critic). My parents, Maurice and Dolores Pengelley, who instilled in me my love of books. Bernadette McSherry, who was there from day one, and suffered through my earliest, truly dreadful efforts. Dennis Seguin, for being a brutal critic. Lorraine Seguin, just because. Sheryl Dunn of Shelfstealers, for some excellent advice. The baristas, bartenders, and habitués of the several cafés and bars in and around Kensington Market, where so much of the novel was written—Ronnie's Local, Free Times, Pamenar, and Q Space. Quattro Books of Toronto—Allan Briesmaster, John Calabro, and Luciano Iacobelli will always have a place in my pantheon of personal gods. Sarah Beaudin, Maddy Curry, and Lynsey Morandin, thank you! My wonderful agent, Sam Hiyate of The Rights Factory, and my editor at Random House, the awesome Kate Miciak—the two people who have truly launched Ayesha Ryder into the world.

IF YOU ENJOYED *RYDER*, READ ON FOR A
PREVIEW OF AYESHA RYDER'S NEXT ADVENTURE IN

RYDER: AMERICAN TREASURE

Nick Pengelley

CHAPTER 1

The child, a girl, was sprawled on her back in the gutter, a teddy bear clutched in one tiny hand. One of its legs had been ripped off by the force of the explosion. Her frilly pink dress was shredded and daubed in the blood that seeped from too many wounds to count. Even as Ayesha watched, the child's little chest heaved once, then stilled forever. The child's mother, her own face a mask of blood, scooped her up, keening an unnatural high-pitched sound that tore Ayesha's heart. She took a step toward the woman and her dead daughter.

"I'm sorry—" The words caught in her throat as the woman swung her shocked gaze in Ayesha's direction. "We didn't mean—"

"Pardon me, Dr. Ryder?"

Her heart pounding, Ayesha stared into the face of the young man, a footman dressed in the royal livery, who held out a silver tray laden with champagne glasses. She frowned, her mind grappling for the present, for something to hold on to. The room swam. She closed her eyes, then opened them. Memory returned. The past receded.

"Yes, please." She forced a smile. She lifted a glass from the tray. Drank deeply. Then, as the footman moved away, she checked the time on an ornate clock, a gift from Kaiser Wilhelm II to Queen Victoria. She sighed. Royal protocol demanded she stay for another half hour. She threaded her way across the crowded reception chamber and took up a position in front of a large painting, a Rembrandt, one of the queen's collection. It depicted a middle-aged man and a woman dressed in dark garb, against a dark background. Ayesha hoped her own black Dolce & Gabbana suit, heels, and hair might blend with the scene so a casual observer would fail to notice her.

A touch on her arm destroyed that hope.

"Imogen." Ayesha liked the auburn-haired head of MI5, the United Kingdom's internal security service, although she unsettled her. It was hard to get by the fact Imogen Worsley was one of the small number of people who knew about Ayesha's past as a member of the Palestinian fedayeen. She'd thought that past buried, along with the dead—friends and enemies—and the guilt. Recent events had proved otherwise.

"I wondered where you'd got to." Dame Imogen Worsley accepted a glass of wine from a footman. "What are you doing skulking in the shadows? This is your party, you should be enjoying yourself. You deserve it," she added, with a nod in the direction of the slim black box tucked under Ayesha's arm. It contained the George Cross, the nation's highest honor for civilian gallantry, with which she'd just been honored by the Queen.

Ayesha turned away, embarrassed by the praise. Her gaze lighted on two men on the far side of the chamber. They were looking her way. She knew one of them: Noel Malcolm, the deputy prime minister. The other, a florid-faced man with short-cropped fair hair, was a stranger. A woman, blond, very tall, striking looking and clearly athletic, joined them.

"Do you know them?" Dame Imogen asked her.

"Noel Malcolm. I don't know the other one, or the woman."

"The man's name is Yael Strenger."

"And?"

"He's with the Embassy of the Holy Land. According to them he's a diplomat."

"But you know different?" *The Holy Land.* Even now, six months after the creation of the new federal state from what had been Israel and Palestine, Ayesha mentally pinched herself whenever she heard the words. That the world equated her with the deed was something she found hard to accept. *It was Lawrence. All I did was find his treaty.*

"Strenger was Mossad. One of their best field agents. Ruthless. I'm betting he's theLondon station chief for the Holy Land's new foreign intelligence service."

"Why would he be talking with Malcolm?" Mossad, short for HaMossad leModi'in uleTafkidim Meyu adim, Israel's Institute for Intelligence and Special Operations. Long ago Ayesha had matched wits with their operatives.

"Why indeed?" Dame Imogen's gaze flicked past Ayesha's shoulder. "Our prime minister approaches," she warned.

At five foot ten, Susannah Armstrong stood almost as tall as Ayesha, her long dark hair a match for her own, although where her skin was a light olive, the prime minister's was pale white, reflecting her Welsh heritage. She was accompanied by a woman whose honey-blond hair was cut into an internationally known bob. Dressed in a canary-yellow Jackie Kennedy–style suit complete with pillbox hat, Diana Longshore, the U.S. secretary of state, turned heads wherever she went.

"Dame Imogen." Susannah Armstrong nodded to the head of MI5, then rested a hand on the secretary of state's arm and turned her hazel-eyed gaze on Ayesha, eyes that always seemed to hold a glimmer of amusement. "I don't think you've met Diana Longshore, have you?" she asked.

"Actually Dr. Ryder and I have met before." The American stared at Ayesha with the direct gaze before whom even heads of state had been known to quail. "Although we weren't properly introduced. Last December, at the Tower of London. Do you remember?"

Ayesha did remember their encounter at the Tower. Forcing her way through the crowd of VIPs surrounding Israel's prime minister, desperate to prevent his assassination by *Shamir* terrorists, she'd shoved Diana Longshore out of the way and knocked her to the ground.

The American held her gaze for a moment longer, then her mouth broke into a warm smile that spread to her eyes. She extended her hand. "It's an honor to meet you properly, Dr. Ryder. I hope you've recovered from your injuries."

Ayesha accepted the handshake and opened her mouth to reply, but the secretary hadn't finished. "I'd like to offer you a job," Longshore said.

Ayesha frowned. "I already have a job."

"Ayesha, please," Susannah Armstrong cut in. "I know you can't wait to get out of here and look for the Ark, but I'd like you to hear Diana out."

Ayesha bit her lip. She was annoyed the prime minister had

mentioned the Ark in front of the American. Dame Imogen also knew about the hunt that consumed her every waking moment. But Ayesha didn't want to widen the circle.

"The Ark?" Diana Longshore asked Ayesha.

"The Ark of the Covenant." The prime minister ignored the black look Ayesha shot her.

"The biblical Ark? I thought that was just a story."

"No. It really existed. Still exists, Ayesha thinks."

"Amazing! So where is it?"

"It was hidden below the Church of the Nativity in Bethlehem," Ayesha got in before her prime minister could divulge anything she didn't want known. "But it was moved."

"To where?" Longshore was fascinated.

"That's what I'm trying to discover." She had no intention of telling the American about the clue she possessed to the whereabouts of the Ark. *Lot of good it's done me.* Weeks of puzzling over it and she'd got nowhere.

"I hope you find it," Diana Longshore said firmly. "I really do. The job I'd like you to take on is also a treasure hunt."

"What sort of treasure?"

"The treasure the British looted from Washington in 1814."

"I don't—"

"You *do* know what I mean?"

"Yes, but . . ." Ayesha had read the news report. A British Museum curator had discovered an artifact that could only have come from the Capitol Building in Washington, D.C.—the capitol the British had looted and burned in 1814, during the War of 1812, when Britain and the young United States had fought a particularly pointless war.

RYDER

"Is it true no one knows what happened to the treasure?" Dame Imogen asked.

"It's a two-hundred-year old mystery," Longshore replied. "Most people who've looked into it think it's at the bottom of the sea, lost after the ship carrying it to England sank during a storm. This discovery might change all that. If one object has turned up in London perhaps there's more."

"I can see why you'd be excited," Dame Imogen said.

"I am!" Diana Longshore's eyes sparkled. "If it still exists, the treasure could include priceless artifacts of early American history. Things from the White House belonging to George Washington and the early presidents. Books, papers—who knows what else?"

"Why me?" Ayesha asked. *Shit!* "Why would you think I'd have any idea how to find this treasure? I'm a Middle East specialist. I know little about the history of your country." There'd been a mistake, she told herself. She'd set them right and they'd leave her alone.

"May I?" Susannah Armstrong touched Diana Longshore's sleeve.

Ayesha had become close to her prime minister since that day at the Tower of London when she'd saved the life of Israel's prime minister not once, but twice, allowing him and Sayyed Khalidi, the Palestinian leader, to declare the new joint state of the Holy Land. She'd never seen Susannah this excited. It had to do with the American, Longshore. Susannah kept glancing at her and smiling. *She wants Longshore to be president.* If the 1814 treasure was found and returned to the United States, it would be a great boost to her in the forthcoming primaries, and the election itself.

"You may not know anything about the Washington treasure,"

the prime minister said, "but you are an expert on Lord Kitchener, aren't you?"

"Kitchener?" What could the great field marshal of the British Empire, Queen Victoria's hero general, have to do with the treasure of 1814? Kitchener had become world famous when he'd avenged the death of General Gordon in the Sudan, at the Battle of Omdurman in 1898, where Winston Churchill had participated in the world's last great cavalry charge. Commander in chief of the British Army in India. Nemesis of the Boers, during the South African War at the end of the nineteenth century when, less famously, he had created the concentration camp to help control the rebellious population. *Sirdar*—commander in chief of British forces in Egypt. Then, as the Great War had broken out across Europe in 1914, he was appointed secretary of war, from which imperial position he had almost single-handedly created "Kitchener's Army," the all-volunteer British force that had helped stem the German tide as it washed across France, before it was halted at the very gates of Paris. Kitchener's heavily mustachioed visage, finger pointing at the viewer, had adorned thousands of recruiting posters over the admonition, BRITONS! JOIN YOUR COUNTRY'S ARMY! Still did, in multiple iconic replications. She had one framed on her own office wall at the Walsingham Institute.

"Yes," Ayesha replied. "I've published several papers on Kitchener. He had a major influence on the modern history of the Middle East. The United States though?" She shook her head. Kitchener hadn't been born until half a century after the end of the War of 1812. "I don't understand."

"You've read about the artifact found by Peter Hendry, the British Museum curator?" Diana Longshore asked her.

"It's been all over the news. Nobody's saying what it is."

"We're keeping it quiet for now. It was in the Capitol at the time the British burned Washington—that's certain. Hendry found it in a box of personal belongings that had been sealed up for nearly a hundred years." Diana Longshore smiled. "Kitchener's personal belongings."

Ayesha's heart sank. She was trapped.

CHAPTER 2

Ayesha stood before the door that bore Peter Hendry's name-plate. She was not in the least enthusiastic about the task before her. She wanted to resume her search for the Ark. Instead, she was at the British Museum on what would no doubt turn out to be a wild goose chase. *Most people would say the same about the Ark.* She checked the time. With luck the interview with the curator would be quick, then, duty done, she could get back to the Walsingham and what she really wanted to be doing.

"Miss Ryder?" The curator rose from behind a desk piled high with papers. They reminded Ayesha of the stratified look of ancient cities exposed in an archaeological dig. The papers on top were crisp and white but the older layers were shades of yellow and the deepest, those closest to the surface of the desk, were brown.

Hendry was in his mid-sixties, although he looked younger. A pale blue silk handkerchief flowed from the breast pocket of his navy blue pinstriped suit. A gold watch chain looped across his waistcoat. There was a glint in his eyes as he bid her sit down, which she did, after shifting more papers from a leather armchair to the floor beside it.

Hendry rested his backside against a corner of his desk, gingerly, so as not to disturb the papers—although they were likely accreted in place—and looked down at Ayesha from his superior height.

She was familiar with the look. It was common to the old men who dominated her own field, jealously guarding their preserves and wary of one, like her, who broke the rules—a woman especially. Even her George Cross wouldn't be enough, in their minds, to counter the photographs of her that adorned the lurid magazine covers at supermarket checkouts. She was used to the condescension; it came out in various ways—like Hendry's failure just now to call her "Doctor" when greeting her. It might have been an oversight, but she doubted it. Such things had never concerned her. She had learned, growing up in the alleys of Gaza, that she was as good as any man; better than most.

She crossed one long silk-stockinged leg over the other with studied indifference. Hendry's eyes followed the movement, lingered on her thighs. She suppressed the urge to get up and leave, wishing she'd had time to change into something less provocative. The prime minister had seen that she was bundled into an official car and on her way to the British Museum as soon as she'd agreed to look into the mystery of the Washington treasure. *Afraid I'd change my mind.*

"So you think you can find the 1814 treasure?" The curator had managed to drag his eyes from her legs to her face, although they hesitated at her breasts.

Hendry was defensive. He regarded the treasure the British had stolen from Washington as his baby. He'd made the initial find. He wanted the glory of making the big discovery. She couldn't fault him for that.

"I wouldn't have the faintest idea where to start." She feigned the shadow of a smile. "My involvement was suggested by the prime minister, because of my knowledge of Kitchener. I understand you found this mysterious artifact we've been reading about in the papers in a box of his personal belongings. I doubt there's anything I can suggest you haven't already thought of."

"Politicians." Hendry sniffed. He seemed mollified by her attitude. "Always interfering."

"I can understand them getting excited. The Americans particularly. If the treasure is found it could mean a great deal to them."

Hendry laughed. The sound was harsh. "You're more right than you know."

"Oh?"

"There's a story that one of the things James Madison left behind in the White House when the British burned it was a letter. Supposedly it was hidden inside a secret compartment in a clock in the president's office. Even Dolley Madison didn't know it was there."

A two-hundred-year-old presidential letter would be of great interest to students of American history and politics. Ayesha couldn't care less.

The curator stared at her. Then, seeming to make up his mind, he said, "A persistent legend has it that someone high up in President Madison's administration was in British pay—a traitor. If proof of that was found, well, think of the implications."

"I see." She did see. She just didn't regard the revelation with the same importance as Hendry did. Doubtless every scholar of American history would get to write and publish new articles and books. Bully for them. She suppressed a yawn, wondered if she could leave now. She remembered her promise to Susannah Armstrong.

"This isn't just something of academic interest, you know," the curator persisted.

"How so?"

"There's a political angle. The White House chief of staff, Thomas Madison, is a direct descendant of President Madison. He's a probable contender in the forthcoming U.S. elections. If something is found that reflects well on his ancestor, he'll get a bump in the polls. Conversely . . ." Hendry looked at her with raised eyebrows.

"I see." As if she gave a damn about American politics. It was time to move things along. "Will you tell me what makes you think the 1814 treasure came to England?"

Hendry opened a drawer in his desk and withdrew a square metal box. He lifted the lid and held the box out so she could see its contents.

Inside the box, nestled in cotton wool, was a small object. Cylindrical, but curved inward in the center, making it rather like an hourglass in shape. About two and a half inches in length and an inch and a half in diameter. It was yellowish and showed a number of cracks.

"What is it?"

"Pick it up," Hendry urged.

She extracted the small cylinder. It fit neatly into her palm but its weight belied its appearance; it was quite heavy. "Ivory." She turned it over to look at the ends. These were metal and very worn.

A device was stamped into one end. She held it up for a closer look. "The American eagle?"

"They're almost worn down," Hendry said, "but if you look with a magnifying glass you can make out words beneath the eagle."

She squinted, but could barely discern the characters with the naked eye. "What do they say?"

"Senate of the United States of America."

"What is it?"

"It's a gavel. The original Senate gavel used by John Adams." She waited.

"Before he was president, John Adams was the first vice president of the United States and president of the Senate. From 1789 to 1797."

"And we know this was his how?"

"His name's on it."

She frowned. Hendry really had found something important. Whether it was a clue that would lead to the rest of the 1814 treasure remained to be seen. She thought with longing of the library at the Walsingham Institute. The Ark would have to wait.

Larry Cohn whistled softly as he pushed through the gate in the black cast iron fence at One Seething Lane and walked toward the Elizabethan mansion that housed the Walsingham Institute for Oriental Studies. He stopped at the entrance, adjusted the navy blue overalls he wore with the initials *BT* emblazoned in yellow across the front, then, picturing the plans Strenger had made him memorize, he turned the heavy brass handle, pushed opened the massive front door, and stepped inside.

In silence now, his expert gaze swept the entrance hall: Its wood-paneled walls hung with ancient paintings, the ornate brass chandelier overhead, the absence of security cameras. Everything was a match with Strenger's plan. The man was a bastard, but he was meticulous.

A carved Jacobean desk occupied the space in the center of the hall. One look at the uniformed security guard who sat behind it, his head bent over the *Times* crossword, and Cohn relaxed. This would be easy. The guard was in his mid-sixties, fat and lazy. Retired army or police, Cohn decided, hefting the hard plastic toolbox he carried in one hand.

"British Telecom," Cohn said, when the guard looked up from his newspaper. "Got a job to do in your library."

"No one told me." The guard sighed. "Not that they ever do."

"Tell me about it."

"What's the job?"

"Problem with your wireless routers. The flux capacitor's out of alignment."

"Gibberish to me, mate." The guard nodded toward the hall behind his desk. "Library's that way. Go across the courtyard at the end of the hall. It's the building in front of you. Everyone's left for the day but I haven't locked up yet. Will you be long?"

"Nah. Ten minutes should do it."

"Right then. Do what you need to."

"Ta, mate." Cohn whistled as he headed down the hall. *Candy from a baby.* He glanced at his watch. Even be time for a pint after. Before the next job.